A Cotswold
Christmas Mystery

By Rebecca Tope

THE COTSWOLD MYSTERIES

A Cotswold Killing • A Cotswold Ordeal
Death in the Cotswolds • A Cotswold Mystery
Blood in the Cotswolds • Slaughter in the Cotswolds
Fear in the Cotswolds • A Grave in the Cotswolds
Deception in the Cotswolds • Malice in the Cotswolds
Shadows in the Cotswolds • Trouble in the Cotswolds
Revenge in the Cotswolds • Guilt in the Cotswolds
Peril in the Cotswolds • Crisis in the Cotswolds
Secrets in the Cotswolds • A Cotswold Christmas Mystery
A Cotswold Casebook ♦ Echoes in the Cotswolds

THE LAKE DISTRICT MYSTERIES

The Windermere Witness • The Ambleside Alibi
The Coniston Case • The Troutbeck Testimony
The Hawkshead Hostage • The Bowness Bequest
The Staveley Suspect • The Grasmere Grudge
The Patterdale Plot ♦ The Ullswater Undertaking

THE WEST COUNTRY MYSTERIES
A Dirty Death • Dark Undertakings
Death of a Friend • Grave Concerns
A Death to Record • The Sting of Death
A Market for Murder

A Cotswold
Christmas Mystery

REBECCA TOPE

The paper used for this Allison & Busby publication
has been produced from trees that have been legally sourced
from well-managed and credibly certified forests.

Printed and bound by
CPI Group (UK) Ltd, Croydon, CR0 4YY

Allison & Busby Limited
11 Wardour Mews
London W1F 8AN
allisonandbusby.com

First published in Great Britain by Allison & Busby in 2020.
This paperback edition published by Allison & Busby in 2021.

A CIP catalogue record for this book is available from
the British Library.

10 9 8 7 6 5 4 3 2 1

ISBN 978-0-7490-2642-4

Typeset in 10.5/15.5 pt Sabon LT Pro by
Allison & Busby Ltd.

For Dave and Tasia

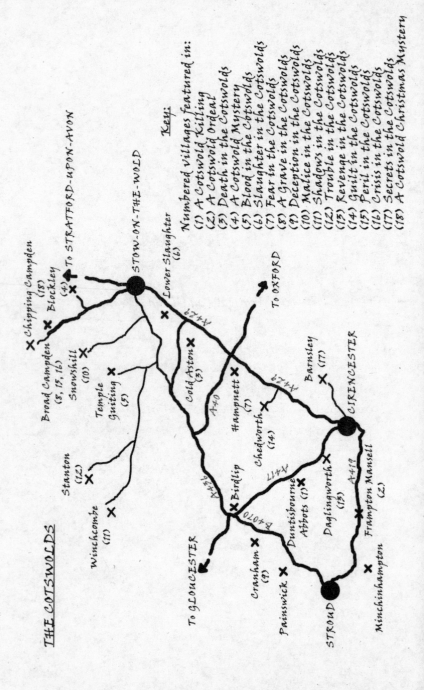

THE COTSWOLDS

STOW-ON-THE-WOLD

To STRATFORD-UPON-AVON

Chipping Campden (18)
Blockley (4)
Broad Campden (8, 15, 16)
Snowshill (10)
Temple Guiting (5)
Stanton (12)
Winchcombe (11)
Lower Slaughter (6)
Cold Aston (3)
A429
Birdlip
A436
A40
Hampnett (7)
Chedworth (14)
A417
Barnsley (17)
A429
To OXFORD
CIRENCESTER
Cranham (9)
Painswick
A4070
Duntisbourne Abbots (1)
Daglingworth (13)
A417
Frampton Mansell (2)
To GLOUCESTER
Minchinhampton
STROUD

Key:

Numbered villages featured in:
(1) A Cotswold Killing
(2) A Cotswold Ordeal
(3) Death in the Cotswolds
(4) A Cotswold Mystery
(5) Blood in the Cotswolds
(6) Slaughter in the Cotswolds
(7) Fear in the Cotswolds
(8) A Grave in the Cotswolds
(9) Deception in the Cotswolds
(10) Malice in the Cotswolds
(11) Shadows in the Cotswolds
(12) Trouble in the Cotswolds
(13) Revenge in the Cotswolds
(14) Guilt in the Cotswolds
(15) Peril in the Cotswolds
(16) Crisis in the Cotswolds
(17) Secrets in the Cotswolds
(18) A Cotswold Christmas Mystery

Author's Note

As with other titles in this series, the action is set in a real village. But the individual houses are invented – and in this case liberties have been taken with the layout of roads and properties to the south-west of Chipping Campden.

Prologue

One whole week to go until Christmas. Four more days at school. Stephanie and Timmy were both close to bursting with anticipation.

'We can walk over to see Ant,' said Thea. 'You two need to get out for a bit.'

'Three,' Stephanie corrected her. 'Don't forget Hepzie.'

'When do I ever forget Hepzie?' laughed Thea, giving her spaniel a quick ear-tickle.

The walk took them up onto high ground to the west of their village, and across a small road to a large estate where the Frowse family lived in a dilapidated old cottage that was actually a converted stable block on a large rural estate. The route was a section of the Monarch's Way footpath, which ran for hundreds of miles and was much loved by walkers.

On this uninviting Sunday afternoon, however, there were very few examples of this species of humanity. Grey clouds drifted heavily not far above the wolds, but it was not quite raining. Nor was it particularly cold. Gloves and scarves had not been called for, but all three wore woolly hats.

The procedure for gaining access to the Frowses' cottage was entertaining in itself. The owner of the estate surrounding the little house had caused an intimidating electrified fence to be erected between his own large mansion and the small residence of his tenants. On their first visit, this had plunged Thea and Stephanie into great confusion. Once you left the road, there was a paved driveway that soon branched off in two directions. If you carried straight on, you encountered a large wrought-iron gate, which had a high wire fence on one side, and a good-sized patch of woodland on the other. The road itself veered sharply away, circling the wood to the west. But if you were visiting the Frowses, you took the smaller branch, which also had an entry gate. This one was more like an ordinary farm gate, but it was equally difficult to pass through. The high fence ran across your path, with the gate an integral part of it. The purpose quickly became clear, as you were confronted by this barrier. The Old Stables was enclosed by a security fence worthy of any prison. Its occupants could only enter or leave via this electronic gate, and the same went for any visitors. There was no back way, other than walking across fields from another larger road to the north. Even then, the fence would prevent access. When challenged about this outrage, the landlord insisted it was intended as added security, deterring intruders, which included deer and foxes. Two of his fields had been enclosed along with the cottage, which he claimed to be the main reason for the fence.

Ant's parents, Beverley and Digby, scoffed at this piece of blatant dishonesty. 'What's so special about the fields?' Digby demanded. 'All he keeps in them is those dozy alpacas.' The alpacas had been a whim on the part of the landlord's wife, and had rapidly become sadly neglected. One of the employees was required to feed them every day, but beyond that nobody gave them any attention. They would run to greet anyone who managed to negotiate the gate, eager for diversion.

Arriving at the gate, pedestrian visitors, as well as those in vehicles, were obliged to request entry by a telephone kept in a small weatherproof box mounted on a post close by. Unless, that is, they knew the passcode; then they could use the keypad that was also in the box. Or so the landlord believed. In fact, Digby Frowse had employed unsuspected computer skills to hack into the software governing this arrangement, so that the mere act of lifting the phone bypassed the code and opened the gate without further ado. Nobody in the family or amongst his friends could understand how he did it, but it worked.

Stephanie delighted in this act of rebellion. Ant had sworn her and the others to secrecy. 'Old Rufus still thinks it works his way,' he chuckled. 'He can't see the gate from the house, luckily. And the camera only shows cars or people standing a bit further away.' The CCTV cameras were another outrageous intrusion on the privacy of the Frowse family.

Beverley met them at the door and welcomed them in. Stephanie gave her a hug, as always, and Timmy stood shyly back and was excused from making a similar gesture. Thea was no more demonstrative than he was. 'Digby's upstairs and Ant's walking the dog,' said Beverley. 'He'll be back in a minute.' She was a sturdy woman of few words, in her early sixties. Stephanie knew little about her, other than that her daughter had been murdered in America, not very many years ago. This gave her an aura of tragedy, as it did her husband too. It made them seem slightly distant, as if wrapped in an invisible cloak of misery that they could not shake off, even when chatting and smiling.

Beverley gave them drinks and mince pies and asked one or two questions about Christmas, while they waited for her son and Percy the dog. Digby came downstairs to join them.

'People!' he said with a twinkly smile. 'Good to see you.'

Stephanie settled into a rather doggy chair and observed the scene. The kitchen was immensely untidy, with bottles, boxes, papers, old tin cans, jam jars, utensils, a radio, and many other objects cluttering the central table and much of the floor. Beverley carelessly cleared a small space for the plate of mince pies, but otherwise left everyone to fend for themselves.

Ant and Percy were soon back, as promised. The young man – who was their real friend out of the Frowse family – hung a grey jacket on the back of the door leading to the rest of the house, where it joined several others. The dog flopped down on a muddy piece of material in a corner, which comprised his bed.

'The daughters are here,' said Ant. 'Two of them, anyway.'

'Already!' Beverley groaned. 'Christmas isn't for another week.'

'Carla's going to be sick of them by then,' said Digby.

'And Rufus even more so,' laughed Ant. 'All they want to do is spend his money.'

'They deserve each other,' Beverley snarled. 'Rotten, the whole lot of them.'

Stephanie was startled at the venom in the woman's voice. Usually she kept things light when the landlord was under discussion. Everyone fell silent for a moment.

'Don't let them get to you, pet,' said Digby wearily, as if he'd said the same thing a thousand times. 'We'll beat them in the end, you'll see.'

Chapter One

Stephanie Slocombe, aged eleven and three-quarters, had completed the first term at her new school. The last day had just ended and she was going home to wait for Christmas. Her schoolbag was pulling on her shoulder and making her walk crookedly because it was packed with cards and presents from just about everyone in her class. Even nasty Millie Forster, who hated her, had dropped a card for her into the classroom postbox. Stephanie had opened it in horror, aware that she had not sent the girl one herself. There was no time left to post one now, either, unless she could persuade Thea to drive her to the post office to catch the last collection, which was vanishingly unlikely. It was all a great worry, but at least there were a few boys who hadn't remembered her, which balanced things out a bit.

14

The special Last Day Lunch was still weighing almost as heavily in her stomach as the schoolbag on her shoulder, mainly because at least three of her friends hated Christmas pudding, so she had helped them to finish theirs.

But she did not feel at all overburdened. Instead she skipped lightly up the driveway to the waiting car, driven by her stepmother, Thea. Millie had probably sent the card with the clear intention of embarrassing her, she decided, and could therefore be safely forgotten. It would be stupid to let her spoil these thrilling days before Christmas Day itself.

Thea looked to be in a reasonably good mood. This was not always the case. By a frustrating twist of Local Authority rules, Stephanie was not allowed onto the school bus that went right through Broad Campden and on to more outlying villages. She lived nearly two miles away from school, which everyone said was perfectly walkable for someone at a secondary school. Two miles, and the bus might have taken her. So Thea or Dad, who did not think it walkable at all, had to drive her to school in the morning and bring her back in the afternoon. There had been talk of sharing with other parents, but there was nobody in Broad Campden who seemed to fit the bill. Two Year Ten girls and a boy in the sixth form were the only ones who lived anywhere near the Slocombes.

Thea complained quite a lot about this extra driving. 'Another nine years of this,' she moaned, having worked out that Timmy would be at school for that long. 'It's a life sentence.'

'Don't be so melodramatic,' her husband had reproached

her. 'It's only for another year or two. They can walk it when there's two of them, at least in the summer. And I already take her some mornings.'

'I know you do—' Stephanie was sure Thea had been going to start sounding off about having to answer the phone when Drew was out, which was nearly as bad as driving back and forth to school. Thea's restless nature was all too familiar after a year and a bit of living with her. Things had not gone nearly as smoothly as everyone had thought they would when there'd been a funny little wedding with hardly any people and a sort-of party in a pub afterwards. Stephanie still remembered how her mum had always been around, even before she got so ill and could hardly get out of bed. Thea was a lot more restless, never altogether satisfied. But at least she loved Dad. The special smile she reserved just for him was enough to keep Stephanie on her side. Dad was lucky in that respect, although he didn't always seem to remember it. Sometimes he forgot to smile back, and Thea would shake her head about it, and look cross. Stephanie always wanted to explain about the way his mind worked; how he could only do one thing at a time, and you just had to wait your turn for his attention. Thea wasn't good at waiting. It was like having a semi-wild animal in the family – or maybe a selkie. A creature that was always yearning to be somewhere else, however much she might love the people she lived with. The story of the beautiful fisherman's wife who was actually a transformed seal had gripped Stephanie in Year Six, not least because she could see how close to her own family life it was. One night she actually had a dream that Thea turned back into a seal and swam away for ever.

Stories about stepmothers were much less easy to relate to. Thea wasn't wicked or jealous or cruel. She was clever and funny and pretty, and kind most of the time. She helped with homework and suggested projects. And she was really good at birthdays. She had interesting relations, as well, like Auntie Jocelyn and her five children, all older than Stephanie. That was because Thea was quite a lot older than Dad, which was another thing that made them unusual.

'Have you done the Christmas tree?' she asked now.

'Not yet. I was waiting for you. I thought you'd want to help.'

Stephanie sighed. She had hoped that Dad would explain properly to Thea that it had been a tradition, ever since Stephanie was born, for the adults to decorate the tree in secret and then make a big thing of revealing it, a few days before Christmas Eve. That had evolved into the last day of term, once Stephanie started school. There had been two wonderful exciting Christmases before Mum got really ill and then it didn't happen in quite the same way after that. At least, Drew had done it instead, which had been good enough in the circumstances. 'Tell her, Dad,' Stephanie had urged him. 'It was such rubbish last year, we need to get it right this time. We have to keep it the same as it used to be.' And he had promised he would.

'I got some new baubles and things for it, months ago, in Poundland, remember?'

There was every reason to go along with Thea, and trust her, Stephanie told herself, despite the appeals to Drew. If this Christmas turned out to be different, it was still

Christmas. The only element missing was a crib. She would have liked a crib, similar to the one they had in the window of one of the houses in the village. She mentioned it to her father.

'I don't really do religion,' he said. 'You know that.'

This had become something of an issue over the past few months. 'But you sometimes have a vicar for the funerals,' she reminded him. 'That's religion.'

'That's my *job*,' he argued. 'I do what the families want, whether it fits with my own beliefs or not.'

'But this is what Christmas is all about. I mean – Jesus being born. It seems wrong to just ignore that altogether.'

'Most people in this country do,' he assured her. 'They focus on food, and bright shiny decorations, and presents and family togetherness. Isn't that enough for you?'

'Not necessarily in that order,' interrupted Thea, who'd been listening in. 'Personally, the food comes last.'

She wasn't religious either. Stephanie had never heard her say a single thing about God or Jesus or heaven, as far as she could remember. There was a sense of a pent-up need to have some sort of conversation about it, if not with her parents, then with somebody.

But there was so much magic in the very fact of Christmas itself, after all – enough to keep everybody happy. 'Yes,' she said now, about the decorations. 'They're brilliant. Has Dad been busy today?'

'Fairly.' Thea had no problem with the change of subject. 'People seem to die quite a lot around Christmas. Usually just after, actually, but there was a new one today. Dad's been doing office stuff mostly.'

Drew Slocombe was an undertaker, running his own alternative burial ground in a field not far from the house. Assisted by Andrew Emerson, he performed every aspect of the work in a simple no-frills style that appealed to a dependable minority of people. A familiar face at hospices in the area, he provided a friendly, affordable service that ensured a regular stream of customers. As prices rose steadily for mainstream funerals, Drew kept his remarkably low. As a result, the Slocombes had very little cash to spare. If Thea hadn't sold the house she had owned in Oxfordshire, they'd have needed state benefits and free school dinners. But now there was also a plan to sell the original Slocombe burial field back in Somerset, where Drew and his family had lived before he met Thea. Stephanie was unsure as to how she felt about this, suspecting that if she had been ten years older, Dad would have let her run it for him. As it was, his one-time partner Maggs had let them all down by deciding she wanted to follow a different line of business from then on. Without her, Peaceful Repose was more trouble than it was worth. As the memories faded, Stephanie found it easy enough to deal with the loss of her one-time home. Timmy was even less concerned than she was. There was so much going on here in Broad Campden – the new school, new friends, even a new cousin – that the past just slid away unregretted.

Stephanie liked Andrew well enough, not thinking of him as a substitute for Maggs, because he was so completely different. He hardly seemed to notice her, for one thing. When he did come to the house, it was always Timmy he concentrated on. He had been a farmer until a couple of years ago, but he had seemed delighted to have given that up and gone into the funeral business instead. He knew the Cotswolds well, and had a lot of useful friends scattered across the villages.

They were home in no time, the conversation scarcely started before they were lugging bags out of the car. 'People shouldn't die at Christmas,' Stephanie said. 'There should be a law.'

Thea laughed. 'I agree with you there,' she said.

The schoolbag was upended onto the kitchen table and the cards scrupulously pinned to the long tape festooning the living room, almost doubling the display. 'All these presents have to go under the tree,' said Stephanie. 'I'll open them on the day.'

Timmy had been home for barely ten minutes when his sister and stepmother got back. Still at the primary school, he qualified for a place on the bus, which dropped him at the top of the lane where they lived. His haul of Christmas greetings cards and gifts was considerably smaller than Stephanie's. In fact, the only actual present was from his friend Caleb. 'Boys don't bother with that stuff so much,' said Stephanie kindly. 'Mine are all going to be nail polish and snazzy socks, I expect.'

'Mm,' said the boy with a shrug.

The living room certainly looked very festive. Thea had produced a box of tinsel and red candles and artificial holly, saved from the previous year. 'I've had this stuff for ages. I guess it's looking a bit sad now,' she admitted. Drew discovered that his own similar box had not survived the move from Somerset. 'I must have chucked it out,' he said, scratching his head. 'I've no idea when I last saw it.'

So Thea had thrown herself into the whole business, getting great armfuls of silver and gold and red decorations from Poundland and other places, pinning them all over the room in a gaudy exhibition of Christmas spirit that made the room seem small and magical, like a fairy's cave. Or so Stephanie observed, in wholehearted admiration when Thea ushered everybody in to admire her handiwork. 'Worth waiting for – right?' she said.

'Do fairies live in caves?' wondered Timmy.

'Grottoes,' said Drew.

'That's the same thing,' said his pedantic daughter.

Drew was making an effort as well. He had gone on his own private shopping expedition two weekends ago and come back with a large bag bulging in intriguing ways. 'Don't look!' he ordered and hurried through to his office at the back of the house.

The air was crackling with anticipation. So many new things were going to happen, one after another. For a start, Andrew and Fiona Emerson had been invited to join the Slocombes for drinks the next evening. Their daughter, who usually did the honours by having them to stay for several days around Christmas, had a new baby and was letting her in-laws take the strain. As an added novelty, Thea's brother Damien had announced, with no consultation, that he and his wife and small daughter would be paying a visit to Broad Campden on the day after Boxing Day, hoping to stay overnight.

'What!' shrieked Thea, when he phoned. 'What brought that on?'

'It's high time you got to know your niece. You've barely even laid eyes on her all year.'

'I've been busy,' Thea protested feebly.

'It'll be good to catch up,' he said, brooking no argument. He was the eldest in the family and nobody had ever got the hang of arguing with him. Thea conveyed the news to the others with trepidation. 'It'll be like a state visit,' she groaned.

'It'll be great,' her husband assured her. 'And Stephanie's going to love the baby, aren't you, pet?'

Stephanie had blithely agreed that she would definitely relish the company of a baby step-cousin.

'Not such a baby now,' Thea reminded them. 'She must be over two. Same age as Meredith.'

'It'll be great,' said Drew again, as if saying it would make it so. Stephanie's faith in him never wavered for a moment.

For a family with very few close friends, the Slocombes were suddenly feeling alarmingly popular. Maggs and Den Cooper were coming at New Year, and Thea's mother was making noises about hardly ever seeing her, with the clear implication that a visit was imminent.

And then there was Jessica.

Chapter Two

Stephanie was the first to throw herself at the young woman who arrived the next morning, closely followed by the spaniel. Having parked her car some distance away, her appearance took them all by surprise. She stood there, big and fair, much more like her aunt Jocelyn in appearance than her mother. 'It's not even eleven o'clock yet,' said Thea.

'I left soon after eight. Nice quick drive,' said Jessica. 'The M6 wasn't too bad, considering everybody's meant to be driving somewhere today. Not a single accident for a change. It was a bit slow, but at least it kept moving. Give us a kiss, Mum – if I can get out of this bear hug.' She gave Stephanie a squeeze and then edged her aside so as to embrace Thea. 'Happy Christmas, everybody.' She crouched down to fondle Hepzie's long, soft ears.

'Same as always, doggie-doos.'

Stephanie giggled. 'That's not very nice. Doggie-doos is rude.'

'It's chaos here already,' said Thea. 'But we finally got the tree decorated, didn't we, Steph?'

Jessica smiled vaguely. 'I've got loads of things in the car. I left it by the church – was that right?'

'You can probably squeeze it in next to the hearse, actually. There won't be any more funerals till next week now.'

'No hurry,' said Jessica. 'I just want to slob out for a bit.'

'Come and see the tree,' Stephanie urged. 'It's amazing.'

'Where's Timmy?'

'In there. He's counting the minutes.'

'What?'

'Till seven o'clock on Christmas morning. That's when we get our stockings. Dad brings them up to us. Tim's working out how many minutes are left till then.'

'Sweet,' said Jessica with a little sigh.

'You look tired,' said Drew, appearing from his room at the back of the house. 'Too many Christmas parties?'

'Hardly any, actually. I feel perfectly all right – not really tired, just ready for a break, that's all.'

'Well, you can have a nice lie-in tomorrow. We're all going to be charging our batteries before the onslaught. That's the plan, anyway.'

Jessica gave him a knowing look. 'Don't tempt fate. Your job's like mine – you never know what the next phone call is going to bring.'

'People aren't allowed to die at Christmas,' said Stephanie firmly. 'We decided that already.'

'Quite right,' smiled her stepsister. 'The undertaker's closed for the holiday, and so is the police officer.'

'Are you a sergeant yet?'

'First week of January. Quicker than I thought. Takes me a step closer to moving up to CID.'

'Hey! You never told me that,' said Thea. 'When did that happen?'

'They only told me this week. Came as quite a surprise, what with one thing and another.' Both women glanced at the child, careful to avoid saying too much. 'I just hope I'll be up to it.'

'It'll be fine,' Thea assured her, characteristically optimistic to the point where she often refused to face real trouble. Even Stephanie found this attitude irksome at times, half aware that it was uncomfortably close to laziness. It took a certain kind of energy to accept and deal with problems, which Thea seemed to lack when it concerned her own family. Drew once observed that she could throw herself into amateur detective work when house-sitting without a second thought. But when it came to their own domestic concerns, all she could do was offer bland statements that things would work themselves out. All of which caused Stephanie to worry that there might be some secret reason to be concerned about Jessica's promotion. Something in the air had changed when it was mentioned.

'I brought food,' said Jessica. 'Nuts, figs, crystallised ginger – that sort of thing. And some decorations.'

25

'Thanks,' said Thea. 'I only managed a box of dates and some satsumas.'

Drew and Stephanie both looked at her in alarm. 'You're not serious?' said Drew.

'I mean – as the special extras. You know perfectly well I've got a turkey and mountains of vegetables. And stuffing. And wine.'

'Mince pies?' Again, father and daughter seemed anxious. 'We finished the ones you bought before,' explained Stephanie. A very subtle stress on the word *bought* conveyed an awareness of how things had changed since Karen had been in charge. A brilliant and enthusiastic cook, Drew's first wife had made everything herself. Not just the pies, but the mincemeat that went inside them – as well as the pudding, stuffing, brandy butter, gravy and bread sauce. Thea just got everything from the supermarket. And last year she didn't even bother with bread sauce.

'I've got some of them as well,' said Jessica. 'We're going to have a perfect old-fashioned Christmas with all the trimmings – you'll see.'

Before they knew it, the day was more than half over. Thea provided sausages and mash for lunch, followed by ice cream. Timmy talked about Pokémon and Drew lit the log fire. There was a sense of suspension, waiting for the day to be over. Stephanie buried herself in *Through the Looking-Glass*, which she was reading for the third time. She could recite 'Jabberwocky' as well as 'The Walrus and the Carpenter', which Thea said would have been old-fashioned even when she was a child. Stephanie had never even tried to describe the powerful sense of wonderment and delight she derived from the book. It didn't fade with repeated readings – the opposite, if anything. Small details that she had previously missed came vividly to life. The knitting sheep, the alarming Red Queen, the elusive references to the game of chess, all held her in thrall. It was in every way infinitely superior to *Alice's Adventures in Wonderland*, which seemed childish and thin by comparison.

True to her word, Jessica slumped passively in the warm sitting room, toying with her phone now and then, but showing no signs of restlessness. 'You still haven't moved your car,' said Thea, at three o'clock.

'And nobody's walked the dog,' said Drew.

'I took her out after breakfast, actually,' his wife corrected him. 'She doesn't need anything more than that.'

It was already getting dark. None of the immediate neighbours had put Christmas lights outside, so there was little sense of festivity until you walked along the main street of Broad Campden. There, one or two houses had decorated their windows with snowflake patterns, and wound coloured lights round their garden trees. The pub had a lovely big Christmas tree as well.

'I'll go and bring my car down, then,' said Jessica.

'I'll come with you,' said Stephanie, allowing no scope for argument.

They walked up the short lane to where the car was tucked neatly beside the church wall. Everything was quiet. It was December the twenty-second. 'Shortest day yesterday – or maybe today. I'm never altogether sure,' said Jessica. 'That's why they put Christmas at this time of year. By the twenty-fifth, they must have noticed that the sun was

27

setting a minute or two later, and the seasons were turning again.'

'I know. It was all pagan before the Christians came and monopolised it. Even the churches were mostly built on old pagan sites.'

Jessica laughed. 'I suppose you would know all about that sort of thing, living in a place like this.'

'Why?' Stephanie was genuinely bemused.

'Oh – well, doesn't it all seem incredibly *ancient* here? These rolling hills – wolds, or whatever they're called. They seem like the graves of giants and prehistoric gods to me. Even the trees look about a thousand years old.'

'More like two hundred. But there is a lot of history round here,' Stephanie acknowledged. 'Thea's always going on about it.'

'What about that one, then?' Jessica was pointing at the very prominent tree growing on a grassy mound near the church. 'It looks as if it's been there for ever.'

The tree was in shadow, only illuminated by faint light coming from the houses behind it. 'That?' scoffed Stephanie. 'That's a cherry. They don't live very long at all.'

'I stand corrected,' said Jessica. 'Now let's get back. Mum might be making some tea by now.'

She drove cautiously down the lane, and managed to manoeuvre the car into the scanty space in front of Drew's hearse. 'He's sure he won't need it, then?' she asked.

'If there's an urgent removal, he'll take Andrew's van. That doesn't live here. We're very organised,' Stephanie boasted.

'You keep bodies here, do you?'

Stephanie gave her stepsister a look, that was lost in the gloom of the back garden. 'You know we do. But you can't reach them from the house. You have to go outside and in again. There are regulations.' She waved at the additional structure attached to the back of the house. It had been a utility room or scullery before the Slocombes moved in, but minor alterations had turned it into a very small mortuary. Drew was still tinkering with it, in the hope of finding space for better storage.

'I suppose you get used to it,' said Jessica, with a little shiver.

'There's absolutely nothing to worry about,' said the child earnestly. 'The dead really are no trouble at all. And besides, there's nobody there now. We're having a holiday from funerals – we told you that already.'

Jessica was lifting a large cardboard box from the boot. 'Here – you can give me a hand,' she puffed. 'Take that bag, will you? And shut the boot for me.'

Stephanie gave her usual competent assistance and started to walk round to the front of the house. 'Oh!' she yelped, as she stepped out into the lane. 'Who's that?'

A figure was moving quickly towards the field that opened out at the end of the drivable roadway. All she could see was a silhouette – which appeared to be a person with three legs. It proceeded purposefully without looking back, and was soon out of sight. 'Did you see?' she asked Jessica.

'What? I can't see anything over this box. I'm going to trip over something if I'm not careful.'

'Somebody went down there. They didn't want to be seen. They've gone now.'

'Are you sure? Wait a minute. Let's get inside and put everything down.'

Stephanie tried to quell the feeling of panic, telling herself that anybody was allowed to walk along the lane, even if it didn't lead anywhere. There were two more houses between theirs and the field – but she was sure the person hadn't belonged to either of them. It wasn't Mr Shipley from opposite, either. And it was *dark*. Nobody went out for walks in fields when it was dark – even if it was only four o'clock.

Nobody wanted to listen to her thin little story, once they were back in the house. An hour or two passed in a kind of quiet aimlessness. Jessica forced Tim into a belated hug and another long discussion about Pokémon. As far as Stephanie was concerned, Pokémon was yesterday's passion and anybody still obsessed with it was embarrassing. Thea was faffing about in the kitchen, rummaging in Jessica's box of goodies and muttering to herself. Drew was – incredibly – on the phone to somebody in his room at the back. The dining room had been turned into his office, with a filing cabinet and shelves and phone and computer. Hepzibah was running back and forth, counting feet and making sure everybody knew she was there. Stephanie hovered in the hallway, trying to forget the figure she'd seen outside. After all, life was full of such moments, where there was an impenetrable adult logic to whatever was going on, and to reveal bewilderment was often to invite derision. Grown-ups didn't mind the dark, especially in the countryside, she supposed. Except that they generally carried a torch – and wasn't there a very strong suggestion that activities carried out in darkness were almost always unlawful, or at least suspicious? There was something horrible called lamping, for a start. And something even more ghastly called dogging that a boy at school had sniggered about only a few days ago.

But it was that third leg that bothered her most of all. Because it was very likely to have been a gun – one with a long muzzle that was undoubtedly intended to shoot something. Or someone. Because wasn't that the whole point of guns?

In the Old Stables on the Crossfield Estate, at eight o'clock on Friday evening, the Frowse family found itself reduced to two. 'Where's your mother?' asked Digby. 'I haven't seen her at all today. Or yesterday, come to think of it. Did she say she was going somewhere?'

'She didn't say anything to me,' returned his son. 'I guess she just took the car and went. She's sure to have told you where and you've forgotten.'

'What a weird lot we are,' sighed Digby. 'You'd think we'd have missed her before now. It did occur to me to wonder last night when there wasn't any supper.'

'She's been out every evening this week, pretty much. I just assumed she was having a drink with some pals. There was all that stuff in the fridge, after all, for us to make supper with. Didn't she come home to sleep?'

'Didn't hear her.' The Frowses all had separate bedrooms, and unusually separate lives, although Ant couldn't recall a time when it had taken a whole day, or longer, before noticing someone was unaccountably absent.

'If she's taken the car, that just leaves us with the van,' said Digby crossly.

'That's okay, surely? Where do you want to go?'

'I might fancy meeting a few mates for a Christmas tipple.'

'If you were going to do that, you'd have gone by now. Look – the chances are Mum said where she was going, but neither of us listened when she mentioned it. I do remember something about a quick trip to London – but that was a week ago. Could be she was always meaning to go yesterday.'

'Not very likely,' said his father, with a small frown. 'The roads are sure to be awful, and won't London be absolute bedlam? Not her sort of thing at all, this time of year. It'd take all day to get there and back. I wish we knew exactly *when* she went.'

'She might have gone on the train. The car's probably at the station.' Ant was finding his father's attitude contradictory. He appeared vaguely worried, while at the same time taking an entirely selfish line. 'Why does it matter what time she went, anyway?'

Digby sighed and pinched his nose. 'Oh, I don't know. I mean – I know she's unpredictable, but doesn't this seem a bit . . . *unusual*, even for her?'

Antares looked around the disorderly house. Their constantly critical landlord did have a point – they did live like Gypsies. Or rather, like the old-fashioned, politically dubious idea people once had of Gypsies. The people the

Irish referred to as 'tinkers', who set up camp in lay-bys and strewed a wide area with bits of scrap metal and other detritus. They set up washing lines and tied up ponies and dogs. Ant had seen just such a habitation in County Wicklow, when he was about eight. They'd been visiting Digby's brother, who had moved to Ireland in his twenties. When he glanced out of the kitchen window now to view the front garden, the similarities were inescapable. Digby was a magpie, visiting local auction rooms and car boot sales and coming home with every kind of junk. Most of it was set down on the patch of grass between the house and the driveway and never attended to again.

Inside was not much better. Digby and Beverley had moved into separate bedrooms around the time Aldebaran had died, and filled each room with paraphernalia. In Digby's there was a computer, scores of books, stacks of printed-out text and boxes of junk that would decay or disintegrate if left outside. In the past year he had drifted into selling as well as buying, setting up his own car boot two or three days a week, weather and work obligations permitting. 'This is my stock,' he would say, waving vaguely at the boxes. He had begun to focus on old Bakelite radios and telephones, along with table lamps and car mascots. 'People collect this sort of thing, you know,' he asserted. Some of the lamps were so old they were fuelled by oil.

In Beverley's room there was also a laptop and books, but her studies were much more focused. She was teaching herself law, with special regard to property rights, tenantry laws and council responsibilities. Nobody would have been surprised if she had suddenly announced an intention to go into local politics.

'She's probably just sick of this house,' said Ant now. 'Carla's daughters will have been the final straw.'

'You could be right. It's like being under surveillance by the Stasi – even if we have worked out how to dodge the cameras.'

The CCTV cameras, ostensibly intended to deter burglars and other intruders, overlooked the Frowses' cottage at the front. If the family left by the main door, walked down to the small parking area and drove down the drive, every step would be captured. But they had soon devised a system whereby they left through the back door, walked in a loop around the side of the house, and reached their vehicles without being seen. Little by little, they had shifted the parking area out of range, too. But there was no avoiding the camera down at the electric gate. The only satisfaction there was that the landlord couldn't see who was inside the car as it drove away.

To Ant, this was mostly just a game. He didn't let it affect him emotionally, beyond the concern he felt at the way it upset his parents. His mother was right in saying it was definite harassment and intimidation, and she wrote regular letters to the Housing Department to say exactly that. She kept a detailed dossier with every tiny event logged, and a copy of every letter. She was talking about buying a 'dashcam' to set up inside their car, so that any physical approaches that occurred in the driveway could be recorded. This was because there had been one occasion when Rufus Blackwood had stopped her at the gate and started accusing her of letting their dog Percy trespass on forbidden ground. Carla owned a precious pedigree Pekinese, of all things, and the existence of other dogs presented a direct threat to its welfare, apparently.

'They'll be too busy with Christmas to bother about us,' said Ant. 'They've kept at a distance so far, anyway.'

Digby said nothing and Ant went on, 'I'm going to try and phone Mum and see what's she's up to.'

But when he did just that, the phone was unresponsive. 'She's switched it off,' he said.

'What's new?' said Digby.

Ant himself had plans for the evening. Although not considering himself to be in a committed relationship, he did have a female friend whose company he enjoyed. Alice Whitworth lived in Chipping Campden with her young daughter and two corgis. Because of the child, Ant was never permitted to stay overnight – except when young Lydia was sleeping at her father's, which did not happen very often, because he lived in Birmingham. Alice and Ant had known each other since school, off and on, and had an easy understanding that never developed into anything serious.

'I'm going over to see Alice,' he said. 'I'll probably be late back. I'll go on the bike, so it won't matter if I drink.'

'Lydia not at her dad's for Christmas, then?'

'Certainly not. But she is going there for New Year's Day, I think. Staying a night or two.'

'Ah well. She's right, you know. Best not to confuse the kid,' said Digby, as he had said many times before. Ant didn't argue. They had all seen enough bewildered children

35

from broken families to understand the pitfalls. 'It's not as if you're aiming to marry her, now is it?'

'Doesn't look like it,' sighed Ant, who was beginning to resign himself to perpetual bachelorhood. 'If I do, it won't be till Lydia's about sixteen.'

'Well, don't worry about me,' said Digby. 'I'm going to see if I can get that radio to work. I think if I give it a better aerial, I might get somewhere. And your mother's sure to be back before bedtime.'

'Maybe clean the place up a bit, as well,' said Ant, with a cheeky grin.

'I might just do that,' said his father.

Chapter Three

Thea Slocombe was doing her best to concentrate on Christmas. She owed it to Drew and his children to make the best possible effort. The year before, everyone had been finding their feet and wondering how this newly formed family was going to work out. They had all been treading carefully, wary of hurting each other's feelings or trampling on sacrosanct ground, so that Christmas had turned into a somewhat scrappy event, with everybody going through the motions with far too much care. It was more relaxed now, but expectations were higher. Memories of Karen were inevitably more vivid at such a time, her special Christmas touches still important to her children. The tree was a prime example. Drew had explained it, with some embarrassment, leaving it to Thea to decide whether or not to adhere to the ritual established by his first wife. 'That's not fair,' she had wailed. 'Can't you take an executive decision and then explain it to them?'

'I might if I knew what the decision was,' he said reasonably.

'Oh, I don't know. I'll do my best, I suppose, to keep things as they were. There's no sense in making changes for the sake of it. The trouble is, I know I won't make such a good job of it. We've already established that Karen put a lot more into the whole thing than I'm ever going to.'

'They're still very young,' he had pleaded. 'Just give it three or four more years. Stockings, treasure hunt, mince pie for Santa. It's all quite ordinary, really.'

'Treasure hunt?' Thea had echoed worriedly.

'Little presents hidden round the house. We bought them with money that Karen's relations sent. Wrapped in colour-coded paper, red for Tim and yellow for Stephanie.'

'Well, let's cut that one out, at least,' Thea said. 'Not least because it doesn't seem likely that the relatives – whoever they are – are still going to send any money.'

'They didn't last year, come to think of it. They must think that now I've got you, they can forget all about me and my kids.'

There were further details, such as roasted chestnuts, mistletoe hung from a door frame, and the exact kind of satsuma. 'The ones that are really easy to peel,' Drew specified.

It wasn't, she acknowledged, that these were especially outlandish requests. They were much the same as she and

Carl had included in their own Christmases. But that had been a long time ago and since Carl died, she had foisted herself on Jocelyn most years, leaving her sister to construct whatever festive frolics took her fancy.

Thea herself liked Christmas well enough, recognising that without it the dark days of winter would be intolerable. December flew by in a whirl of preparations, so that by the time the decorations came down the evenings were lighter by a few minutes and there was hope for better days. She liked the excitement of children and the coloured lights everywhere. What she did not like was the expense and the relentless advertising. She had assumed that Drew felt the same, and was largely reassured in that respect. He did, however, insist on spending unreasonable sums of money on his children. The previous year had seen them both in receipt of lavish toys, which had been all too quickly abandoned, the money wasted. Although he was taking more care this year to fit the gift to the individual child, he was still spending far more than Thea thought necessary. From force of habit he continued to take charge of their clothes, making a special outing to select new outfits, letting them have whatever they wanted. Thea stepped back, thankful that at least one aspect of their maintenance could be avoided. Drew also saw to their haircuts, rather to Thea's amusement.

'You don't have to get them anything,' he had told her, regarding the Christmas presents. 'These are from both of us.'

'That's something, I suppose,' she sighed, eyeing the purchases with disfavour. 'But they really don't need such big things, you know.'

'So you keep telling me. I happen to disagree.' His firm stand was enough to silence her, at least for that year.

Her share of the labour, as always, came down to food and household management – making beds, putting up decorations.

'Is there anything else we need?' she asked the girls, later on Friday afternoon. 'Speak now, if there is, because I really don't want to go to the shops again after tomorrow.'

Jessica and Stephanie exchanged looks. 'Cranberry sauce?' said Jessica.

'Got it.'

'A present for everyone – that's me, Drew, two kids.'

Thea pretended to be horrified. 'You mean I have to get *you* something?'

'And Hepzie,' said Stephanie.

'Absolutely not. Dogs don't do Christmas. Everyone knows that.'

'You've got things for everybody, have you, Steph?' Jessica asked.

'*Ages* ago.'

'She's not exaggerating,' said Thea, rolling her eyes. 'She had most of them wrapped by the end of October.'

'Aunt Emily always did them in September,' laughed Jessica. 'Is she still the same?'

'Not quite. I think she's still a bit wobbly.' Thea's older sister's life had taken a knock in recent years, making her withdrawn and uncommunicative.

'And Damien will bring his presents – assuming there are any – when he comes on Wednesday.' She sighed, as she often did at any mention of her brother.

Andrew Emerson and his wife Fiona arrived at seven on Friday evening, having been warned by Drew that they could only expect drinks and nibbles, rather than a full-scale meal. This was perfectly acceptable, it seemed, as Fiona made clear from the outset. 'Saving ourselves for Christmas,' she said. 'We signed up for a big meal with all the trimmings at the hotel in town. You know – Chipping Campden House. I've got out of the habit of cooking.'

'Lucky you,' laughed Thea, heady with relief at not being required to provide serious quantities of food.

Stephanie liked Fiona a lot. She and Timmy were staying up until the visitors had gone, which seemed only right and proper. 'They won't stay later than nine anyway,' said Drew.

But Drew was oddly distracted throughout the whole visit. One by one, the others noticed, though long after Stephanie had become aware that he wasn't right. It had started with the phone call before supper. He had come out of his office into the disorganised preparations for a scanty supper, before the visitors arrived. There had been no opportunity for a coherent conversation. 'Can you feed the dog for me?' Thea had asked him.

'Can you bring some more logs in?' was the next request.

'Dad – what time *exactly* will you bring the stockings up on Christmas morning?' Timmy wanted to know.

'Drew – when are you going to take me down to look at your burial field?' Jessica wondered.

They ate quickly, and washed everything up, while Stephanie continued to observe her father and his obvious preoccupation. She was none the wiser when the Emersons arrived.

Andrew was the next person to realise something was awry. 'What's up, mate?' he asked, in his plain-speaking fashion.

Drew flinched, and forced a smile. 'What? Oh – nothing. Worrying about whether everyone's going to like the presents I've got them. Families and all that sort of thing.'

Andrew gave this some thought. He was nearly twenty years older than Drew, a lifelong farmer driven out of business by TB in his cattle, and a fatal loss of hope for the future of agriculture. He and Fiona had sold their farm near Chedworth and accepted Drew's offer of low-paid sporadic work as his assistant in the undertaking business. Fiona had remained in her job at the council, increasing her hours and enjoying the absence of livestock. 'Everyone said we would miss the cows and sheep, but they were wrong,' she repeated regularly, with a liberated laugh. The money they had managed to salvage from the sale would see them through to old age, even after buying a small bungalow on a new estate in the area.

'You've got your family right here in front of you,' said Andrew.

'The most important ones, yes,' said Drew. Only Stephanie overheard this remark, and wondered what it meant. She found herself sliding into a meditation about herself and Timmy and how they were Drew's real family, more than Thea and Jessica were. And that brought her to the subject of Drew and Timmy, and their clumsy attempts to love each other. Because Timmy really wasn't an irritating person. He was thin and small for his age, but he wasn't stupid or mean or fussy about food. His very existence seemed to be the problem – a conclusion that Thea had once accidentally confirmed, when Stephanie heard her say, 'You can't blame him for being born, Drew. You've really got to try harder with him, you know you have.' They'd been in their bedroom, and hadn't seen Stephanie outside on the landing. Drew had groaned and agreed, saying, 'Yes, I know.' Nothing much had changed, though.

Except it had got better in the past week or so, because of Christmas. Timmy made a modest list of the presents he would like, all very serious stuff, and Drew had gone over it with him and told him he was very advanced in his grasp of history and maps and that sort of thing. He even said Timmy's mother would have been proud of him, which was particularly kind, because Karen dying had probably been worse for Timmy than for anyone else.

Jessica was being kind to him now, as well. She let him go on about Pokémon for ages, and then said she'd read to him when he went to bed. Two more sleeps till Christmas Eve and she suggested a whole lot of things to do that would please him most. 'Stephanie and Thea can see to the food, and we'll go out for a walk,' she said. 'With the dog.'

'That sounds great,' Thea had said with a smile. 'It'll be good to have you out of the house for a bit. It's all going to be terribly busy, with school breaking up so close to Christmas. I don't know what they were thinking – the poor teachers must have hated it.'

Nobody cared about the teachers, and Stephanie was of the opinion that it was quite a good idea to jump straight from school to the main business of the holiday, without lots of boring days to wait for something to happen. She shook herself, and returned her attention to Andrew, who was watching her face.

'No new funerals, then?' he asked Drew. 'Or have you turned the phone off?'

'Just the one that came through yesterday. Luckily, the hospital's keeping him for me until Wednesday, which is very decent of them. And the phone stays on. Anything that happens from now till Wednesday will have to wait, but at least they can call and tell us about it. Although we could do a removal on Tuesday, I suppose, if we absolutely had to.'

'No problem,' Andrew nodded. 'I'm not going anywhere.'

'We could do a burial Thursday or Friday, at a push,' Drew went on. 'But I have a feeling we're not going to have any new business before the end of the week.'

'People aren't allowed to die at Christmas, are they, Dad?' said Stephanie, pushing up under his arm, and gazing into his face. She wanted him to remember she was there, at his side, *on* his side, if it came to a disagreement. She was acting like a much younger child, clinging to the magic of Christmas in the face of a threat that growing up meant losing her grasp of all that part of it.

'Right,' said Drew, with a sigh. 'Although not everybody sticks to that particular rule, sad to say.'

'Anybody you know?' asked Andrew astutely.

Drew made a gesture that meant *Hush!* and quickly changed the subject. 'Timmy's counting the minutes till Christmas. It's still quite a lot, eh, Tim?'

The child was not far away, sitting next to Jessica on

the sofa. Fiona Emerson was leaning over the back of the couch, joining in a three-way conversation about the various animals you could keep as pets. 'My sister's got rats,' said Fiona. 'She absolutely adores them.'

Timmy heard his father and looked across at him. 'What?' he said.

'Counting the minutes,' Stephanie explained. 'Dad's telling Andrew about it.'

'Oh.' Even Timmy understood that his father had just been making conversation for the sake of it. The pet rats were a lot more interesting.

Andrew came to the rescue. 'I gather there's been some bother up at Crossfield,' he said. 'Some priceless bit of jewellery's gone missing. We heard about it yesterday.'

Drew seized on this with alacrity. 'Really? No, haven't heard anything. Thea – did you know there's some ructions at Crossfield? You were there a few days ago, weren't you?'

Thea had been circulating with bowls of crisps and peanuts. 'What sort of ructions?'

Andrew shrugged. 'The Blackwood bloke was in the post office in Chipping Campden, shouting about a mislaid package that had been sent special delivery from London, and never turned up. They told him he would have to try tracking it online, and he said he'd done that and the fools insisted it had been delivered and signed for. The signature was one of those done with your finger, which always looks like a bit of meaningless scribble. He said the delivery man must have stolen it, which was going too far for the woman in the post office. She turned her back on him. It was rather fine, actually. That man's a complete bully.'

'It was Sunday when we were there. This must have happened since then. Or else the Frowses didn't know about it.' Thea regarded Stephanie. 'They didn't say anything, did they?'

Stephanie shook her head. 'Ant just said there were two daughters visiting and Beverley was annoyed about that.'

Thea nodded. 'Right – I remember. It's dreadful the way those people make them live. The Frowses, I mean. I'm sure there must be a law against it, but Beverley says it's all very complicated and inexact. And Ant says it's the wife that's the real pig. Rufus wasn't too bad before he married her.'

Stephanie absorbed the new story about the necklace with interest. A fight in the local post office must have been quite a drama. And priceless jewellery sounded like something out of a book. Jessica seemed to think so too. 'Have they reported the loss of the jewellery to the police?' she asked.

Andrew spread his hands in a display of ignorance. 'No idea,' he said. 'Although I would guess not, the way he was talking.'

'He probably will, though,' Thea said. 'Those sort of people won't let anything go. They're very likely thinking it was Ant or one of his parents who nicked the thing. They'll use any excuse to persecute them.'

'Nasty,' said Andrew.

'They *are* nasty,' said Stephanie fervently. 'Nasty rich people.'

Everyone laughed at that, which made her feel silly and ridiculously young.

Then it was nine o'clock, and the Emersons were going home, and Thea was clearing up glasses and the dog was gleaning crumbs from the carpet. Jessica stretched and said what a lovely lazy day it had been, and still two more to go before Christmas. Timmy groaned and said it felt as if Christmas would *never* come. Drew sat in one of the armchairs, watching them all with a weirdly distant expression.

'Bed, you two,' ordered Thea. 'Dad can read to you tonight. It must be his turn.'

And he did, briefly, and with very poor expression. Because the children were in the same room while Jessica was staying, one story did for them both. It was *Martin's Mice* by Dick King-Smith, which was childish and funny and familiar. Drew had owned the book since he was eight, and the cover was badly torn. When he picked it up before starting to read, he went very quiet, until Timmy said, 'Dad? We're waiting.'

Then they got the hurried chapter, and a perfunctory kiss, before being left to their own devices. 'Weird,' said Timmy.

'He's worried about something,' said Stephanie. 'I think somebody he knows must have died.'

'So why doesn't he tell us? Has he told Thea?'

'No,' said Stephanie with certainty. 'He hasn't. He's probably going to do it now.'

'She might not listen,' said Timmy, to Stephanie's surprise. 'She often doesn't.'

Stephanie found herself pulled in two directions. She wanted to defend her stepmother, who was being really good about Christmas, and staying cheerful and keeping it all going. But her deeper sympathies were with her father. He just wasn't very good at getting to the point, when he wanted something. He had a very poor grasp of timing; it made Stephanie wince when he would broach an important topic when it was obvious that Thea was juggling five other things already. And he would regularly start in the wrong place, jumping into the middle of a story that needed much more careful introduction. Thea would stop him, often irritably, saying, 'I can't read your mind, Drew. You need to explain what you're talking about.'

'She will if he says it properly,' she told Timmy.

'If,' said her brother sombrely.

Next morning, it soon became apparent that no meaningful conversation had taken place between the adults. Thea was still in domestic mode, making lists and teasing Timmy about his minute-counting. 'Just under forty-eight hours to go,' she calculated. 'We're getting there.'

Jessica had got up early and was on her mobile. Nobody asked who she was texting or why, but she volunteered the information anyway. 'I have to be back bright and early on Wednesday,' she announced. 'I was hoping I could have the morning off. I'm on duty all over New Year as well.'

'Do you get paid double time for that?' Thea asked.

Jessica shrugged. She was well known for being careless with money, haphazard with direct debits and credit cards. 'You'll never be able to buy your own house if you don't pay more attention,' Thea repeatedly warned her.

'That doesn't worry me at all,' came the blithe reply.

'So who's keeping you informed about the work rota?'

'Sandy. My flatmate. She's working right up to the end of tomorrow. She's CID and they've got a new case. Not sure what it is, but it's having an effect on the shifts, apparently.'

Drew wandered into the kitchen. 'I've got to make a phone call, but first I need to tell you something,' he said to the room in general. 'I'm going to have to be out all day today and part of tomorrow. Lucky Jessica's here – you can use her car if you need to.'

'Why? What are you talking about?' Thea seemed breathless with surprise.

'I had a phone call yesterday afternoon from my mother. My father died on Thursday night. She wants me to go up and see her.'

Chapter Four

Antares was slow to wake on Saturday, after drinking quite a lot of wine with Alice the previous evening. It was half past eight and he was supposed to be selling Christmas trees in Chipping Campden. The final day of a punishing three weeks, which had left him exhausted. It was several minutes before he remembered his absent mother. Her car had not been there when he returned home, which had bothered him at the time, but not enough to prevent him from slipping into a deep sleep the moment he lay down.

But now he was pierced by a feeling of acute concern. Where *was* his mother? While she was undeniably a woman of fierce independence, and even fiercer obstinacy, she would never leave for such a long time without explanation. He tried to think of reasons why she might so abruptly disappear. Something to do with Christmas seemed the most persuasive idea. An enforced two days of sitting around the house eating too much and bickering might have struck her as unbearable. Or perhaps the lurking presence of Carla Blackwood's two daughters, just over the fence, had felt insupportable. There was, after all, no absolute requirement for Beverley to remain at home and understandable reasons why she might choose not to.

But where would she go and why wouldn't she tell her husband and son?

For several years now, she had gone her own way, treating the bonds of marriage as of diminishing significance. Digby had been forced to accommodate himself to it until he discovered that he was himself liberated by this loose arrangement. Beverley had been an entirely adequate mother to her two children, until they finished school. Then she had swiped her hands together, given them beaming smiles and told them she intended to devote the rest of her life to pleasing herself. 'In the nicest possible way,' she had added with a laugh.

But she had been civilised about it. She mounted a large cork board on the wall and embellished it with dozens of drawing pins, several of them holding clean white sheets of paper. 'Just write your movements up here,' she instructed. 'Dates and places.'

'Wouldn't a simple calendar suffice?' asked her husband. 'Or one of those boards you can wipe clean?'

'Or stick notes onto the fridge with magnets?' suggested Ant.

'This way's best,' his mother insisted. 'Work from left to

right, see. There's space for all kinds of information, and we can refer back if necessary.'

Two years after that, Aldebaran had grabbed a felt tip, and written 'I'm off to America. See y'all. Deb.'

And she had gone, a month later, never to be seen again. Her note was still on the board, after ten years' absence. Ant peered at it now. Cluttered, dusty scraps of paper curling at the edges, they still used it once in a while. Nothing recent, though. Nothing from Beverley to explain where she'd gone so suddenly.

The approach of Christmas had seen all three of them scrambling to take advantage of the increased commerce that came with the festival. Digby had been running his stalls at a dozen different village hall sales, offering poinsettias, hyacinths, wreaths, mistletoe, holly, as well as keeping his regular market stall going, selling bric-a-brac and general junk. The van was permanently crammed with plants, packaging and fancy pots. Beverley went with him now and then, but her own activities centred more around textiles. She made rugs and wall hangings, blankets and bags, which she sold to pretentious emporiums all around the Cotswolds. She spun and dyed the wool herself, as well as running classes in a whole range of handicrafts. The Frowses were always busy.

'Didn't she have a row with old Blackwood a couple of days ago?' Ant said slowly. 'Was that Wednesday? She was upset about it that evening.'

'Bloody swine,' said Digby, automatically. He was a heavy man, whose past life had been full of incident, if his stories could be believed. Now in his late sixties, he had once been the manager of the whole estate, when it had been a fruit farm. Four hundred acres of apples, pears, plums, apricots and cherries had been grown there. The gates had been open to the public, who came to pick their own, or buy in bulk. But then it had failed, largely thanks to EU regulations and various social changes, and Digby had been out of work. Not, however, out of a home. The cottage was 'tied' and the family had a perfect right to stay in it for the rest of their lives. The entire estate had been sold, eighteen years earlier, to a millionaire who fancied a rural Cotswold lifestyle, but was appalled at the presence of a ramshackle cottage only yards from his own handsome Georgian home.

The landlord's name was Rufus Blackwood, and he was the owner of the whole Crossfield Estate, now amounting to six hundred acres on the edge of Broad Campden. It had ceased to function as a fruit farm years before, and all the apple and plum trees had been rooted out. Now it was grazing land, maintained more as a decorative park than a working farm. Alpacas and Highland cattle strolled over the close-cropped acres, a few fields were given over to growing lavender, a few more to fast-growing willows intended for biofuel. Blackwood was exceedingly rich, but he still enjoyed exploiting whatever government subsidies might be there for the taking. The Old Stables were a perpetual thorn in his side, the very sight of which enraged him. He and his Russian-born wife had decided to try to persuade the Frowses to leave by a campaign of harassment that had Beverley especially in a constant state of vigilance. She wrote down every detail of every underhand act, preparing herself for a legal defence that might never be needed.

The electrified fence around the whole property, with the gates and the keypads that had to be operated to open them, were several steps too far, as anybody would agree. Even though Digby had so cleverly circumvented the need for a code, the outrage persisted. The moment anyone lifted the phone, they were automatically connected, and the gate would swing open as if by magic. It was immensely satisfying, and a very good joke against the Blackwoods – but there was no denying the original intention to harass and intimidate. The landlord still believed he was making life difficult for his unwanted tenants. If he ever discovered the subterfuge, he would make a point of installing something even more draconian to make the Frowses' lives difficult.

The landlord's own visitors mostly arrived by helicopter, or fancy cars with special electronic devices that opened the big wrought-iron gate with ease. His wife had three daughters who showed up from time to time. Their father had been a Russian oil magnate. Carla had quickly found a rich Brit to marry when the rich Russian died in a freak accident. And Carla had been horrified at the eyesore that was the Old Stables when she first moved into Crossfield. Digby's van, his heaps of junk and the awful old caravan, and Beverley's untidy heaps of dyed wool drying in the sunshine – it all produced an impression starkly at odds with the mansion Carla had so enthusiastically come to live in.

Crossfield House was indeed a mansion. Covered in ivy, dating to around 1760, modernised and beautiful, it suffered terribly from its scruffy little neighbour, in Carla's eyes. 'My father would simply have had it demolished without a second thought,' she had said. 'Surely you can do that?'

'Sadly not,' sighed her new husband. 'I'd most likely end up with a prison sentence.' But he shared her contempt for the slobbish Frowses and their stubborn refusal to take increasingly heavy hints. The house was deliberately allowed to fall into disrepair, with Rufus ducking out of his obligations to keep roof and windows watertight. The tenants paid such a minimal rent that he felt entirely justified in neglecting them. He had much more important things to do, such as entertaining CEOs of large corporations and discussing investments with fund managers. He also had to keep Carla happy with lengthy trips in his yacht. The lodge they owned in Aspen had to be visited two or three times a year, as well.

Beverley, her husband and son suspected, made everything worse by her attitude. Every time the rent was reviewed, she wrote a long letter to the authorities listing the reasons why the house was uninhabitable as it was, and any rent was extortion. Even more self-defeating, she refused to allow Digby to make any sort of improvements himself. 'It's not our property – we're not responsible for the maintenance,' she repeated over and over. And so the plaster flaked off, the plumbing was full of airlocks and the kitchen was an absolute mess.

And yet Beverley loved Christmas. She would hang up great sprigs of Digby's holly and mistletoe, send handmade cards to everybody she had ever known, and kept a secret cupboard well stocked with surprise presents. On the day itself she would prepare a lavish meal with turkey and every imaginable accompaniment. More than once she had invited random strays to join them.

'What was the row about?' Digby wondered now. 'Did she say?'

'Something to do with a package that's gone missing. I didn't take very much notice, but apparently Rufus sent up for some priceless piece of jewellery for Carla, and it never arrived.'

'What? He had it sent through the post? That doesn't sound very likely.'

'I might have got it wrong. He accused Mum of having it, anyway. That was on Wednesday afternoon, when she was down by the gate. She was absolutely livid about it. You can't have missed the whole thing. You were right here when she came to tell us about it.'

His father grimaced. 'I remember bits of it. She wasn't really talking to me, was she? I was on the computer, as I recall.'

One of Digby's many methods of distracting himself from what he had feared would be long days of retirement was discussing the American Civil War with a large group of like-minded aficionados on his laptop – which he generally brought downstairs during the day, sitting at a small table in a corner of the living room and ignoring everything going on around him. He had been to the battlefields once, long ago, and never lost the interest. When he was on one of his forums, a bomb could go off next to him and he wouldn't notice.

Ant tried to remember more detail. 'I admit it didn't

make a lot of sense. You know how she talks in shorthand. But now I'm wondering—'

'What?'

'It might not have been the usual sort of thing. He was *accusing* her of something. Stealing, even. But just as I was starting to think it might be important, Jason phoned and I had to set him straight about the trees and we never got back to it. Mum went upstairs and the rest of the day seemed fairly normal. She made that lamb stew, remember, and went to bed early? And I don't think I've seen her since then.'

'Oh,' said Digby with a sigh. 'Well, I haven't either. D'you think we ought to do something about it?'

Mr and Mrs Frowse did not share a bedroom. When their daughter died, they agreed that her room should not be kept as any kind of shrine to her, except for a framed photograph of her. And on a corner shelf there stood a lidded urn made of porcelain in which Aldebaran's ashes were stored. 'I want her to be buried with me when I go,' said Beverley.

She had moved into the empty room and had been there ever since, with Digby making very little objection. 'Can I be in the grave with you as well?' was all he said. As far as Ant could tell, there were no conjugal encounters between his parents. Not one of the family could claim any activity of that kind. Only the dog enjoyed any sort of sex life, and that had been two years ago when Percy had fathered a litter of crossbreed puppies and suffered the extreme punishment of losing his gonads as a result.

'I'll try her phone again,' said Ant with no sense of

optimism. His mother did in theory carry a mobile with her, but generally it languished in the glove compartment of her car, the battery dead. 'Why would I want to be pursued by a telephone, when I've hated them all my life?' she would demand, with scant originality. When family or friends insisted, 'But they're so useful,' Beverley just laughed.

It was not that she was a deliberate rebel, going against the flow in any way. She was simply unaware most of the time that there *was* a flow. She barely noticed the news, had absolutely no grasp of current affairs, and only concerned herself with events inside her own small circle. She had not always been like this, however. The brutal and unsolved murder of her daughter Aldebaran had been the cause of her withdrawal from the world. 'If I can't do anything to change it, then I have no choice but to ignore it,' summed up her existence. 'I would rather not engage with this stinking world,' was what she said at the time. Digby's grief had also smothered most of his emotional life in a dense grey blanket. Both parents seemed to Ant to have drifted away from normal social intercourse, even with him, their only surviving child.

But he made his second phone call anyway and left a voicemail to the effect that he and his father were wondering what had become of her. 'I have to go,' he realised, five minutes later. 'One final push. I can hardly wait for tomorrow. Did you find the Christmas carols?'

'I did. It'll be playing all day, just as always.'

There was one special CD they always put on for Christmas Eve, and which always concealed itself in one or other pile of junk throughout the rest of the year. 'Where was it this time?' asked Ant.

'Top shelf, above the telly. Quite logical, really. Probably put it there myself.'

'Don't forget to take the dog for a quickie before you go out. If Mum's not back soon, he's going to have a boring day, poor old lad.'

The dog was Ant's, officially, and he was diligent in exercising and entertaining him as a rule. But Christmas chaos ensured that very few of the usual rules pertained.

'I'll have to wait for you to get home, won't I? I'll need the van.'

'So you will.' Ant sighed. 'You'll have to take him up to the footpath or somewhere. He ought to get a run.'

'Why can't you do it?' Digby whined. 'Where are you planning to be this afternoon?'

'Nowhere special,' Ant admitted. 'Once I've taken the tree to the hotel, I thought I'd set up the rest in the usual lay-by and catch a few last-minute customers. I could pack that in by about two, and get back then.'

'That'll do, then,' said Digby, in a disinterested tone. 'I may as well make the effort, even if it only fetches a few quid.' He had signed up for an evening stall in Blockley High Street, the last attempt to make some sales before Christmas. The whole family had agreed that they would stay at home on Christmas Eve regardless of what final business opportunities might present themselves.

'So just take the dog down to the gate and back for now. Don't forget.'

'I won't,' said Digby. 'But Bev's sure to be back sometime today. Isn't she?'

An hour after Drew's bombshell, during which he had answered countless questions and made an attempt at explaining his fractured relationship with his parents, Stephanie found herself stupidly feeling as if she had caused her unknown grandfather's death. Was that possible simply by the way she had recently been thinking about how her blood relations seemed so distant? She had been critical of them, in her own mind, and resentful of the way they seldom made contact. Or had she telepathically read Drew's mind, when he went so quiet after the phone call? In either case, she felt overwhelmed with concern for him, as she watched his face. Strange pouches had appeared beneath his eyes, and he couldn't look at any of them.

'Christ, Drew,' said Thea. 'Tomorrow's Christmas Eve.'

'I know it is. But if I don't go now, I won't be able to get away for days. She begged me. What could I say?'

Thea and Jessica both knew what it was to lose a father – though not one who had been entirely estranged for over twenty years. Stephanie and Timmy had lost their mother. Everyone understood how much such an event mattered. Timmy spoke up. 'Who's your father, Daddy?' he asked with a frown.

'Oh, Tim.' Drew pulled the child to him, and buried his face in the small shoulder. Again, Stephanie had a dreadful sense of having somehow made all this happen, by the power of her thoughts. 'You never met him.' Drew lifted his head. 'I'm so sorry about that. It was very wrong, and now it's too late. We never even had a name for you to call him. Your grandfather – that's who he was. His name was Peter James Slocombe, and he was seventy-six years old.'

'That's not very old to die,' said Stephanie, well aware of how many of their burials were of people over ninety.

'No,' said Drew emphatically. 'I always thought there'd be time to patch things up with them, and take you two to see them.' He was holding himself tight, pinching his nose to stave off the tears. 'I thought I might not tell you about it until after Christmas. I didn't want to spoil it.'

'Oh, Drew.' Thea was at his side, hesitantly patting his arm. 'We won't let it spoil anything. How far is it from here? County Durham – right? Can you get there and back in a day?'

'Barely. It must be four hours each way, at least.'

'What does she want from you? Will you have to go back again for the funeral? What about those cousins in Liverpool? Or wherever it is.'

He gave her a very rueful smile. 'That's the other thing. Apparently, she's been following my career more closely than I realised. She likes the idea of a natural burial for him, and wants me to see to it for her. She says it's the least I can do after abandoning them the way I did. It's all my fault, in her view. I'm stubborn and selfish and a big disappointment.' He looked up, misery and anger fighting for dominance. 'She always said she hated the idea of my being an undertaker. Now she's completely changed her mind about it – without ever telling me.'

'She doesn't know what she's saying,' said Jessica. 'If

she's just lost her husband she'll be in shock.'

'Yes,' said Drew impatiently, managing to convey the obvious fact that as an undertaker he knew quite a lot about newly bereaved people. 'But she knows I'm going to have to do as she wants. Aren't I? She's still my mother.'

'She can't possibly want you to bury him here.' Thea looked round at her daughter and stepchildren. 'Can she?'

'No, no. She's never been anywhere near the Cotswolds. But apparently there are two or three natural burial grounds within reach of Barnard Castle, and she wants me to see to the whole thing, because I "know the ropes", as she puts it.'

'She said all this on the phone yesterday and you sat through the whole evening without a word? You've taken all this time to tell us about it.' She was not so much accusing as bewildered.

'You were all so jolly, it wasn't too difficult to stay quiet.'

'If anybody's selfish, it's me,' said Thea sadly. 'I should have given you more attention, instead of worrying about potatoes and custard.'

'Potatoes and custard!' snorted Timmy. 'Yuk!'

'There was more,' said Drew, giving his son an oddly speculative look. Everyone went quiet. 'She said it was very wrong of me to keep her grandchildren away, and not even ask her to our wedding last year. I never even told her about it until last Christmas.'

'You were scared of what she might say,' Thea nodded. 'Too many stories of terrible mothers turning up at weddings like wicked fairies.'

'Well, anyway – she said I should bring them with me tomorrow. It would be a consolation, when she's got such a miserable Christmas in store for her.'

Thea gave a small shriek. 'Don't tell me – she wants you to bring her back here tomorrow night. She wants to have Christmas with us. Doesn't she?'

'Would that be so awful?'

'*Yes!* Call me selfish as much as you like, but yes, it would be awful. A woman I've never met, just widowed, with a mountain of baggage on her shoulder, sitting like a dead elephant at the dinner table. Besides, there's nowhere for her to sleep, if she's still here when Damien comes. No, Drew, it's impossible.'

She looked from face to face, puzzled to see a variety of grins looking back at her. 'What?'

'Dead elephant,' giggled Timmy. 'You said she was like a dead elephant.'

'Did I? You know what I mean – people say there's a dead elephant in the room. That's what she would be.'

'Elephant in the room, Mum. Nobody ever says it's a dead one,' Jessica told her.

'Oh. Right. Well, anyway, I'm not having her and that's that.'

'She doesn't want to come, actually,' said Drew. 'But she does want me to take the kids with me tomorrow. I thought maybe just Timmy . . . Stephanie's got to entertain Jessica. I thought it might be nice just to have him . . .' He tailed off awkwardly.

Another silence filled the room. 'Me?' said Timmy eventually, with a frown. The idea was so new, it took some effort to process. Stephanie felt a rising anger at being excluded. However alarming and confusing this sudden development might be, she didn't want to miss any of it. *What about me?* she wanted to whine. But she was eleven and old enough to bite back the words. In any other situation she would have been happy for father and son to spend time together, confident of her own favoured place in Drew's heart. But this was different – this was a Significant Moment. That much was obvious already. Timmy would remember it all his life; he would be the first to meet their grandmother. He might even see their dead grandfather in his coffin. Dead bodies in coffins were nothing strange to either of them, after all.

'Are you sure?' asked Thea, bending over the little boy. 'He's very young.'

'He's nine. What do you think, Tim?'

'It's fine,' he shrugged. 'So long as we get back for Christmas.'

'I promise we will.'

'The roads are going to be dreadful,' Jessica reminded him. 'Everybody starts rushing around on Christmas Eve.'

'I think it's a bit silly, to be honest,' said Thea. 'You'll be a wreck by Monday, just when you should be on top form.'

'If we leave this afternoon and stay overnight somewhere like Sheffield, then start early tomorrow, we'd easily be there by half past ten or so. Then stay till teatime and be home again by bedtime tomorrow.'

'More like midnight, if the traffic's as bad as Jessica thinks,' Thea corrected him. 'And you can't just *go*, like that. You've got to pack if you're staying overnight.'

'Which would take five minutes.'

'Where are you going to stay?'

'Find a Premier Inn or one of those places they have on the motorway. Look – it's all perfectly feasible. We could even go now, and be there by dark – but I don't think she wants us staying there overnight. I've worked it all out. Don't argue with me, okay?' He spoke to Tim. 'Go upstairs with Mum and help her to pack your things.'

It was not the first time he'd done it – referring to Thea as 'Mum' – but it always jarred the whole family. It was obvious that he had conflated his two wives in a forgetful moment, and that offended everyone, even Karen's ghost. Especially Karen's ghost, in Stephanie's opinion. And now he was being uncharacteristically masterful, brooking no disagreement, which didn't seem fair. He'd had the whole night to work out what he wanted to do, while the rest of them were still trying to digest the news of the grandfather's death. But he was obviously right in thinking the trip could work. If anyone could construct an effective itinerary, it was Drew Slocombe. His logistical calculations were born of his days as a conventional undertaker, where there might be five funerals in a day, with limousines and hearses to be scheduled with absolute precision, flowers delivered and ministers arranged. It soon became second nature, even for one of the lesser employees, to compulsively work out routes and timings.

'Wow!' exclaimed Jessica. 'He can be decisive when he tries, can't he!'

Thea abandoned any further argument and took Timmy upstairs to choose clothes for the next day and pack pyjamas and a toothbrush. Stephanie watched with a mixture of sadness and envy. Poor Timmy – his first night in a hotel, and it was all too much of a rush for him to enjoy it. Hours and hours in a car, then a meeting with a grandmother who sounded like something close to a witch. 'Be nice to him, Daddy,' she said impulsively. 'Nine isn't very old, you know.'

'You think I won't be?' He really seemed to want to know.

'You might forget about him,' she said bravely. 'With everything else that's going on. It's all a bit *surprising*, isn't it? I mean – he hasn't had time to understand what's happening. You need to look after him,' she urged. 'Like you look after me.'

'Oh, Steffie.' Their eyes met in a long gaze of mutual understanding. 'What did I do to deserve you?'

Jessica made a pretend-coughing noise. 'God – you two! Don't worry, Steph, Tim'll be fine. They'll be back again before you know it, and we're going to be mega-busy tomorrow. Your dad says you have to entertain me, remember.'

It was around eleven that morning by the time Ant was parking his van in a narrow Chipping Campden street, where only the slenderest of vehicles could squeeze past him. He was only going to be two minutes, and the street was a minor one. 'Should be okay,' he muttered to himself.

'You'll get a ticket,' came a female voice at his shoulder. Turning he saw Bronya, the eldest of Carla Blackwood's three daughters. Beside her was one of her sisters; he wasn't sure which.

'Oh, hello,' he said, startled not just at her sudden appearance but at the relatively friendly look on her face. 'Down here for Christmas, are you?'

'That's right. Just me and Annika this time. Olga had a better offer from a man in Scotland.' She laughed. 'Mama isn't pleased about it.'

The trio of sisters were Russian by birth, but had acquired a near-perfect mastery of English. Bronya in particular was inclined to be talkative, despite a degree of hostility acquired from her mother. 'Oh,' said Ant feebly. 'Well, I'd better crack on, or you'll be proved right about that parking ticket.'

'What are you doing?' asked Bronya curiously.

'Taking a Christmas tree to the hotel just along there.' He pointed to the front door of the Campden House Hotel. 'Something happened to the first one, and they want a replacement.'

'Why not take it around the back? There's a big car park there, you know.' It was the other sister speaking. Annika was smaller and younger and quieter than Bronya. It surprised him to realise she had such a good grasp of the town's confusing geography.

'I know – but this is quicker,' he said. 'It's quite a walk from the car park to the building, and the tree's pretty heavy.'

'We stayed here when Mama and Rufus got married,' Bronya explained. 'With a lot of other guests.'

'Oh,' said Ant again. The Frowses had been only vaguely aware of the scale of the Blackwood wedding, three years earlier. They had not been invited, and only discovered that it was happening at all from town gossip a week or so before the event. Guests filled the main hotels, big expensive cars filled the local parks and helicopters landed at Crossfield in greater numbers than usual.

'Rufus is so good to her,' Annika suddenly gushed. 'She has been so lucky with him. A much better man than our father, it must be said.'

Bronya nodded her big golden head, her expression sceptical. She had Eastern European looks, with plump cheeks and a lot of yellow hair. She wore a fur coat that looked heavy and rather too warm for an English winter. Ant was torn between 'cracking on' as he termed it, and staying to encourage whatever further indiscretions might be on offer. It was highly unusual for anyone from the big house to make conversation like this. *Must be Christmas*, he thought. The mellow attitude was oddly seductive, so he hesitated, waiting for more.

'But this week has been quite troubled,' Annika went on, pulling a face to indicate chagrin. 'A package has got lost somehow, and Rufus was frantic about it. Quite frantic. Saying somebody has robbed him and the police have to be called.' She gave Ant a searching look. 'He thinks perhaps it was wrongly delivered to your cottage, and was saying he would go and ask your mother about it.'

'Or your father,' added Bronya. She nudged her sister. 'All that was days ago now. We haven't even seen Rufus since Thursday. He had to go away for some reason.' She shrugged, lifting the heavy coat with strong shoulders. 'He's always dashing off to some crisis or other. Mama is worried he won't get back for Christmas.' Her mastery of the English language was noticeably better than Annika's, which made Ant wish he knew more about their early lives. While entirely unfamiliar with the works of Russian literature, he had a sense that they remained exotic and intriguing by virtue of their birthplace.

'We haven't had any deliveries,' said Ant quickly. 'We did hear there'd been a lost package, but it's nothing to do with us. We've only had the usual Christmas cards. Nobody ever sends us parcels.' Not strictly true, he silently corrected himself. Digby routinely ordered books and other things online, which various delivery services brought to the door.

'It's his present to Mama, you see,' Bronya explained. 'A very valuable piece of jewellery. The parcel was supposed to be registered and sent by special delivery, but somehow it hasn't arrived.'

From one moment to the next, Ant understood that there had never been anything mellow or benign about the sisters' approach, here in the street. They had been playing with him, pretending to be friendly before leaping into accusations. Both pairs of eyes narrowed and each woman stepped a little closer to him. The fact of their Russian origins felt significant in a much more threatening way. They were going to stab him with a deadly toxin or carry him off to a prison somewhere in order to beat him senseless. The clichés crowded his mind, born of James Bond stories and decades-old paranoia. And yet, it was real. There was malice vivid on both faces.

'What are you accusing me of?' he asked, much too loudly. A woman passing by gave him a worried look.

'Leave me alone. I've got work to do.'

'We're not keeping you, are we?' said Bronya with appalling sweetness. 'Carry on, why don't you? Deliver your tree and go home to your Gypsy parents. They'll be worrying about you, little boy.'

It was horrible. The 'Gypsy' was meant as an insult that carried special resonance for a Russian. The 'little boy' was even more insulting, since he was pretty sure both women were marginally younger than he was. They were referring to the fact that he still lived at home, barely a fully functioning adult as a result. He was happy to be a Gypsy, but he did not want to be thought of as immature or childish.

He pulled away and went to the back of the van. But before he could lift out the large tree, he got a surprise phone call. Letting go of the heavy trunk, he extracted the phone from his jacket pocket.

'It's me,' breathed his mother. 'I'm phoning to say I'm really all right, but I don't think I'm going to be home for Christmas.' He could hear an unfamiliar hint of emotion in her voice. He gazed unseeingly at the street around him, the Russian girls walking arrogantly away from him.

'For God's sake! What's happened? Can't I come and get you from wherever you are?'

'No, love. Don't do that. It's all horribly complicated. He's dead, you see. Ant – do you hear me? He's dead and I won't be able to come home.'

Ant was balancing a large tree half in and half out of his van. People were tutting loudly at the obstruction he was causing. The narrow pavement was unsuited to such manoeuvres, and with the phone in one hand, he was further impeded. A woman pushed at him impatiently. When he tried to lift the tree out of her way, it brushed the top of her head and caught in her hair. His van was also causing trouble, its back doors open. 'What?' he called down the phone. 'Is this some kind of a joke?' He grimaced apologetically at the woman and a handful of others who were finding him a nuisance.

His mother's voice was growing faint. 'The battery's going and I haven't got the charger. Ant, I think there's going to be trouble. I'm in Win—' and her voice disappeared, partly thanks to a loud horn honking in the street, but mainly because his mother's mobile was dying. Helplessly, he shook his phone and called her name. Then he pocketed his device, shouldered the tree and marched along the pavement. Then he turned left into the front door of the Campden House Hotel and dumped the tree. He was detained for a further three minutes, while the manager came out of his office to shake his hand and present him with a ready-wrapped package. 'We were expecting you,' he said. 'This is for all your work this year – it's for your mum as well.' He went on with a formal little speech that Ant barely had the patience to hear.

'Gosh, thanks,' Ant panted, when he finished. 'Have a good Christmas. Sorry! I can't stop any longer – I'm parked on the pavement.' And he ran back to his van.

He called his mother back, in desperation, but her phone remained unresponsive.

Win? Where was Win? Winchcombe, probably. But there was also Winchester or Windermere or Windsor. And

71

Winchmore Hill in North London was a place, as well. In a fit of hysteria, he even considered Winnipeg as a possibility.

Then, with pounding heart and clammy palms, he called his father.

Chapter Five

Ant abandoned his plan to sell his remaining trees in a lay-by, and went home to talk to Digby. The words his mother had spoken on the phone echoed and whirled around his head, making less sense with every passing minute. He needed Digby to explain them to him.

'Should I call the police?' he wondered, having described the bizarre conversation.

'Don't be so bloody daft. I don't see what's so alarming in what she said, anyway.' Digby was alternately impatient and reflective, taking a long time to respond to his son's evident panic and confusion. 'Listen – she said she was all right, didn't she? Why would the police take any interest in it, if you did call them? She's a grown woman, perfectly capable of looking after herself.'

'Have you been listening to me at all?' Ant shouted. 'She said somebody's dead, and she's scared to come home. Who's dead? What did she mean? Has she done something terrible? Run someone over and not stopped? Or what? Dad – you have to take this seriously. There's something really weird going on.'

'I'll grant you that,' said Digby, still infuriatingly calm. 'But it sounds to me as if she's working it out in her own way. We'll just have to wait for her to get over it and come home. Might not be till after Christmas, though, by the sound of it. Pity about that.' He rubbed the head of the dog sitting at his side. 'Percy's going to miss her,' he added, with a little grunt of amusement.

Ant was still breathing hard and quelling an urge to thump his father in the chest out of sheer frustration, when someone knocked on the front door. 'Who's that?' said Digby. 'Go and see, there's a good lad.'

The tone was intolerably patronising, and brought to mind the 'little boy' comment made by Bronya that very morning. 'I am *not* a lad,' he snarled. 'I'm thirty-five years old.'

'Just answer the door,' said his father, with a sigh.

A duo of uniformed constables was standing there, looking irritated and puzzled after struggling with the electric gate. 'We didn't have to speak to anyone before it opened,' said one, waving back down the driveway.

'Don't worry about it,' advised Ant.

The other man was staring wide-eyed at the obvious mismatch between the main house and the battered converted stable. 'We've just come from talking to Mrs

Blackwood,' he said. 'She told us we would have to phone you to gain access.'

Ant simply waited for them to explain their presence. The materialisation of police officers, when he had only just been suggesting he call them, felt like some sort of magic trick. And then as if by more magic, his father was at his elbow. 'Morning, lads,' he said, rather loudly. 'What can we do for you, then?'

'It's concerning an item of jewellery that appears to have been misappropriated,' said the first man stiffly. 'It has been reported by the lady of the big house, who suggested we speak to you about it. In particular she mentioned Mrs Beverley Frowse.'

'She's not here,' said Digby. 'We heard that poor old Rufus lost track of his wife's Christmas present. He'll be in the doghouse, sure enough.'

Ant was slowly processing his father's behaviour. The hail-fellow-well-met delivery was one of his favoured methods of addressing those in authority; a refusal to show any sort of deference. It was not that so much as the words, and the haste with which he spoke them. The implication was that Digby did not want his son to reveal the truth about Beverley's disappearance and subsequent phone call. Ant was strongly tempted to ignore these wishes and dump all his worries onto official shoulders.

He's dead, you see, and I won't be able to come home. Beverley's words repeated endlessly inside his head, until it had reached the point where they had become almost meaningless. He wanted somebody to explain them to him in a way that would not mean trouble. Because on the face of it, they were very troubling indeed.

But the police had come about the stupid Blackwoods and their missing package. 'Oh, yes,' he said. 'Her daughters spoke to me about that this morning. I bumped into them in town.'

'You never mentioned that to me, son,' said Digby. He smiled at the policemen. 'Busy time, as you'll appreciate. Trying to earn an honest crust in these last few days before the big event. Plenty of parcels and so forth going missing, I shouldn't wonder. Shame you got called out for something so unimportant when you must have plenty of better things to do.'

This comment was allowed to drop without response. 'We have to ask you, sir, whether you have any knowledge of the whereabouts of the item in question?'

Digby widened his eyes. 'I don't even know what the darned item *is*. Some tasteless piece of female ornament, I assume. Wasn't it insured? Is Mrs Blackwood accusing us of taking it? That's a bit rich, wouldn't you say, son?' He turned his wide-eyed gaze onto Ant.

'We haven't seen it, whatever it is,' said Ant. 'We'd be pretty stupid to steal something from our own landlord, don't you think?'

It was impossible to misinterpret the look that passed between the two officers. *People who live like this are capable of anything* it said. The word 'Gypsies' was silently circling around. All four men were standing in the cluttered hallway of the Old Stables, the dog gazing suspiciously at the intruders.

Ant was still far more concerned about his mother than

76

he was about some missing gewgaw. It seemed ludicrous to remain silent on the subject, when he had the police right there in front of him. They could find her, probably with ease, once they knew her car registration number. But now she had been named as a likely thief, it was all even more complicated, and he said nothing. They were perfectly capable of interpreting her words – assuming he quoted them, which he probably wouldn't – as a confession to a killing. And if he didn't quote them, there was hardly anything meaningful to say.

'Well, then,' the first officer finally concluded, 'we won't disturb you any longer. You'll notify us if you happen to locate the item, won't you?'

'Of course. But that isn't going to happen, is it?' said Digby. 'Now, have a happy Christmas, lads, and don't worry about that infernal gate. It'll open if you just push the red button.'

When they'd gone, Digby slumped back into his chair with a groan. 'Takes more out of me than it used to – play-acting like that. Bloody Blackwoods, accusing us of taking their stuff. As if we ever would!'

'You didn't want me to mention Mum, then?'

'Absolutely not. You did well, son. I was worried for a minute.'

Ant went back to obsessing about his mother's phone call. He squeezed every conceivable interpretation from her words as the day wore on. She had killed someone and was afraid of being caught. She had been living a double life, married to two men at the same time, and the one who wasn't Digby had died. The dead person had been suffering from Ebola and Beverley was afraid to contaminate her loved ones. Or it wasn't a person at all, but a dog she had accidentally run over – a highly valuable pedigree dog whose owner would seek revenge.

Digby appeared to be much less concerned. He immersed himself in his Internet discussions until mid-afternoon, when he began to prepare for his evening stall in Blockley. 'Last-minute presents – that's the thing,' he muttered to himself. 'Plants, knick-knacks, soap. Didn't we have a boxful of soap somewhere?'

Ant made no attempt to help. His father would have welcomed him as assistant stallholder but would never think to ask. While appearing to the outside world as a classic father–son team, in reality they had opted for quite different means of earning a living. Ant's chief occupation was as jobbing gardener, with a regular part-time position at a large garden centre. Digby was a wheeler-dealer of the old school, with fingers in a bewildering number of pies. He went to auctions and house clearance sales, did private deals with men and women who lived much the same as he did himself. Only at Christmas did their activities overlap.

'What a weird day,' Ant said at one point. 'And I can't help feeling there's more trouble to come.' This feeling, he realised, arose mainly from Digby's strange reaction to the disappearance of his wife. It almost seemed as if he knew where she was and why she'd gone, so unworried did he appear. At last, he blurted a direct challenge. 'You know where she is, don't you? You know what's going on. Why won't you tell me?'

Digby straightened from the cardboard tray he was

filling with Christmas cacti and met his son's accusing gaze. 'No, I don't know where she is. All I know is she's safe enough, and she'll come back when she's ready. She's got some crackpot idea in her head, and all we can do is wait for her to work it out in her own way.'

'Crackpot idea? Like what?'

But his father would only shake his head and said no more.

In despair, Ant decided there was only one thing he could do – and that was to phone his friend Thea Slocombe and talk the whole thing over with her.

There was a big meal at the Slocombe house that Saturday lunchtime, composed of all the things Thea assumed would not be wanted when Christmas actually arrived. She had been forced to reorganise the freezer a few days earlier to accommodate the extra food that would be needed for their entertaining, so there was stewing steak and pork chops in the fridge, urgently requiring to be eaten. Evidently the beef had been transformed into a nice casserole earlier in the day, because suddenly there it was, with some carrots and broccoli that were also due for consumption. Drew and Timmy were scheduled to leave mid-afternoon, on their adventurous trek north. 'Of course, we could get there all in one go, but it doesn't seem right to turn up halfway through the evening, does it? I doubt if she'll want to put us up overnight,' said Drew again.

'Stop agonising about it,' said Thea briskly. 'It's all decided now. She's expecting you tomorrow morning. You stay four or five hours, and get back here for bedtime. Minimal disruption for all concerned.'

'Don't forget I need to hang up my stocking,' said Timmy. 'What if we get back too late for that?'

'There's no such thing as too late for that,' said Thea. 'But if you set out by three o'clock, you should be back by eight or nine. That leaves plenty of time.'

The child seemed to have difficulty grasping the details. He looked round the kitchen in search of assistance and plainly had a new and unconnected thought. 'Are we going to have Christmas dinner in here?'

'Where else?' asked Thea, slightly snappishly. 'Surely we don't have to rearrange furniture for Christmas as well as all the rest of it?'

There was a silence as the three Slocombes remembered the succession of small disappointments that the previous Christmas had thrown up.

'Why don't we take this table into the living room, and push it up to the one in there?' said Drew. 'If we covered it with a big cloth, it would look all right. Then we can have candles and a centrepiece, and be beside the tree and the decorations.' He smiled. 'We could do it on Christmas morning, after we've opened the presents. It could be quite Dickensian.'

'With my mum as Scrooge,' laughed Jessica, not quite kindly.

'I can make a centrepiece with holly berries and ivy and some silver spray.' Drew rubbed his hands together. 'I used to love doing that. Except I don't suppose there's time now.'

'Actually,' said Jessica, 'I brought one with me. I wasn't going to produce it until Monday.'

'You brought a centrepiece?' Everybody stared at her. 'Really?'

'Why is that so surprising?' She looked at her mother. 'Dad and I made one every year, remember? I'm just carrying on the tradition. Isn't that the whole point of Christmas? Families creating their own special traditions and keeping them going?'

'Yes!' said Stephanie, despite not being entirely sure of herself. 'Can we see it now?'

'If you insist. It took me ages to make it. Had to drive out to some woods and find all the doings.' Again she fixed her gaze on Thea. 'It was funny doing it without Dad, but it felt as if he was there with me, in a way.'

'That's nice. Carl was always so good at that sort of thing.'

Stephanie tried to get a sense of the father and husband whose death balanced that of her own mother. He sounded nice, taking his daughter out to pick berries and nuts and things and showing her how to make a decoration out of them. Drew had never done that.

'No, don't get it now,' said Timmy. 'It'll spoil it if you do. Wait till Christmas Day. It'll be a nice surprise then.'

There was general enthusiasm for this plan. 'Good thinking, Tim,' said Thea with a sweet smile. Watching her, Stephanie understood that she was making a real effort to play the part of a devoted wife and mother, determined to create the perfect Christmas for her family. She was being noticeably more *present*, compared to usual. Having Jessica there was a big help, too. On the face of it, Thea had nothing and nobody beyond their four walls to worry about. Even the imminent visit by Damien and his family was keeping her focused on the house, and all the tasks required to feed and accommodate the extra people. Stephanie welcomed the effort her stepmother was making, and hoped her father was equally appreciative. Of course, now it was him who was spoiling it, rushing off to see a mother he had barely mentioned or considered for the past ten years.

But Jessica was still the real centre of attention. 'I have got a few more things that I can show you now,' she said, and went to her half-emptied box. A moment later, she flourished a gold-coloured tin labelled *Fortnum and Mason spiced Christmas tea* and proposed that they try some there and then, having almost finished lunch. 'Even the kids might like it,' she said.

Nobody objected, and the only teapot in the house was commandeered. Even a tea strainer was located at the back of a drawer. Jessica ritualistically infused the tea leaves, to Stephanie's great fascination. She lowered her face over the steam and inhaled ecstatically. 'It smells heavenly,' she said. 'Like a magic land where they eat nothing but Christmas food all year round. Oranges and chestnuts and even a whiff of chocolate.'

'Steady on!' laughed Jessica. 'You'll be dreadfully disappointed when you taste it at this rate.'

But everyone sipped it, as if at a solemn ceremony involving Mongolians or American Indians, and judged it at least . . . *interesting*, and at best delicious. 'Where did you get it?' asked Thea.

'It was my present from Secret Santa at work. Lucky me, eh?'

The merry atmosphere continued for the next half-hour, giving Stephanie a swelling optimism for the entire coming week. So many good things were going to happen once Dad and Tim came back again from their trip, all combining to make her feel infinitely light and warm inside. Boxing Day would be spent playing with her presents – whatever they turned out to be. Uncle Damien and his family would create great additional diversion, as well. And after that there was still *ages* before they had to go back to school. She squashed next to Timmy on the sofa, where he was doing one last calculation of the minutes before having to get ready for the drive northwards, and gave him an excited little punch. 'Not long now!' she whispered.

He gave a cheery smile, which further improved Stephanie's day.

But then there were coats and an overnight bag, and the dog casting anxious looks at the obvious signs of departure. Stephanie was suddenly filled with anxiety, too. What if they had a crash, or the car broke down, or Drew decided he had to stay with his mother all over Christmas? 'You will come back tomorrow, won't you?' she said, her voice wobbling.

He gazed at her blankly. 'What? Of course we will. Why should you doubt it?'

'I don't know. No reason, really. Just . . .'

'Things happen,' said Jessica understandingly. 'You should realise that by now, Drew. Nobody in this family is ever going to take anything for granted, are they?'

'What's this heavy talk?' Thea demanded. 'Trying to jinx it, or what?'

'Only Steph having a moment,' said Jessica, putting her arm around the girl's shoulders. 'Don't worry, pet. They'll be back in no time. The weather's good, look. No rain or ice. And think of the story Tim's going to be telling us when he comes home.'

Timmy himself was looking doubtful, as if he was seeing himself as a brave hero venturing into a dangerous unknown realm without adequate preparation. 'Will I?' he faltered. 'I'm not very good at stories.'

'An experience,' Jessica clarified. 'You're going to have an *experience*. That's always a good thing.'

'I'll go instead, if you don't want to,' Stephanie offered, well aware that this was not a realistic option. Drew had already decided which child he was taking.

'Enough talk,' said Drew loudly. 'We're off.' And after a brief exchange of kisses, they were gone.

It was less than half an hour later that Ant Frowse made his phone call to Thea. He had gone outside to do it, not wanting his father to hear him. 'Are you busy?' he asked his friend. 'Have you got time to talk?'

'Loads of time,' she assured him. 'What's the problem?'

'It's going to sound silly, but my mother's gone missing,' he began. 'And so has some precious trinket belonging to old Blackwood.'

'Oh – we heard about that. He was making a fuss at the post office about it. I should think the whole of

Chipping Campden knows about it by now. They think Beverley took it, do they?'

'No, not exactly. Nobody knows she's gone off. There's not really any connection. I think.'

'Start at the beginning,' she told him.

So he did, leaving nothing out. He described the episode in town that morning, with the Russian sisters making veiled threats and the visit from the police a little while later. 'Dad did his usual injured peasant act, running rings round them, so they didn't know what to say.'

'Did you tell them it was just Carla doing her usual harassment?'

'Actually, no. We might have missed a chance there.'

'Beverley would probably say so.'

'We mostly leave all that up to her. She's taught herself the legal stuff and knows exactly what to say to them.' He made a small sound of frustration. 'But where *is* she? Somewhere beginning with "Win", apparently. I'm going mad trying to figure it all out – and Dad's not helping at all. He says he's got no idea where she is, but he doesn't seem a bit worried. What if she doesn't come back for Christmas?' he wailed, like a much younger person.

'Cook the turkey yourself,' she said unfeelingly. 'It's not very difficult.'

'It's a goose. And I don't think we could face it without her. Christmas is never very jolly here at the best of times, even though Mum does make an effort to keep it all going.'

'She's probably just exhausted, then. Can't face another year of that. Gone off to Windsor or Wincanton for a break by herself.'

'I never thought of Wincanton,' he said. 'Where is it?'

'Somerset. Not terribly far, but unless she knows someone there, it's pretty unlikely, isn't it?'

'The point is – why couldn't she just *tell* us? Why the secrecy?'

'Scared you'd talk her out of it, presumably. I don't know, Ant. She's your mother, not mine. People do funny things. But she did phone you, so you know she's alive. That's the main thing.'

'You sound just like Dad,' he said glumly.

'And you sound like a lost little boy crying for his mother,' she said brutally. 'I bet you she'll show up tomorrow evening and you'll have a lovely roast goose, after all.'

The call finished with Ant feeling even worse than before. Did Thea privately think that Beverley actually had nicked the Blackwoods' trinket and run off with it somewhere? Or was she so accustomed to violent murders and convoluted police investigations that a simple case of a missing woman carried little to interest her? Ahead lay the rest of Saturday, and then the whole of Christmas Eve. His plan had been to tidy the house, walk the dog, and wrap the presents he'd got for his parents. None of that seemed to have any point now, except for his faithful and long-suffering Percy.

Chapter Six

The afternoon was passing rather aimlessly at the Slocombe house. Thea built up the log fire, and all four females settled down in front of it, letting the warmth seep into them and relishing the peace. The scent of the tree in the corner was faint but real, spreading the smell of Christmas, adding to Stephanie's blissful condition.

Thea was looking and feeling rather less blissful. 'When are we going to move the table?' she said suddenly. Drew's belated suggestion about the dining table was as unusual as it was irritating.

'When Drew comes back,' said Jessica. 'It won't take a minute.'

'I suppose I'm in charge of the funerals while he's gone. He never even thought about that, did he? I can't leave the house until he gets back. What if I have other things to do?'

'Like what?'

'Like trying to help Ant and Digby,' she muttered. 'Sounds as if there's a problem over there.' Drew's sudden dash north to gratify his mother's wishes seemed to Thea to justify a few hours devoted to the mysterious disappearance of Beverley Frowse. But her phone was not linked to the business line, which effectively meant she would have to stay in the house just in case, the whole time Drew was away. Unanswered calls would be diverted to his mobile – which he would be unable to answer if driving.

'They'll be fine,' said Jessica airily, on the basis of no real knowledge.

'That's where you're wrong. Ant's really worried about his mother,' Thea snapped. Then she noticed Stephanie's alarmed expression, and modified her tone. 'But it is what it is,' she added with a sigh. 'I don't suppose it's anything much. And there's always a possibility someone will phone about a funeral.' Despite she and Stephanie having agreed that people really should not die at Christmas, the fact remained that they did. Their relatives might well expect a suitable response, even from an alternative undertaker with limited facilities and a young family. 'So I'll try to be good and stick by the phone.'

'We should play a game,' Stephanie said a minute or two later, anxious not to let any of this magical time go to waste, as well as hoping to improve Thea's mood. The spaniel was snuggled against her on the big armchair, and the firelight was dancing on the shiny surfaces of the decorations hanging from the ceiling.

'Good idea,' said Jessica. 'But nothing too noisy or competitive.'

'Most things need an even number of people,' said Thea, clearly not wanting to get up from her place on the sofa. But then she gave herself a slap. 'Listen to me, making difficulties as usual. A game would be brilliant.'

'Snakes and ladders,' said Stephanie. 'That's all down to chance. Anybody can win, from the age of two to a hundred. It says so on the box. And it doesn't matter how many players there are.'

'Where is it?' wondered Thea.

'Middle drawer,' Stephanie told her with total certainty. And it was. 'And we should have candles,' she added. 'I love candles.'

'Tomorrow. We'll put one in every window, to welcome Dad and Timmy home again.'

'And mulled wine,' said Jessica. 'And did you get some crackers?'

'Obviously,' said her mother, with a sigh that suggested contentment as well as the long list of tasks ahead of her. 'Charles Dickens has a lot to answer for, you know.'

'It can't all be down to him.'

'The tree was Prince Albert's idea,' said Stephanie. An annoying idea occurred to her. 'I suppose it's quite bad for the environment, cutting down all these trees?'

'They say not, because they grow them specially, so they don't count,' said Thea quickly.

'That makes no sense at all,' Jessica laughed. 'But just at the moment I can't pretend to care.'

They played snakes and ladders, the dice consistently favouring Stephanie. Thea accused her of cheating and fetched a plastic cup to use as a shaker. The rattle it made was loud in the peaceful room. 'It is fairer like that. Her little hands don't turn it around properly,' Thea insisted.

But still Stephanie got fives and sixes, dodging the snakes almost every time.

'We forgot the carols,' said Jessica, as the game came to a finish. 'I knew there was something missing.'

'The quiet's nice, though,' said Stephanie.

'It is,' Jessica agreed. 'We can have the CD playing all day tomorrow – and the next two days, if we don't get sick of it by then.'

'Right,' said Thea. 'I do love the quiet.' She got up and put more logs on the fire. They crackled softly and added another scent to that of pine needles. For another twenty minutes, everything remained tranquil. Then it was teatime, and Thea remembered the washing-up hadn't been done after lunch and there was an urgent need to make another batch of mince pies, and the dog wanted to go out.

At the Old Stables, Digby and Ant were scraping a small meal together, much as the Slocombes were, but with considerably less appetite. Ant was sinking further into despair, seeing no way out of the morass surrounding him on all sides. His dog was squatting beside him, its nose on his leg, conveying bucketsful of sympathy and concern. Any idiot canine could detect an anxious atmosphere in that kitchen.

'Better get a move on,' said Digby. 'I should start setting

up by five. The punters turn up at six.'

'Nice evening for it,' said Ant listlessly.

'Buck up, son. I don't like to leave you in this mood. Come with me, why don't you?'

Ant shook his head. 'You're better on your own. I'd just put people off, the state I'm in. I'll try Mum's phone again, and see if I can raise her. Although I'm not holding my breath.'

'I was thinking,' Digby started slowly. 'Maybe she's more upset than we realised about that spat you told me she had with Blackwood. When was it? Wednesday?'

'Right. When he first started flapping about that parcel and laid into her at the gate about it. He might have accused her of taking it, to her face.'

'She would have said something.'

'She did say something. She came back in a rage about it.'

Digby blinked. 'Did she? Well, it looks as if they've all decided it was one of us that took it, now. Sending the cops over is a bit of a giveaway. Real harassment, that is.'

Ant wondered why he hadn't connected the events together before this. 'That must be it,' he said, with a much brighter expression. 'She's scared she'll do something she'll regret if she stays around here.' Then he thought again. 'But that doesn't explain who's dead, does it?'

'It strikes me you might have misheard her there,' said Digby. 'Nobody's dead, are they? We'd know about it by now if they were.'

Ant had no answer to that.

Digby went on, 'Mind you, I don't think I've seen the old bugger for a couple of days. Last thing I can remember is Carla yelling at him about something in the parterre. Must have been Wednesday, as well.'

He pronounced the word *parterre* with fully rounded contempt. When the Frowses had first lived there, the area concerned had been a perfectly ordinary yard. The Blackwoods had taken a JCB to it, shipped in soil and turf and low-growing shrubs and transformed it into a mock-Tudor garden with a seat and a sundial. Beverley had found it particularly offensive in its poor positioning and total mismatch with the rest of the house. It was the closest point to the Old Stables, visible from an upstairs window.

'Shouldn't that be *on* the parterre?' queried Ant. 'Maybe not. Mum would know.' He paused. 'What was his missus shouting, then?'

'I don't know. Probably something trivial. Maybe she wanted to be the one to accuse us of pinching her bauble. She would have enjoyed that. You know how much she loathes us.'

'Well, we never got a Christmas card – again.'

'Nor an invitation to a festive glass of sherry.'

The attempt at banter felt woefully flat. 'I'm going to try her phone again,' said Ant tiredly. 'Sometimes the battery revives a little bit, if you leave it a while.'

'I don't believe that,' said Digby. 'But it doesn't hurt to try.'

The phone reported itself as being out of commission and the two men picked forlornly at their simple meal. 'Some Christmas this is turning out to be,' grumbled Digby. 'Deserted by wife, harassed by landlord and invaded by the forces of the law. God knows what we'll do with ourselves tomorrow.'

'She might have turned up by then,' said Ant with unconvincing optimism.

Instead, a different woman turned up, just as the men were tidying away their plates, Percy having consumed quite a lot of the food that had been on them. A double knock on the door sent the dog barking and Digby almost tripping over his own feet in his haste to answer it.

It was Carla Blackwood, the witch herself. Her expression was a bizarre combination of accusation and embarrassed reluctance to engage with her tenants at all. 'Have you seen my husband?' she blurted, without any preamble.

'Several times,' quipped Digby, unable to help himself. 'Do you mean on one specific occasion?'

'Since Thursday. Three days ago. Have you seen him?'

'Careful,' murmured Ant very softly in his father's ear. Digby blinked and merely shook his head.

'Why – have you lost him?' Ant asked, with exaggerated concern.

'He must have gone on a business trip, I think. Though perhaps not, so close to Christmas. I haven't been able to contact him.'

'Oh dear! But why in the world would you think *we* might know where he is? We have no dealings with either of you, as you know quite well.'

'He had a disagreement with your wife last week. I thought . . .' When it came to it, she could not bring herself to make a direct accusation. 'Is she here? Perhaps she could shed some light on his disappearance.'

'No, no. She's out just now,' said Digby airily. 'But I can promise you she's got absolutely no idea where he might be. We move in such different circles, you see.'

They could almost hear her gnashing her teeth – or at least grinding them. She was dressed in a luxurious costume comprising silk and leather and real fur at the edges. Her face was elaborately made up, and her hair sleek and glossy. It would not take anybody long to guess at her Russian origins. 'Well, it is very strange. And worrying. He always keeps me informed of his movements, and said nothing about going away. Especially seeing that it's *Christmas*.' This detail was clearly important. She looked up at the sky, as if expecting snow to start falling, or Santa Claus to come sweeping down in his sleigh.

'Oh dear,' said Digby, noncommittally.

'The police were here earlier, you know,' said Ant. 'Didn't you ask them to send out a search party for him? Instead of trying to get us arrested for stealing your missing parcel? Could be that Rufus has got it with him, all along, and couldn't face telling you. Does he know you reported it to the police?'

'That's none of your business,' she flashed.

'Well, he's bound to turn up,' said Digby. 'Maybe you could send those daughters of yours out to search for him. He might have had a heart attack.'

She shook her head emphatically. 'He is in perfect health, thanks to our excellent doctor. His pacemaker is the best in the world. There must be another explanation.'

Ant and Digby had heard about the state-of-the-art

pacemaker before, when Rufus had spent a week in an expensive London clinic having it implanted.

Carla went on, 'But I must ask you to inform me if you—' She broke off, evidently realising how unlikely her request was to be honoured. 'Well, I mean, if you see or hear anything,' she finished bravely.

'That isn't going to happen, is it?' Ant was brutal. 'Even if he's lying dead in one of your beautifully kept ditches, it won't be any of us who find him. Seeing as how we're not allowed into any of your fields.'

Carla Blackwood turned pale. 'If he isn't back by tomorrow, I'll have to contact the police – again.' She clenched her jaw. 'Well, that's all,' she said, and turned on her heel. 'Goodbye.'

'And a happy Christmas to you, too,' said Ant, rather loudly.

It gave them an uncomfortable amount to talk about, when she'd gone, despite Digby's need to leave for Blockley within the next twenty minutes. The implications of Carla's visit were all too starkly obvious. 'So what do we do?' said Ant, for the fifth time. 'If Mrs B contacts the police, we'll have to own up that Mum's disappeared, even if we don't say exactly what she told us about the argument with Blackwood.' He had another thought. 'I did tell Thea about it, though. And she's matey with one of the top CID people.'

'No sense in worrying about who tells who what,' Digby insisted. 'I can't see bloody Carla bothering the cops again so soon, either. It's the same thing as we said before – there's never much concern about a healthy adult going off for a bit. Especially at Christmas.'

New thoughts were exploding in Ant's poor head. 'You don't think . . . ? What if . . . ? I mean, they haven't gone off *together*, have they?'

Digby gave a loud guffaw at this idea. 'What – your mother and Rufus Blackwood? I hardly think so. She hates his guts.'

'Right.' It had reached the point where Ant thought he could believe almost anything. After all, Blackwood was rich, and fairly handsome. He and Beverley had been almost friendly years ago. But it was an awful thought, even so.

'I've got to go,' said Digby, moving towards the door. 'They'll put me right at the end of the street if I'm not careful.'

Ant still had things he wanted to say. 'But what if . . . ?' he started. 'I mean, it *does* look bad for Mum, on the face of it. She said – *he's dead and I can't come home*. And now a man she hates has gone missing at the same time as she has. What's anybody going to think?'

'She hasn't killed Rufus Blackwood, Ant. Don't be ridiculous.'

'Well, I just wish she'd come back and tell us that for herself.'

'She will. We'll talk about it a bit more when I get back. Shouldn't be too late. These things don't last very long as a rule. Wish me luck.' And he made his escape, driving off with a vanful of Christmas goodies.

Ant's thoughts revolved even more rapidly without

his father there to bounce them off. Perhaps the apparent disappearance of Blackwood was a good thing, if Carla reported it. The police would quickly clock the fact that something odd was happening at Crossfield, and maybe they should have a look round. And they might equally quickly come up with a harmless explanation. Except that they might just as easily find something dreadful. It was hard to avoid the conclusion that Beverley didn't want to be found – she wasn't answering her phone, after all. But she couldn't know that Ant had only caught the first syllable of her place of exile. She might have assumed he knew she was in Winchcombe or Wincanton or wherever.

He tried to imagine himself in his mother's situation, with great difficulty. The major stumbling block was her assertion that somebody was dead. Without knowing who – or what – that was, nothing made the slightest sense. There had been an implication that she felt herself to be responsible in some way, or at least liable to be blamed. Everything appeared to have started with the mysterious parcel that both the Blackwoods obviously regarded as precious and important. Counting that item, the list of missing people and things amounted to three. 'What next?' Ant murmured to his attentive dog. A dog, he remembered, who had barely been outside the house all day.

'Sorry, Perce. Just a quickie out in the garden for now. It's too dark to go any further.' He opened the front door, and let the animal wander out. The Frowses did not believe in picking up dog droppings, whether on their own premises or someone else's. For years, Beverley had insisted that the plastic bags used to collect it caused far greater damage than a bit of muck walked into the house or car. Finally, she pointed out, the world was starting to agree with her.

Everything outside was quiet. The security lights had come on, as always, so Ant went around the house closing the curtains. He was still thinking hard, now including his oddly unconcerned father. A short while after he'd first reported Bev's phone call, stressing the words about someone being dead, Digby had jumped into an extended and not entirely serious brainstorm to try to explain what she might have meant. 'If there really is a dead person – and not a dog or cat or aged uncle – we'll find out soon enough,' he had concluded.

'An uncle's a person,' snapped Ant. 'And we don't have any of those now the one in Ireland's dead.'

'Oh, there's sure to be one or two lurking in the woodpile. Didn't Bev's dad have a younger brother who went to the bad? He'd be an aged uncle by now.'

'Should we go through her letter drawer and see what we can find? Has it got to that point yet?'

Digby had coughed, expressing his discomfort with this idea. He also went slightly red. 'Better not,' he said quickly. 'She would really hate us doing that.'

Ant had still been in panic mode. 'Dad, we ought to be doing more to find her. Aren't you scared for her?'

His father gave this some thought. 'Not *scared* exactly. Worried, confused – that sort of thing. It's all too complicated for my simple mind.'

Ant was not fooled by that. Digby's mind was far from simple. The whole day had felt unreliable, his father acting one role after another, with none of it striking Ant as genuine. The suspicion that Digby knew a great deal more than he was admitting came back repeatedly. Something had happened that Ant had missed – or, more likely, several things.

Blackwood getting himself lost as well was another point that kept niggling at him. There surely had to be a connection with Beverley. Carla must have been pretty panicked to swallow her disgust and come knocking on their door. It made Ant wonder what sort of sinister outfits Blackwood might be involved with. What if his mother had blundered into something really nasty?

Then he snorted at his own fanciful notions. Was he thinking of Russian spies? That Carla had links with some underground political goings-on, and Rufus had got on the wrong side of them, dragging Ant's wretched mother with him somehow?

'It's not impossible,' he muttered to himself. 'Unlikely, though. And if there was any whiff of that kind of thing, the police would be onto it, and be taking us a whole lot more seriously.'

The recollection of the police brought another person to mind. The person he had already concluded was his only hope in this whole messy business. When Percy came back in, looking reproachful at the lack of a walk, Ant said aloud, 'We'll just have to hope that Thea Slocombe can get things moving for us, won't we?'

Chapter Seven

Jessica took charge of bedtime that evening. She read a story, not very well, and Thea stayed downstairs with the dog, banging pans a bit in the kitchen. 'It's so funny without Daddy here,' said Stephanie. 'Usually it's Thea who goes away. I can't remember a time when he's been out all night.'

'Must be his turn, then.'

'I suppose. I don't like it, though. Did Thea go away a lot when you were my age?'

Jessica gave this some thought. 'Not really. We used to all go together, visiting my grandparents and uncles and aunts. And we had some nice holidays. My dad loved wide open spaces, like the Yorkshire Dales and Dartmoor. He really wanted us to sleep in a tent, but Mum was never very keen on that. We did it once or twice, but it rained and was quite miserable.'

'Thea always knows what's the best thing to do,' said Stephanie, as if this was an obvious truth. 'And she's very brave.'

'Is she?'

'Oh, yes. She stays in houses where somebody's just been murdered, and she goes round asking people questions, and gets stranded in the snow. All sorts of things like that, and it always turns out right for her.'

'She's been lucky. She should be more careful now she's got you Slocombes to think about.'

'Mm. It seems a bit unfair, though, having to think about us when she wants to be having adventures. And Dad doesn't really get it sometimes. He thinks all he has to do is make enough money, so he sits in his office when he could be cooking or something. He leaves all the house stuff to her, and she doesn't like it.'

'Why doesn't she tell him, then?'

'Maybe because it sounds like moaning. And anyway, he's been better lately. Ever since she came back and cried all over him, in the summer holidays.'

Jessica did not request further details, but got off the bed and leant down to kiss her little stepsister. 'Christmas Eve tomorrow,' she said, as if the idea was every bit as magical and amazing to her as it was to Stephanie. 'Night night, kiddo.'

Just before she eventually fell asleep – which took much longer than usual – Stephanie remembered the man she had seen, with the gun that looked as if he had a third leg. Half asleep, she saw him again, much larger than life-size, pointing his gun through the bedroom window at her. The muffled cry she gave went unnoticed by Thea and Jessica downstairs, but she heard Hepzie give a sympathetic little yelp. That was enough to reassure her and she sank into a dreamless sleep.

'They're in Sheffield!' Thea announced next morning, staring at her phone in disbelief. 'At least, they were when Drew sent this. They got there at eight-thirty last night, in spite of dreadfully slow traffic. It's a hundred and fifteen miles. They'll be halfway to Durham by now.' It was nearly nine o'clock; they had got up shamefully slowly. But now they bustled through breakfast.

'Are you telling us you've only just picked up his text?' Jessica asked accusingly. 'If it'd been me, I'd have checked it at 7 a.m.'

'I was up till nearly midnight, I'll have you know. I didn't open my eyes until half past eight.'

'Oh, well – none of my business, I guess. Where did they stay the night?'

'Holiday Inn. Forty-five pounds. All perfectly easy, apparently.'

'Is Timmy okay?' asked Stephanie.

'Presumably,' Thea told her. 'He's probably having a brilliant time. Now who's going to walk the dog?'

Jessica and Stephanie took Hepzie out into the chilly morning, where everything was very quiet and still. A dove cooed somewhere and a plane hummed high in the sky, but there was no sound of human activity. 'Gosh, this place is weird,' said Jessica, not for the first time. 'Where are all the people?'

'Don't know,' said Stephanie vaguely. 'Which way shall we go?'

'The field, I suppose. She can run free there.'

'She can run free anywhere. She's very sensible.'

They turned right at the front gate and followed the narrow lane to the point where it simply stopped at the edge of a field. A characterful old house marked the final navigable point, with a sturdy Land Rover Discovery parked outside to prove it. The field had been shaved late in the year, the grass now thin and patchy with outcrops of small stones all across it. 'They made hay here in the summer,' said Stephanie. 'We watched them cutting it.'

'Probably due to be ploughed soon,' said Jessica, uncertainly. 'I used to know all this stuff, but I've forgotten most of it. My dad used to take me for long walks, showing me all the plants and different sorts of corn. His grandfather was a farmer, about a hundred years ago.'

'Your dad died, didn't he?'

'Right. You knew that already. Five years ago now, or nearly. Seems ages. He was a really nice man.'

'Like my dad, then.'

'A bit like him, yes. My mother seems to have a taste for a particular kind of man. She likes the quiet type, no rages or sudden passions. Steady, I suppose. Reliable. Not especially adventurous.'

The word *boring* hovered in Stephanie's acute mental ear. 'Thea's very adventurous,' she said, echoing the previous evening's conversation. 'She likes it when things get exciting.'

'It takes all sorts,' said Jessica carefully. 'Didn't we

say all this last night?'

That felt like a put-down to Stephanie. 'Not really,' she said. 'Not all of it.'

'We'd never manage all of it. There's a quote – something about containing multitudes. A poem, I think. It's true, though. One single person is fantastically complicated. And we never properly understand each other.' She sighed. 'And that makes life very difficult a lot of the time.'

'Yes,' said Stephanie warily. 'I don't think Daddy understands Thea very well, sometimes.'

'I expect they're fine, really. They're a good fit. They seem to know what they're doing. Not like me. I've been pathetic in my choice of men.' She gave Stephanie's hand a little shake. 'But you don't want to hear about my problems. I'm hoping I'll know better another time.'

'Boyfriend trouble,' said Stephanie, hoping she sounded understanding and sympathetic, while aware that they were on dangerous ground.

'Not any more,' said Jessica. 'All that's behind me now.'

The spaniel was running aimlessly around the edge of the field, pausing to sniff at the wintry undergrowth, her plumy tail slowly wagging. Jessica watched her with a nostalgic little smile. 'I remember when Mum first got her,' she said. 'She said it was a substitute for me, because I was doing my A-levels and would be leaving for college before long. My dad suggested a spaniel because he had one when he was young. He said they were the easiest of all dogs, because they didn't have any vices.'

'He was right. I wish she could have some puppies, though. I think puppies are brilliant.'

'I imagine they'd be a lot of work. And it must be sad when they all go. Besides, wouldn't you worry about them – wondering if the new people were being kind to them?'

Stephanie gave this some thought. 'People are usually quite kind to their dogs,' she concluded. 'I think it'd be all right.'

'Ah – such a trusting little soul,' said Jessica with all the wisdom of a newly promoted police sergeant. 'You should see some of the things I've seen. Except – no, you shouldn't. Not until you're at least twenty-one.'

They ambled after the dog, not saying very much more. Stephanie had a sense of holding in the delicious awareness that it was the day before Christmas. It was like having a lovely secret, or knowing something that everyone else had forgotten. The very air shimmered with it. She couldn't remember spending so much time with Jessica before, having her all to herself. If Timmy was allowed to meet their mysterious grandmother, then she was going to find out all she could about their stepsister. It would keep things in balance.

They had walked around two sides of the big field, and were a quarter of the way along the third before Stephanie found the courage to ask, 'So you haven't got a boyfriend now?'

'Didn't I just tell you I haven't?' The tone was a lot less friendly than it had been three minutes before. 'Has my mother been saying something about that?'

'No, not at all. You . . . I mean, just now . . .'

'Oh God, I'm sorry. It's all right, Steph. I didn't mean to snap. You touched a raw nerve, that's all. I had some trouble, back in the summer. It's all sorted now, no harm done. Nothing for you to worry about.'

Every word of which served to heighten Stephanie's curiosity. 'Tell me,' she pleaded.

'I can't. You're too young. You wouldn't understand.'

'I'm nearly twelve. That's old enough.'

'You're still only eleven. Your father would kill me if I started talking about the sort of stuff that can happen when you're daft enough to fall for the wrong man. Especially at Christmas. Ask me again when you're about eighteen, and I promise I'll fill you in on all the gory details. It'll be a warning to you. I intend to do everything I can to stop you getting as hurt as I was. I wouldn't wish that on anybody.'

'Oh.' The world went a shade darker for a few minutes. Stephanie knew that people died, and that they sometimes actually killed each other. She knew that planes crashed and earthquakes happened, and there was an element of risk in everything you did. She knew that her own stepmother had been involved at close quarters with a lot of unpleasantness, often because she wilfully sought it out. But she hadn't bargained for her own dear Jessica to be hurt by somebody she loved. That was definitely unfair.

'I've said too much,' Jessica realised. 'Listen, Steph – don't worry about it for a second. I'm fine now. Your dad and Timmy will be back tonight and we'll have a fabulous Christmas. We'll go back now and make some more mince pies or something. Mum's never been much of a cook – we'll have to make sure she does everything properly. She's sure to need some last-minute shopping as well, which means we'll have to use my car.'

Stephanie was gazing into the next field, which led into the further end of Chipping Campden, by the church. 'There's that man again,' she said suddenly. 'Look!' She pointed to a figure at least two hundred yards away. 'The one with the gun.' Because he still looked as if he had three legs, as he had two days before.

'What are you talking about?' The morning sun was shining in Jessica's eyes, and despite its December weakness, it was enough to dazzle her. 'I can't see anyone.'

'Over there, look.' The man was in silhouette, with a tall hedge behind him. He seemed to be turned away, offering only his back view. 'By that holly tree.'

'Oh, yes.' Jessica squinted. 'I don't think it's a gun. It's got some sort of bulge on the end. He's waving it about in a funny way.'

'I saw him the day before yesterday, when we'd just unloaded your car. I told you, but you didn't take any notice.'

'Did you? Hey – I know what it is! He's got a metal detector. He's looking for something under that hedge. Nothing to get alarmed about. He's sure to have permission. And even if he hasn't, it's not much of a crime. Let's leave him to get on with it.'

Not a gun – Stephanie felt relief and disappointment. And a flicker of interest, because metal detecting was actually quite exciting. What if he found a hoard of gold coins? After all, the Romans had been all over the Cotswolds – there could be loads of stuff still to discover. 'I hope he finds something,' she said, looking back as Jessica headed for the house. 'That would make him happy for Christmas, wouldn't it?'

'Mm,' said Jessica.

Stephanie gave one last backward look. Even from that distance, she was sure the man needed something to make him happy. He seemed sad to her. Or if not sad, then possibly bad. Something not very nice seemed to emanate from the slouching shoulders. She remembered the vision of the previous evening, when she had thought it was a gun, that he was pointing right at her through her bedroom window.

Shortly before Jessica and Stephanie set out for their walk, the body of Rufus Blackwood was found by the clichéd figure of a man walking his dog. The dog had played no part in the drama, running right past the inert figure lying in the dead leaves without a second glance. The man, however, had been in little doubt as to what he was seeing, from a distance of fifty yards. He paused, aware that he was walking in a private woodland, where no footpaths allowed access to the general public. He liked it for that reason, and saw no good cause to stay out. But this would surely mark the end of his trespassing, and that was every bit as much of a shame as the fact that a man had died here.

He stood over the body, phone in hand, dog forgotten, and made himself take long, slow breaths. There was no obvious blood, but the deceased was lying on his side, with much of his front concealed. His head appeared to be undamaged. No knife was sticking out of his back. 'Are you certain he's dead?' asked the woman at the end of the phone.

'Completely,' said the man. 'His eyes are open and sort of cloudy.'

'Can you feel a pulse on his neck?'

'I'm sorry, dear, but I can assure you I'm not going to try. It's quite obviously unnecessary. I would say he's been dead for some time.'

He gave his name as William Turner, resident of Chipping Campden, aged seventy-four, owner of a sadly unintelligent Irish setter. He mentioned the dog because it seemed to him a significant part of the overall picture. He had at one point in his life worked as a hospital porter, and was a lot less affected than most people would be by the sight of a body in the woods on Christmas Eve. The knowledge that the woods had been for ever spoilt for him was still his primary preoccupation.

'It could very well have been natural causes,' he added. 'There's no sign of violence.' Then he looked closer. 'Although I suspect I'm wrong about that. I neglected to mention that he's wearing pyjamas and a dressing gown. And I repeat that there are signs that he's been here for quite some time.'

That was half past nine. By half past ten a large turnout of police personnel had erected a tent over the body, taken numerous photographs and successfully identified the deceased as local magnate Rufus Blackwood. Two different officers recognised him. 'He's a Freemason,' said one. 'Mega-rich.'

William Turner was taken home by a needlessly solicitous female officer, where his wife told him off for being late and treated his discovery with hurtful indifference. 'That damn dog, I suppose,' she said.

'Not at all. The daft thing never even noticed.'

'Do they know who it is?' she asked idly.

'That Blackwood chap, lives up at Crossfield. I guessed it might be him, and I heard them saying his name just before they brought me home.'

Mrs Turner began to take more interest. 'Good heavens! That's going to make a good story, isn't it! Especially if somebody deliberately killed him.'

Chapter Eight

Thea was not in the kitchen when the girls and spaniel got back, which Jessica appeared to think was a dereliction of duty. 'Shouldn't you be peeling chestnuts or something?' she said.

'Probably. But I've just had a phone call that made all that seem rather beside the point.'

Stephanie wasn't sure what that meant, but it definitely had ominous implications for the lovely magical Christmas she was anticipating. Her stepmother was on the sofa, a weird blank look in her eyes.

'So who phoned?' asked Jessica impatiently. 'It's not Drew, is it?'

Stephanie could feel her insides go cold and her chest turned to iron. They had been talking about Thea's first husband, who died in a car crash. Surely that couldn't possibly happen to her second husband as well? Stephanie's own beloved daddy.

'Oh God, no.' She met Stephanie's gaze. 'No, no. Nothing like that. Don't panic, Steph. It's nothing you need worry about.' She turned to Jessica. 'It was Gladwin who phoned. You know – the police detective. She's been called out to Crossfield, and thought I might be able to help. She knows I'm friendly with the Frowses. There was a case last year . . . well, that's not relevant now. The thing is . . .' She paused and glanced at Stephanie. 'The thing is, they've found a body over there.'

'So?' said Jessica, refusing to be drawn into feeling anything like excitement.

'So Antares phoned me yesterday and said his mother had gone missing. This could be her. Gladwin didn't say anything about an identity. It's all just happened, half an hour ago. All hell's breaking loose as we speak, I shouldn't wonder. Everybody's going to be hopelessly distracted with Christmas.'

'Did you tell Gladwin about yesterday's phone call? Does she want you to identify your friend's mother – or what?'

Thea shook her head. 'She was in a tearing hurry. Just said there was a body at Crossfield and I might turn out to be useful, because I know them there. Barely gave me time to say a word.'

'Hasn't this exact same thing happened before?' asked Jessica suspiciously. 'Probably more than once. Why does it have to be you and how does it make getting ready for tomorrow "beside the point" as you put it?'

'Jessica – these people are my friends. Stephanie and I go there all the time. We were there last weekend, in fact. Ant's got his hands full fending off an extremely unpleasant landlord and his wife. They harass and intimidate the Frowses constantly. I can't just ignore them now there's trouble. Especially not when Gladwin thinks I can be useful.'

Stephanie had heard it all, her eyes darting from face to face, trying to reconcile the two positions. 'They're really nice,' she said now. 'It's not Ant's mother who died, is it?'

'I honestly don't know, darling,' said Thea. 'Let's hope not.'

'From what you say, she's more likely to be the killer,' said Jessica with a little laugh. 'In any case, it sounds as if the landlord needs to be interviewed pretty soon. Where does *he* live?'

'Right there. It's a big fancy estate with a fence all round it and electric gates and security lights. The Frowses have got a ramshackle tied cottage in the middle of the whole property and the landlord wants to get rid of them.' Thea was pulling on her trainers and barely thinking of what she was saying. 'We'll have to go in your car. Steph – you'd better come as well.'

'Hey – hang on!' Jessica objected. 'We can't just barge into a crime scene, if that's what it is. I can't believe that's what your detective person was suggesting.'

'We can go to the cottage. They'll be in a state. They'll be glad to see us.'

'Go by yourself. You can drive my car easily enough.'

Thea hesitated. 'No,' she decided. 'I don't want to leave you two without knowing how long I'll be, or what exactly happened. If it's bedlam over there, you can just drop me and come back again.'

Jessica stood with her back to the door, preventing her mother from leaving the house. 'This is ridiculous,' she said firmly. 'You've got no idea what's been found, or what possible part you might have to play. You can't take a child into that. What's the hurry, anyway? I don't imagine anybody's going anywhere. Let the dust settle a bit, and at least find out who's dead. Even your precious Gladwin must realise that's the least she should be telling you.'

Thea gave way with reasonable grace. 'You're probably right,' she said. 'Gladwin was a lot less coherent than usual, I must admit. She was banking on having the whole Christmas holiday off work, so this must have thrown her.'

'Well don't let her offload it all onto you,' snapped Jessica. 'Which I get the impression she's rather inclined to do at times.'

'I'm useful,' said Thea, with a lift of her chin. 'But she's perfectly professional. She's not going to duck out of anything important.' She sighed. 'Thank goodness Drew's not here. He'd go mental.'

'Which leaves me to take his part, then,' said Jessica, throwing a smile at Stephanie. 'I can see his problem now. You must be a nightmare to live with.'

'It's not that bad,' said Stephanie. 'And the Frowses really are our friends.'

'So let's sit down and talk it over for a bit. You can tell

114

me all about them,' Jessica suggested, moving cautiously away from the door. 'And we can think it out sensibly before rushing off anywhere.'

They all moved into the kitchen, and Thea absently made a pot of tea. She repeated everything she could think of concerning the Frowse family. 'The landlord really has been harassing them for ages,' she insisted. 'Beverley's a bit of a character – called her children Antares and Aldebaran. They're stars, apparently.'

'They are,' said Stephanie in a small voice. 'They're the fourteenth and fifteenth brightest stars, actually.'

'Good Lord – how do you know that?' demanded Jessica.

'Tim likes stars, and makes me listen to him talking about them. Those are two of his favourites.'

'And how did you meet these people?' Jessica wondered.

'It was a year or so ago. When we'd only been here a little while. When—'

'When that woman was murdered,' said Stephanie, matter-of-factly. 'Ant talks about that sometimes.'

'It *was* pretty awful.'

'He likes us because we let him talk about dead people.'

'His sister!' Thea had obviously forgotten until then that Aldebaran had died at the hands of a murderer in Texas. 'God – that must make it worse that his mother's disappeared.'

'Explain,' said Jessica.

'That's it. That's all we know. She was older than Ant, I think, and they never found the man who did it. It must have been absolutely terrible for them.'

'Awful,' agreed Jessica, momentarily diverted by this

tragic story. 'So what exactly does your Gladwin friend want you to do? Given that it's Christmas Eve and you don't work for the police and you have a whole lot of people arriving – and your husband's father has just died?'

'Nothing in particular. She was simply telling me about it, because she knows they're our friends. Haven't I said that already?'

'I'm still processing it, given that it's massively unorthodox. She must have a reason for involving you so quickly.'

'She might think I'd have some idea about Beverley.' Thea hesitated, thinking this through. 'Although I don't expect she knows anything about that. Nobody's likely to have told her. Nor about the lost piece of jewellery.'

'You're saying you're ahead of her already.'

Thea nodded, her face rather pink. 'You could say that, I suppose. Look, Jess – I really do want to be there, at least to see who it is that died. Everything's under control here. Most of it can wait until this evening, if it has to. I could have a little look for Beverley, if it's not her.'

'Don't be ridiculous!' Jessica sounded really angry. 'You can't just wander around the countryside in the hope of finding this woman under a hedge somewhere. It doesn't work like that. Either there's a properly organised police search, or you just wait for her to turn up. You wouldn't know where to start.'

Stephanie made a small sound. 'You could start in our burial field – because that's where dead bodies end up. Even when they're not supposed to.'

Jessica stared at her. 'You're joking. You've got to be.'

116

Stephanie could not suppress a giggle. Not only were her words completely true, but it had happened before Drew had even met Thea, before Stephanie herself could remember. There had been a body unofficially buried in Drew's first burial ground, right at the very start. It was a story he told often, along with a lot of boasting about how he had solved the murder almost by himself.

'She won't be dead,' said Jessica with unwarranted certainty. 'She's probably just stressed. Is there a husband?'

'Yes. Digby. He's a bit of a wheeler-dealer, apparently. Involved in house clearances and car boots and all that. Puts his hand to anything. Mends stone walls, if I remember rightly.'

'Metal detecting?' asked Jessica, making a sudden connection.

'Quite probably.'

'Well, text her again now, and see if you can find out any more. But let's forget about showing up for a bit, okay? You'd only add to the confusion. If it's murder, they'll want a clear field for the SOCOs, and lots of peace and quiet.'

'I know,' said Thea meekly. 'I almost wish she'd never told me anything. Just when I was all set to do the perfect family Christmas. You're right about Drew. He won't like it one bit.'

'No, he won't,' said Stephanie. 'But he won't blame you. He'll say Mrs Gladwin should never have brought you into it.'

'And he'll be right,' said Jessica.

There was no reply to Thea's text for almost an hour. Then it came through with a *ping*. 'Deceased is Rufus

Blackwood. Not sure about cause of death. Family in meltdown. Happy Christmas!'

Sonia Gladwin's approach to Christmas was very similar to Thea's. The children's expectations were impossibly high, despite being unable to rely on their mother's presence throughout the holiday. Her husband was the constant parent, his work relatively undemanding and his hours reassuringly predictable. Sonia's income was the higher by far (unlike that of Thea, which had dwindled to nothing) but there was still a sense that the overall household management was down to her. That included finding the ideal presents, sending out cards, ordering the turkey and ensuring there were dozens of mince pies available. This year, with the twins rapidly leaving childhood behind, she resolved to do everything properly, with the right festive spirit. It would be pure magic, she promised herself; a Christmas they would all remember for ever.

But now everything was under threat because a dead man had been found not far from Broad Campden. As she drove north to view the scene for herself, she was being regularly updated. A team had been summoned, including a doctor and enough officers to secure the site and repel sightseers. 'Not that there'll be many of those, this being Christmas Eve,' said the girl who was relaying information. Phoning Thea Slocombe had been an act of sheer selfishness, she admitted to herself as soon as the call was concluded. She had wanted to share her frustration, to elicit support and even sympathy. In justification, she reminded herself that the death was close to Thea's home, the people involved likely to be familiar. But it had been outrageously early, even before the body was officially identified. And she had managed to retain enough professionalism to withhold from Thea the name she'd been given. Already she had breached protocol – and doubtless interrupted Thea's own family Christmas. All before she had any idea what had killed the man and whether there was any mystery attached to his death.

The body was stiff and apparently unmarked. The doctor was still there when Gladwin arrived, his hair tousled and his coat muddy. She knelt down beside him, to get a closer look at the body. 'Please tell me it was a perfectly ordinary coronary,' she begged.

He stirred his hair distractedly. 'Doesn't look like it to me. His colour isn't right. And he's in *pyjamas*. And I'm pretty sure he's been moved – look.' He pointed to a long, narrow groove in the fallen leaves. 'That has every sign of something being dragged along it. It's not a path.'

Gladwin looked around at the handful of officers awaiting her instructions. 'Has anybody had a look to see where it goes?' she asked.

A young constable raised his hand like a schoolboy. 'It leads to the perimeter fence,' he said.

'What perimeter fence?' Gladwin stared at him blankly. 'What do you mean?'

'The Crossfield Estate is just over there.' He pointed to a low ridge only a few yards distant, which might once have been a hedgerow. It had a few straggly trees growing along it, and a stretch of dead bracken. 'He's only five minutes from home. Less, probably.'

She got to her feet. 'Show me,' she said.

The lad took her alongside the scraped track, over the ridge and then stopped. A fence, six feet high, was barely five feet in front of them. It comprised five strands of stout wire strung between metal posts that had been planted every twenty feet or so. 'It's electrified,' said the constable.

'What's the voltage?' asked Gladwin, with a vague sense that this was important.

'Not sure, but the legal maximum is ten thousand.'

'Is that enough to kill someone?'

'Not really. It depends on a whole lot of things. And I would imagine the voltage here is a lot less than the maximum.'

'I'm impressed,' she told him.

'Don't be. I got it off Wikipedia ten minutes ago,' he confessed.

'That's impressive in itself. You were thinking this might be what killed him, were you?'

'I thought it might be. I haven't said it to anybody, though.'

'So let's ask the doctor what he thinks,' she said, turning back into the woods.

Chapter Nine

The path running alongside the woods in which Rufus Blackwood had been found was a popular spot with Ant and Percy. They would amble along it two or three times a week, avoiding going into the woods themselves, but defiantly using the path, making a point of following the perimeter fence as visibly as they could in the hope of irritating the people on the other side. The Crossfield Estate was almost six hundred acres in size, and the Frowses had been expressly forbidden from entering any of it. But the woodside path was an exception. Digby had performed one of his dramatic little scenes, begging for permission to use it as a shortcut to Chipping Campden, if going there on foot. Blackwood had grudgingly acceded to the request.

The electric fence encircled the Frowse cottage, separating

it unambiguously from the main house, but enclosing about an acre of ground, purely because the Blackwoods did not want it too close to their own gardens. Beverley had calculated its length and probable cost when it was first erected, using an arithmetical skill that her husband and son sorely lacked. 'Many thousands of pounds,' she concluded. 'All to intimidate us. Who else do they think is going to invade them?'

'It's all down to Carla,' said Digby. 'Before she turned up, Rufus wasn't really such a bad lad.'

That was true. Carla was fanatical about security. She had introduced the immoderately bright lights beaming down on the gates and yards all night. 'All it does is draw attention to themselves,' sighed Beverley. 'It's hard to credit that people can be so stupid.'

It was past midday before Ant and Digby were made aware of the demise of Rufus. The same police officers from the previous day came to the door with a serious expression. 'Good God – she doesn't still think we took that damned parcel, does she?' Digby burst out, before they could speak.

'This is concerning a different matter,' said one of the men. 'Could I ask you both about your movements over the past two days?' he began.

Slowly the story emerged, albeit very vague and patchy. The policemen had clearly been trained in careful questioning, where the interviewee concerned was given no helpful clues as to why the questions were being asked. 'Is this about my mother?' wondered Ant in confusion.

'Please just answer the question, sir.' He looked first at Digby.

'Well, I didn't go anywhere on Friday. Last night I had a stall in the Christmas market at Blockley. Ant went out selling trees in Chipping Campden yesterday morning. You saw us here yesterday afternoon.'

'Have you taken the dog for any walks?'

Ant snorted. 'Yes, of course. I took him along the ridge today, early on. That was about three hours ago now.'

'The ridge?'

'That's right. Monarch's Way footpath, if you want to look it up on a map. It goes past the Bakers Arms pub in Broad Campden, but we didn't get that far.'

'What's this about?' demanded Digby.

Ant had a sudden insight. 'It's not to do with my mother, is it? You wouldn't be acting so cagey if it was that. Something's happened. Is it Blackwood? His wife came over yesterday to say she couldn't find him.' He watched the officer's face closely. 'That's it! Hey! Has something happened to our esteemed landlord?'

The policeman was confused. Irony had not been mentioned in his training. 'You were fond of him, were you?'

'Well, we'd certainly notice if he wasn't around any more. He's a central part of our lives. And his wife, of course.'

'So when did you last see him?'

Ant exhaled, a long, complicated sigh of relief and gratification and his tongue became strangely loose. 'So it is him. I last saw him . . . let's see . . . must have been nearly a week ago. We coincided at the road gate – might have been Tuesday – and he gave me a short nod of recognition. Very decent of him, I thought, seeing as how he had to concentrate on driving his Jag. He's got four cars, you know, and he takes them out in rotation. Keeps him quite busy, I guess. We're shocked that not one of them's electric, though. Somehow I don't imagine Mrs Blackwood's very interested in toxic emissions and that sort of thing.'

'Ant!' his father scolded. 'Stop talking so much.' He glanced at the policeman, who was clearly floundering. 'We see Mr and Mrs Blackwood quite regularly, Officer. Usually when we meet at the road gate, or when they have a reason to walk past the end of our garden. That isn't very often, and they seldom pause for a chat. We have very little in common to talk about, actually.'

'What's happened to him, then?' asked Ant impatiently. 'It can't hurt to tell us now we've answered your questions. We already knew he'd gone missing, so whatever it is isn't going to come as a very great surprise. Unless someone's killed him, of course.'

The silence spoke for itself. 'Good God!' said Digby, sitting bolt upright in the chair he had not left all morning. 'Is that what's happened?'

'His body was found today, close to the perimeter fence around this property,' the officer informed them, with a small frown.

'Shot? Stabbed? Throttled?' Ant's excitement was impossible to conceal.

'I'm not authorised to reveal any further information.'

'Never mind. Blimey! This is going to shake things up a bit.' Ant stared at his father. 'What'll happen to us, then?' When there was no reply, he faced the policeman. 'Are you sure he's dead?' Then he shook his head. 'Of course you are. And you think it was homicide, as the Americans say.

Homicide . . .' he repeated, his face suddenly drooping. 'That's what they called it when my sister died. And it's never all right, you know. I never thought I'd say this, but I actually feel sorry for the loathsome Carla.'

Digby was also shaking his head in bewilderment. 'But where's my wife?' he asked, his right hand stretching out as if needing to feel her presence. 'I want Beverley.'

'Hush, Dad,' said Ant. 'She'll be back. Everything's going to be all right.'

'Wife, sir?' Both officers were suddenly alert. 'You are unaware of her exact whereabouts?'

Ant snorted at the clumsy sentence. He was still feeling giddy with relief. But Digby was ahead of him, frantically trying to backtrack. 'Oh, gosh, silly me,' he chuckled, in a perfect imitation of an addle-headed old man. 'She went off to the shops, I remember now. Wouldn't let me go with her, said I'd be in the way. Time she was home, though. She'll be wanting to hear the news.'

'We need to speak to her,' said one of the men decisively.

'You won't want to waste time hanging about here,' said Ant, picking up his father's lead. 'The shops must be awful today – all that last-minute panic buying.'

The men exchanged glances. 'Well . . . when she gets back, could you ask her to contact us?' said the more talkative one.

'Of course,' said Digby, with a little bow. 'Excuse me if I don't get up.'

The policemen took their leave, with a few scanty lines in a notebook. Whatever the situation on this peculiar fortified estate, it was beyond their pay grade to understand.

Jessica continued to admonish her mother about her determination to involve herself in the Crossfield business. 'So now you know it's not Beverley,' she repeated, 'you've got much less reason to be concerned.'

'Yes, I know. But it's still a major event. It'll have enormous ramifications for the Frowses. The police are going to be all over them, because you only have to glance at the place to see there's a stand-off between landlord and tenants. There's probably a file on it all somewhere, because Beverley always contests any rent rises. And we still don't know what's become of her – Beverley, I mean.'

'So what're you going to do? It's Christmas Eve, Mother. You've got responsibilities here.'

'I thought I could go and see Ant and his father after lunch. The police activity will have settled down by then. You and Steph can come with me, if you like. We could make a nice walk of it.'

'And Hepzie?' asked Stephanie. 'She likes playing with Percy.'

'Why not?'

Stephanie was feeling very grown-up, the way Thea and Jessica were including her in the whole discussion. While there was no definite suggestion that the Blackwood man had been murdered, there did seem to be a feeling that he might have been. Never before had she been around Thea when something like this had happened. She had only heard short summaries, after everything had been resolved. Now here they were, right in the middle of it from the start. She allowed herself a smug little thought that after all, Timmy was not having all the fun. 'They call him Blackheart, you know,' she said, when the dead man was under discussion.

'What's his real name, again?' asked Jessica.

'Blackwood. Like the magazine,' Thea told her. At Jessica's blank look, Thea sighed. 'Before your time. Before mine, actually. I think it died when I was about ten. But I came across it when I was doing that history course. *Blackwood's Magazine* was an institution. Very radical and satirical. I don't suppose this man is connected in any way, although he is a Scot, I think, and it was an Edinburgh publication.'

'Never heard of it,' said Jessica.

They were eating another of Thea's ad hoc lunches, with bread and bacon and scrambled egg. Jessica had called it 'brunch', which Stephanie found amusing. Another thought struck her – with so much happening, the day was going to fly by, bringing Christmas morning all the sooner.

'So are we going out, then?' Jessica asked. 'Or what?'

Thea was emphatic. 'I don't care what you two do, but there's no way I can just leave it as it is. And this is the only chance we've got. Once Drew gets back, it'll be non-stop here. That leaves about three hours to see what's going on. You don't begrudge me that, do you?'

The stepsisters both looked at her. Stephanie waited for a decision that was completely out of her hands. Thea was small and dark and disgracefully pretty for her age, an unlikely amateur detective, and just as unlikely a stepmother, probably. Then she looked at Jessica – larger and fairer and strangely adult, as if she were the older of the two. 'What are you looking at?' said Thea. 'You seem

127

very judgemental all of a sudden.'

'Sorry,' said Stephanie, not feeling at all repentant.

A short silence ensued, in which all three adjusted their expectations for the afternoon and wondered about the implications.

'So are we going?' nagged Stephanie. 'Or what?'

'Surely we ought to go by car instead of walking?' said Jessica. 'How far away is it?'

'Only about a mile. It'll take half an hour at most, along the footpath. Walking's better, really – and nicer for Hepzie. It's easier on foot, as well – we don't know whether they'd let us drive in through that gate.'

'What gate?'

Thea briefly explained in greater detail than before about the Blackwoods' efforts at security.

'For heaven's sake,' Jessica worried. 'It sounds as if we'll be shot as trespassers if we're not careful.'

'And the fence on both sides of it is electrificated,' said Stephanie.

'Is that a word?' wondered Thea.

'It is now,' said Jess.

They followed the Monarch's Way footpath in a westerly direction, with fields sloping away to their left. 'Lucky it's not windy,' said Jessica. 'It must get quite raw up here at times.'

'Great for flying a kite, though. Timmy's got one and we bring it up here now and then.'

'It never works very well, though,' Stephanie complained. 'We need to be in a field, really, and Dad says we're supposed to stay on the path.'

'Oh, well,' said Jessica vaguely.

There were a few people scattered along the path. It was a Sunday and Christmas Eve and several of the second homes in the area were suddenly occupied by people escaping their urban environment for something quieter. 'Nobody you know?' asked Jessica.

Thea and Stephanie shook their heads. 'Anybody local will be shopping or calling in on each other for sherry. These second-homers bring all their provisions with them, and probably a skivvy to get it all cooked for them. So they're free to come out for a walk and pretend they know their way around.'

'No sign that anybody's heard about a dead man, either,' said Jessica. 'You'd think there'd be snoopers by now.'

'That doesn't seem to happen around here so much,' said Thea.

Jessica watched a couple coming towards them. 'These two look as if they've dressed for the occasion. All very tweedy and shiny new boots,' she murmured.

Thea laughed.

'It's a funny business, when you think about it,' Jessica went on. 'They've got to be seriously rich if they can afford to keep two homes running. It can't be good for the economy here, and it's sure to inflate house prices. Selfish, basically.'

'They think if they've got the money they can do what they like. That's what Ant says,' Stephanie contributed. 'And Blackheart's the worst of the lot. He's got at least two other houses, with nobody living in them. Except housekeepers and people like that.'

'It's quite feudal, in fact,' said Thea. 'The rich have always done whatever they liked. Until the revolution comes and they get their heads chopped off.' She paused, hearing herself. 'Well, he's got his comeuppance now, apparently.'

They soon emerged onto the small road that ran towards Chipping Campden and turned left. 'Here we are,' said Thea, calling her dog to heel. 'We go along the road a little way and it's just off to the right.'

There were two police cars parked on the driveway leading up to the main house, and they glimpsed movement and odd white shapes in the woodland away to their left. 'Come on,' said Thea. 'They won't bother us if we just keep going up this way.'

Jessica was looking all around her, partly out of curiosity and partly from nervousness at the sense of intruding where she shouldn't. She noticed the wording on a handsome signboard planted beside a pair of wrought-iron gates a little way ahead. '"The Crossfield Estate",' she read. 'Those gates aren't electrificated, then?'

'I expect they are, actually. But they're a lot grander than the ones we have to use.' She pointed ahead to where the driveway branched off in two directions. The lesser branch was barred by a plain field gate, with sturdy wire fences either side of it, preventing access via the grassland that lay all around. 'This one leads to the Old Stables. We'll have to pick up the phone.'

'How long has all this been here?'

'At least two years, I think. Since before we came here,

anyway. I popped over for a snoop a year or so ago, when I first got to know Ant. He told me all about it and I wanted to see for myself.'

'It's horrible,' said Jessica in disgust. 'A travesty.'

'It certainly is,' her mother agreed.

There was a phone and an intercom on a post beside the gate, at the right height for a car driver to use it. Thea lifted the phone and prepared to speak into the grille, but before she could do so, the gate whirred and creaked and very slowly began to open. They pushed through as soon as the gap was wide enough, but the gate went on opening. 'Stupid thing,' said Stephanie.

Ant was standing in the doorway of his house as they walked up the driveway towards it. He was wearing a shabby brown jacket and green boots. His large dog was at his side, but when he saw the visitors, he came bounding towards them. The garden belonging to the Old Stables amounted to little more than a stretch of unkempt lawn strewn with rusting equipment, and half a dozen apple trees that Digby had rescued from the fruit farm days. A little old caravan was tucked into one corner, with a clematis growing over it. The winter twigginess of the climber added to the impression of general scruffiness.

Hepzie was off the lead, as she had been throughout the walk, and now leapt to meet her friend Percy. The two performed their usual jerky game, feinting and pouncing on each other. A pair of white alpacas in a field the other side of the driveway watched warily.

'Oh!' cried Stephanie, belatedly spotting them. 'Can I go and stroke them?'

'Definitely not,' said Ant. 'That field is strictly out of bounds to the likes of us.'

There was a large modern barn at the top of the drive. 'Who uses that? I've never noticed it before,' said Thea.

'Local quad bike business. Mowers and stuff, as well. He keeps his surplus stock in there. Blackwood knew him yonks ago, apparently.'

'He hangs onto old friends, then?' said Jessica, with a little tilt of her head. 'Sorry – I'm Thea's daughter. I'm in the police, as it happens.'

Stephanie watched Ant's face as he absorbed this information, thinking that she herself had actually forgotten about Jessica's job, for the moment.

'Better come in,' said Ant, with a nervous glance around. 'It's all kicking off down there. You'll have heard, I suppose? That'll be why you're here.'

'Your landlord died,' said Thea. 'Gladwin told me. Remember her?'

Ant shook his head. 'Remind me.'

'She's the detective superintendent, based in Cirencester. They called her out, presumably, when they found the body.'

Ant frowned. 'Why would they do that? I mean – it must have been before they'd even had a proper look at him.'

'Good question,' said Jessica, giving herself a light smack on the brow. 'Why didn't I ask that? Normally, there'd be all kinds of preliminary work before calling someone that senior.'

'Trying to save time, most likely,' said Thea. 'What with it being Christmas. If they thought she'd have to be called

132

at some stage, they'd have opted to do it sooner rather than later. Don't you think?'

'Makes sense,' said Ant, with a vague little nod.

'So what exactly has been happening up to now?' Thea asked.

'Come in first. I wouldn't put it past Carla or one of her daughters to be spying on us, even now.' He flicked a quick look at a CCTV camera mounted on a high pole, about twenty yards away.

'Surely not?' said Jessica with a little laugh. 'Not when her husband's just been found dead.'

'I promise you,' said Ant. 'They're so desperate to get rid of us, they're gathering any tiny scrap of evidence against us. They'll have persuaded themselves that one of us did the old man in, I shouldn't wonder. It's second nature to them, to fit us up for anything that goes wrong.'

'This is a bit more than something going wrong,' Jessica protested. 'The man's *dead*.'

Ant's face changed abruptly. 'That's what my mother said.' He turned towards the house, stumbling as he went.

Stephanie could see sudden creases under his eyes and round his mouth. It was like looking at a totally different man. 'Are you all right?' she asked him, grabbing his hand.

He pulled her to him. 'Don't worry,' he choked. 'It just hit me, that's all. Funny the way that happens.'

'Oh, yes,' said Stephanie understandingly. 'Delayed shock. I know about that. You should have a mug of sweet tea. Is Digby here?'

They moved into the house, pulling their boots off in the small front porch and filing through to the kitchen, where Digby Frowse sat in a sagging old armchair by a small black stove, both dogs now at his side. The mud on Percy's feet was dry, but Stephanie hoped he wouldn't jump up at her, all the same. The house felt damp and draughty. There were no Christmas decorations; no piles of vegetables waiting to be peeled and chopped; no sign of a turkey or sausage meat or seasonal drinks. 'Don't you do Christmas?' asked Jessica.

'Oh, yes. It's all meant to be happening – but without Bev, everything's on hold. She's put a tree up in the sitting room, and bought a goose last week, and that's about it. Not very spectacular, I know. Doesn't seem so much point when there's no kiddies to enjoy it.' Digby looked at Stephanie with a feeble smile. 'Where's your little lad, then?'

'Oh, he's gone north with Drew. Family crisis,' said Thea shortly.

'Don't tell me. Seems as if there's a lot of it about.'

'Don't joke, Dad.' Ant was scowling. 'Not when there's all this trouble. And we still don't know whether Mum's involved. I don't know about you, but I can feel myself getting into a fair old panic.'

'So tell us the whole story,' said Thea, taking a chair at the pine table. 'Jessica – maybe you could rustle up a nice big pot of tea. Ant won't mind you rummaging in his kitchen, I'm sure.'

'Help yourself,' said Ant, with a very unhappy sigh.

Chapter Ten

The whole story did not take long to tell, especially as Digby left most of it to his son. The older man remained in his ramshackle chair, putting in a few words now and then, sighing and even groaning once or twice. 'Don't forget about the missing jewels,' he interrupted, early on, leaving Ant to explain.

'I told you some of it on the phone yesterday. There was a row with Blackwood last week. Mum took it that he was accusing her of nicking a package that was signed for, apparently, and then just vanished into thin air. But that hasn't got anything to do with her being missing.'

'Do we know exactly what was in the packet?' asked Thea.

'Carla's Christmas present, I think. Some piece of

135

bling. Worth a bit, probably.'

'Okay. Carry on with the story,' ordered Jessica.

Ant obliged, taking two or three minutes to describe events since Thursday, and his feelings of anxiety about his missing mother. He summed up with the words, 'The thing that keeps coming back to me is – it's Christmas. Mum would never willingly stay away from home, knowing how much we depend on her. It's completely incomprehensible.'

'Tell us again what she said on the phone,' said Jessica, sounding rather official all of a sudden.

Ant repeated the familiar words. 'She said she wouldn't be able to come home, because somebody was dead.' Digby moaned gently in the background.

'Right. So what do you think she could possibly have meant? That was yesterday, you said? Presumably Blackwood was still alive then?'

Everybody looked at her. 'You think?' said Thea.

'Carla hasn't seen him for quite a bit longer than that,' Ant remembered. 'And nobody goes into those woods. He could have been there for days.'

'Ah.' Jessica grimaced. 'That's not good. You're telling me that your mother and your landlord might have both disappeared at more or less the same time.'

'Have the police worked that out as well?' wondered Thea.

'They still don't know that Beverley's gone AWOL,' said Digby. 'We've been careful not to tell them.'

'Ah,' said Jessica again, looking even more uncomfortable. 'You'd better put that straight, then. Otherwise you'll be had for concealing evidence.'

'Come on,' said Thea. 'Beverley can't possibly have killed him. I mean – *Beverley*.' She forced a laugh, which nobody echoed.

Jessica sighed. 'All right – you know her and I don't. But from what I can understand, Ant, your mother could have been held up by the unexpected death of somebody she knows, and is upset about it. She phoned to tell you she can't come home. She was about to tell you her whereabouts, when the phone expired. That's the best spin we can put on it, and it still doesn't look very good, does it?'

Ant had already realised that the story had a host of horrible implications. Jessica was forcing him to see that here was a family where the wife went off on her own without telling husband or son where she was going. It was a family that lived in a state of disorder on an estate that was otherwise pristine and evidently extremely affluent, earning their living by buying and selling whatever came to hand, doubtless much of it under the counter and free from tax. They lowered the tone by their very existence. And now the affluent landlord was mysteriously dead, and every reasonable person hearing this story would draw one very obvious conclusion. He clumsily articulated these thoughts, addressing his father in particular.

'We're not tinkers, you know,' Digby protested. 'Whatever it might look like, we're perfectly decent people.'

'Of course you are,' soothed Thea.

Stephanie went from Ant's side to Digby's. 'You're very nice people,' she said. 'And sad because of what happened to Aldebaran.'

Digby clutched her hand, pulling it to his chest. Ant watched, wondering whether this was another piece of play-acting. It showed every sign of being genuine for once. 'You're right, lovey,' Digby said. 'Nobody knows how that feels. You're a good girl for reminding everyone.'

'It must have been awful,' said Jessica, just slightly too briskly. 'But not relevant to the case in hand.'

There was clearly nothing to be said about that. A long time ago, in another country – but not to be lightly dismissed. 'Did you go out there?' the young woman asked.

'We did,' nodded Digby. 'She had made her home there, and we wanted to see it. We had her cremated and brought the ashes back with us.'

'But you're not thinking Beverley might have gone back there now? For Christmas, perhaps? Nothing like that?'

Ant's head went up at this new idea. 'God, no. That wouldn't have occurred to her. Would it, Dad?'

Digby shook his head emphatically. 'She would never have afforded the fare, for a start. And she would tell us. Our daughter is long gone now.' He looked around at them all, gathering himself for an overdue speech. 'The point, you see, is that it never leaves you. Once you know that the worst thing in the world can actually happen, you never really relax again. And when your wife disappears for two days without a word, you get worried.'

Ant was both impressed and confused. 'But you *haven't* been really worried about her, have you? You've been weirdly calm ever since she went. You don't even seem to be taking it seriously now. What if she's charged with killing Blackwood? Then what?'

'I'm worried enough, lad, and don't you doubt it,' said the old man angrily. 'But I know enough to understand that sometimes all a man can do is sit back and wait.'

'For what?' asked Jessica softly. 'Just what are you waiting for, Mr Frowse?'

After that, there seemed to be little to be gained by staying any longer. 'We've got to walk back, and get on with all the Christmas stuff,' said Thea. 'We shouldn't really have come, according to Jessica. But I'm glad we did. Thanks for explaining it all to us.'

'I'm glad too,' said Jessica. 'I'm sorry if I sounded a bit officious. It's really nothing to do with me – you don't have to do anything I say. But I really think the police ought to know about your mother. It's in her own interest, in the long run, to come back and give an account of herself.'

'She'll come back when she's ready,' said Digby, who was making no secret of the offence he had taken. Jessica's challenging attitude had forced him into a renewed silence, which had the effect of making the guests feel they should go.

'Well, I don't suppose much is going to happen before Wednesday now,' said Thea. 'Won't there have to be a post-mortem before there's any real progress? And they won't do that on Christmas Day or Boxing Day, will they?'

'Shouldn't think so,' Jessica agreed. 'All the same—'

Thea cut her off. 'That's enough, Jess. We've heard the story and had our say. We should leave these poor men in peace now.' She addressed Ant. 'Phone any time if you want to talk. If Beverley comes back, I'd love to know what she says. Or just that she's safe. Any time,' she repeated.

'Thanks,' said Ant. 'You're a good friend.'

Digby looked up at that. 'As good as we deserve, anyway. Tinkers like everybody thinks of us – nobody's going to stick up for our rights, are they?' He sighed bitterly. Even Stephanie had no answer to that. The three females all turned to go. The spaniel got up from the hairy blanket she'd been sharing with Percy, and trotted after them.

Unlike the earlier walk, the return home was entirely occupied with talk about the Frowses and the Blackwoods. Stephanie understood that the others were trying to avoid saying anything too grim about the likely outcome, but she had no illusions as to their real opinions. 'You think Mrs Frowse must have murdered him, don't you?' she accused.

'I don't think that at all,' Thea disagreed. 'But I can see that's what the police are going to think.'

'What's she actually like?' Jessica asked. 'Give me an objective picture of her.'

'Gosh! There's a question. Let's see. She's very independent, and doesn't talk very much. I think she had some sort of job when her kids were at school, and probably after that as well. I haven't known them very long, remember. I get the impression they didn't used to be so messy. Things have been going downhill since their daughter was killed. It's a kind of depression, I suppose.'

Jessica waited for more background. When it didn't

come, she prompted, 'This business with the landlord. It must be a worry. What's going to happen ten years from now?'

'You mean when they're in their dotage and can't keep up the fight any longer?'

'Something like that,' said Jessica. 'It doesn't look as if it could have carried on like this indefinitely. So now the landlord's dead, what's going to happen?'

'Who knows? Carla might carry on in much the same way. She'll inherit the whole estate and be able to do as she likes. Not that Rufus stopped her doing anything, anyway.'

'So she's not likely to have killed him?' Jessica spoke lightly, as if making a mild joke. But Thea took it seriously.

'We still don't know for sure that anybody killed him,' she said. 'And we won't know that till next week.'

Jessica turned to Stephanie and grinned. 'Looks as if your Christmas is safe, kid. Let's forget about dead people and think about all that lovely turkey.'

'And the presents. And the games – and everything.' For a moment, Stephanie faltered. What was so great about Christmas anyway, when it came down to the details? Was it just a lot of effort for the adults, with all the cooking and buying things and being nice to everybody? Was it just a way of making the darkest days of winter go by more quickly?

'Gosh, don't you love it!' Jessica cried, throwing her arms wide. 'I might be all grown up, but it still seems like magic to me – and look at this view! What a place to live!'

'Honestly,' tutted Thea, pretending to be annoyed.

'What's come over you, all of a sudden?'

'Just glad to be alive, I guess. Come on Steph, let's run!'

The girls and the spaniel hared along the track, and down the final slope to the road through Broad Campden. The Bakers Arms pub was almost opposite them, festooned with Christmas lights.

'Now listen,' said Thea, as they walked past the church and down to the house. 'Best not say anything about this Blackwood business to Drew. Not yet, anyway.'

'I wasn't going to. He'll have more than enough to deal with without that.'

'Is that okay with you, Steph?' Thea asked. 'I'm not asking you to keep secrets. If he wants to know what we've been doing all day, you can say we went to the Frowses'.'

'It's okay,' said Stephanie. 'I don't suppose we'll be doing the funeral, either.'

Jessica gave a yell of laughter. 'You really are your father's daughter, aren't you? Business first and all that.'

Stephanie didn't know whether to be offended or pleased. 'Well, he is an undertaker, after all,' she said meekly. 'And our field is a lovely place to be buried. Digby says he wants to have a grave there when his time comes.'

'When did he say that?' Thea asked.

'Ages ago,' shrugged Stephanie. 'But he did say as well that he'd have to check with his wife first.'

'No more talk about the Frowse family,' Jessica ordered. 'Let's just be Christmassy for a bit.'

* * *

It was nearly four o'clock. Hepzie flopped down in a dramatic display of exhaustion, and Thea glanced at the mobile phone she had left on the kitchen worktop. She found another text from Drew sent shortly before three. *All gone well. Should be leaving soon. Have the mulled wine ready.*

'I hope the car doesn't conk out,' said Thea. 'It's not used to long journeys. All it has to do now is get them back in good time this evening.'

'All that way for a few hours. It seems pretty daft to me,' said Jessica.

'And me. But it'll be interesting to hear how it went, all the same. I'm still trying to get used to the idea of having a mother-in-law who might actually want to meet me one day.'

'What do you mean – one day? You'll have to go to his father's funeral, won't you? It'll be early in the New Year, presumably.'

Thea took a deep breath. 'That never occurred to me. What about the kids? And the dog? I don't see how I can possibly go all up there, in the depths of winter.'

'What you mean is, you're sure you'll be able to find a cast-iron excuse not to.'

'That's just your nasty suspicious mind.'

Stephanie found herself recoiling from the laughter that seemed unpleasantly heartless to her. These were her grandparents they were making fun of. Her actual blood relatives. 'I might like her,' she said mildly.

'And she'll *adore* you,' said Jessica, with a quick hug. 'There's nothing so wonderful as a granddaughter. She's been an idiot to ignore you for so long.'

'Well, we can make it a New Year Resolution to be nicer to family,' said Thea. 'Starting with Damien, heaven help us.'

'If you can cope with Damien, you can cope with anybody,' said Jessica. 'Even I think he's hard going.'

'He thinks religion gives him an excuse for being terribly rude. He judges and disapproves and makes critical remarks like a Victorian Methodist.'

Stephanie had never met this step-uncle, but was altogether open-minded about him. 'I expect he's perfectly nice, really,' she said reproachfully. 'And Kim's sure to be lovely, like Meredith.'

'Last I heard, she was having mega-tantrums and refusing to eat anything but cheese,' said Jessica. 'But if anybody can charm her into better behaviour, I'm sure it's you, Steph.'

'She can work her charm on Drew's mother, then, when we finally get to meet her,' said Thea. 'Pity we'll never know the grandad as well. Mind you, I've never liked the sound of them, from things Drew has said. They're pretty unreconstructed about nearly everything. I gather they more or less disowned him when he became a nurse. They still think nurses should be female. And the undertaking was probably even worse. They found him embarrassing.'

'But he's so *sweet*. How could anybody deliberately shun him like that?'

'Precisely. They're obviously horrible people.'

Stephanie listened to this with total absorption. The existence of a nasty bigoted grandmother was intriguing and not entirely unwelcome. Her experience of grandparents was patchy anyway. Her mother's parents had paid an extended visit when Karen had first been hurt, and then again when she died, with infrequent appearances in the intervening years. They called themselves Nanna and Gampy, and were alternately sickly sweet and sharply critical. They hadn't approved of the undertaking either, and thought Karen's ways were uncivilised. When the Slocombes moved to the Cotswolds, the grandparents appeared to take this as a sign that they were no longer needed, and promptly took themselves off to live in Portugal. Stephanie remembered them with mixed emotions. 'You never wash those children's faces,' Nanna had complained. Or 'This carrot's still got mud on it,' objected Gampy. Now, from what she was hearing about Drew's mother and father, Stephanie was concluding that he and Karen had a very similar pair of parents.

'But now he's dead, and Dad's mum must be sad,' she said. 'Maybe that'll make her nicer.'

'It's possible,' said Thea doubtfully, 'and she and your dad probably think it's time for a reconciliation, and from here on it's all going to be lovely.' She sighed. 'She'll meet my mother and they'll get along famously, and we'll turn into a classic nuclear family with two grannies.'

'Don't knock it,' said Jessica. 'It's evolved like that for good reasons.'

'Just so long as neither of them wants to move in with us,' said Thea darkly.

A minute passed as all three contemplated the situation in varying ways. Then Thea shook herself.

'I'd better answer Drew's message,' said Thea. 'He'll be

wondering where I am.'

'He'll be on the road by now. Don't make him break the law by answering his phone,' said Jessica.

'Right. Except he's far too law-abiding to do that. He'll give it to Timmy to deal with. I could just send a text, to keep him happy.'

Again, Stephanie was uneasy at the tone, which came over as unduly critical of her dad. The adult currents were harder to ignore when Timmy wasn't there. The hints and references were just as confusing, but the implications were clear. Even at Christmas, there was something not right between Thea and Dad, as well as Thea and her brother. In fact, Thea seemed to be the problem, making everyone cross and just laughing at them instead of trying to understand their feelings.

Thea composed a quick message and continued to hold her mobile. 'I might call Gladwin, as well,' she said thoughtfully. 'There's quite a lot to tell her, after all. Except . . .' She stopped, clearly uncertain as to what to do.

'We've been over all that. The only thing you can usefully tell her is that Beverley's gone off somewhere without telling her menfolk. Speaking as a police officer, I should order you to inform the police about that immediately. But as an uninvolved visitor, anxious for a peaceful family Christmas, I would advise you to leave it all for another day or two. Won't Gladwin herself just want to put the whole thing on hold until Wednesday? Or Tuesday, at the earliest.'

'I'm hungry, after all that walking,' Stephanie interrupted. 'What's for supper?'

'Good God, we've only just had lunch,' said Thea.

'Don't tell me I've got to produce another meal already.'

'Have a biscuit for now,' said Jessica to Stephanie. 'And I'll do some supper later on. How do you fancy potato cakes?'

'You're a star,' sighed Thea gratefully.

'Just keep the mince pies coming and we'll be fine,' breezed Jessica.

'Mulled wine!' Thea said suddenly. 'I promised that Mrs Yacop in the village that I'd take her some. She asked me to get two extra bottles, days ago now, and drop them round to her. I completely forgot.'

'Not too late, is it?'

'I don't know. You'd think she'd phone to remind me if it was important.'

'Maybe she did while you were out. Have you checked the landline for messages?'

It transpired that Mrs Yacop was indeed anxious for her wine, and reproachful at its non-appearance. Thea snatched the bottles from the larder and put her coat back on. 'I won't be long,' she said and left the house at a run. Then she came back, opening the front door again and calling, 'Hey, come and listen. There's music coming from somewhere.'

Jessica and Stephanie went to the door. Outside it was unusually bright and a faint sound of music wafted up the lane. 'Must be having a carol service in the church,' said Stephanie, cocking her head. 'I wouldn't have thought there were enough people to make themselves heard all up here.'

'I don't think it's actual people,' said Jessica. 'More like a radio somewhere.'

'It's coming from Mr Shipley's house,' Stephanie realised. 'How nice.'

'Do we like Mr Shipley?' Jessica asked.

Stephanie shrugged. 'He's okay. He doesn't talk to children if he can help it, but he's not too bad with me and Tim. We invited him here for Sunday lunch once, and he was very nice and polite. His sister died, and Dad did the funeral, which made us friendlier. But he spends a lot of time in London. I wonder why he's here at Christmas? It doesn't look as if he's got any visitors.'

'You'll have to ask him over here, then,' said Jessica, as if there was no possible argument against the idea. 'What about offering him Christmas lunch?'

'I don't think Thea would like that,' sighed Stephanie. 'We've got enough visitors already.'

Chapter Eleven

Thea's thoughts were in a jumble as she trotted along the road to Mrs Yacop's house. It had been a spontaneous burst of neighbourliness that had prompted her to offer, earlier in the week, to get the wine, prompted by the spirit of Christmas and a sense that Drew would approve. The woman had sprained her ankle and was relying on other people to do her shopping for her. Mulled wine, it seemed, was a crucial element of Christmas Eve in her house, but her husband had forgotten to buy the essential ingredients and was now too busy to go back for them. 'Just get the ready-made stuff,' Mrs Yacop had sighed. 'That'll have to do.' And Thea had obediently bought two bottles, taken them home with her own shopping, and promptly forgotten about them.

It wasn't surprising, she told herself. There was far too much to think about already. As she walked, a host of dilemmas preoccupied her. Should she phone Gladwin? If so, how much should she disclose about the Frowses? Should she really keep the whole business from Drew? Should she think again about inviting his mother to come and stay? Had she got enough food for the next two days? Would the children like their stocking presents? Was Jessica going to be all right? Would Damien be as much of a pain as usual?

She lingered only a few minutes over the delivery of the mulled wine. The Yacops were in no state to be hospitable. Their two boys were rampaging, the husband was slamming pans about in the kitchen, and the poor wife was pale and obviously desperate. 'I shouldn't be walking on it,' she worried, looking down at her badly swollen ankle. 'It hurts dreadfully.'

'They say a sprain is more painful than a fracture,' Thea sympathised. 'You need to put it up.'

'Chance would be a fine thing,' said the woman, who was forty-five, but looked and behaved ten years older. Thea did not much like her, but attempted to remain on good terms, if only because Timmy and the two boys were of a similar age and friends were always a good thing. There was always the hope of shared driving to and from the big school, too, once Timmy and the older boy left the primary.

She turned back towards home, but was suddenly in no hurry. Jessica and Stephanie got along well and would probably be glad of some time alone. All that awaited Thea was more work – lighting the fire, feeding the dog, preparing the turkey, and then filling the Christmas stockings. Before that, Drew and Timmy would be back, bringing stories that would have to be listened to. It all made her feel weary.

It was almost dark, but her eyes had adjusted and she could see well enough. A man was walking towards her, carrying something of an awkward shape. 'Gosh – is that a gun?' she asked him, without thinking.

He laughed. 'No, it's not a gun,' he said. 'It's a metal detector.'

When Thea and Hepzie had gone, Jessica proposed a drink and a mince pie, rather than the biscuit she'd originally suggested. 'We should eat some of them now. There'll be so much other food tomorrow, they'll get forgotten and go stale,' she said. 'And Drew and Tim won't want much when they get back – if anything.'

They had two mince pies each, sitting in the kitchen to eat them. 'I don't expect we'll be moving the table into the living room, after all,' said Jessica. 'Too much of an upheaval.'

'It would be nice, though. Candles and crackers and the thing you said you'd brought. It would be much more Christmassy than eating in here.'

'It's a centrepiece. We'll see if we can persuade Thea to do it, then. We could get it done today, all ready for the big day.'

'Better leave it till tomorrow. Thea's going to need it to put things on, isn't she?'

Jessica swigged her tea and let the matter drop.

Stephanie was still not quite free of thoughts of death

and funerals. Instead of shaking them off, she found herself recalling her mother's burial, and the wild emotions it had aroused. Poor Timmy had been inconsolable, and Dad had been a mess. But time had eased nearly all the pain, helped by a determination to talk about Karen without restraint. Now, by association, her thoughts slid to the death of her unknown grandfather. 'Dad must be sad about his father dying,' she said slowly. 'It must be horrible, not seeing him for so long, and now never seeing him again.' Tears filled her eyes at this sudden rush of sympathy. 'We didn't think about it properly, did we?'

'There wasn't time. Everything happened so fast. I think he wanted to try and get it over with before Christmas. But you're right – he might not be very jolly tomorrow. We'll have to remember what's happened and be nice to him.'

'Thea as well,' said Stephanie with a small flicker of anxiety. Her stepmother was not always quite as nice to Drew as she should be. She complained about all the cooking she had to do, and snapped if he mentioned that there was mud in the hallway, which people coming to arrange funerals might see.

'I'll have a word with her,' Jessica promised.

Another abrupt switch took place in Stephanie's mind. 'I wonder if that metal detector man found anything,' she said. 'It was a funny place to be looking, wasn't it?'

'My guess is that he'd dropped something – a watch or a ring – and knew it happened when he was walking round the field. Don't you think?'

The man had seemed sinister when Stephanie had first seen him going down towards the field in near-darkness.

'He was there on Friday as well, don't forget,' she said. 'When it was dark and we were unloading your car.'

'Are you sure it was him? Don't people go past here all the time?'

'Not really. And yes, I am sure. I thought he'd got three legs—' She laughed in self-mockery. 'Then I thought it was a gun. I was quite scared when I went to bed last night, thinking he might be coming to shoot us.'

'God, Steph. You've got quite an imagination, haven't you! Why didn't you say something?'

'I don't know,' she said.

'I suppose there was too much going on, with Drew's dad and everything.'

'He was a bit suspicious, though, don't you think? The man, I mean.'

'Well, not so much. It looked rather innocent to me, actually.'

Stephanie argued. 'Well, I think it's odd. They don't do that sort of thing around here. They walk dogs and watch birds and take pictures, or go in huge walking groups, yomping along the footpaths. That's what Thea calls it – yomping.' She chuckled. 'Isn't that a great word?'

'Typical Mum word, anyway. So this man – maybe he's just lonely, it being Christmas, and stuck for something to do. He might not have anybody to be with, so he decided to try and find some Roman coins or something.'

'Maybe.' Stephanie tried to recapture the whole scene. 'Do you think he'd found a treasure map that had a big X right at that spot where we saw him?' She grinned. 'That's what Timmy would say, anyway.'

'It could be geocaching,' Jessica agreed. 'If you know what that is? Except I don't think that requires a metal detector.'

'I don't know what it is,' Stephanie admitted.

'It's a sort of treasure hunt, in a way. People hide little collections of objects all over the place, and then tell other people the map reference, and they go out looking for the hidden stuff. Something like that, anyway,' she finished vaguely.

'Sounds nice. How do you get into it?'

'No idea. Try Google, I suppose. You probably have to sign up to a website or an app.'

'Right,' said Stephanie weakly. It was an intriguing piece of information, fitting so nicely with the fantasy she'd suggested, but it did not quite ring true. Without quite understanding how it had happened, there now seemed to be almost too much to talk and think about. The calamity that had befallen the Blackwoods and the Frowses, on top of Drew's dash to County Durham and Christmas and Thea and families and whether people would like her presents, and what they were having for supper, and whether she'd see Tim before they got their stockings, and when she would ever catch up with the stories he was surely going to have to tell her.

Jessica seemed to read her mind. 'The Frowses seem like nice people,' she began.

'Ant's nice. He won't have a good Christmas, will he, not knowing where his mother is, and what she's been doing.'

'I guess not. Did you have any thoughts about that –

anything you tried to say but couldn't make us listen?'

Stephanie shook her head. 'Not really. Nothing sensible, anyway.'

'So tell me something unsensible.'

'Well – it's really stupid, but that parcel. The one the landlord said was lost. It's all part of the mystery, isn't it? I just thought it could be that the metal detector man might have been looking for it.'

'That really is bonkers, Steph. The field is nowhere near the Frowse place. I mean – it might make a bit of sense if we'd seen him *burying* something. But he was trying to *find* something. Wasn't he?'

'I know. I said it was stupid. Things don't have to connect like that. I mean – they really don't connect. But in my head, they sort of do. And there is a bit of a straight line from there to here, with a kink in the middle where you go along the road. And we do *know* the Frowses, and there aren't many places where nobody could see you from a house if you were doing something secret. Even on the big footpath there are always people and dogs everywhere. So it wouldn't be such a huge coincidence, really.' She paused for breath, wondering where all those thoughts had come from. Most of them had been hidden until she started talking.

Before Jessica could reply, the front door opened, letting a gust of cold air into the house, along with Thea, Hepzibah and a man who Stephanie instantly recognised.

When their visitors had gone, Ant and Digby found themselves at a loss as to how to go on. Things had been said that they were both beginning to regret. 'We ought not to have told Thea and that daughter of hers so much about your mum,' said Digby. 'It won't have done any good.'

'Can't do any harm,' Ant argued.

'We'll have to see, won't we? Things are different now.'

'I know that!' Ant was suddenly angry. 'They were bad enough before, and now we've got to worry about being charged with killing our landlord. I'd say that was quite a big difference. And even if he died of a heart attack, we've still got more than enough to worry about. It's a rock and a hard place, if you ask me. Either Carla stays on and ups the intimidation stakes, or she sells the place and we've got a whole new set of problems.'

'Could be we get someone with a liberal social conscience, who has no problem with tenants who pay their rent regularly and don't cause any nuisance.'

'Dream on,' said Ant bitterly.

It was almost dark when they were disturbed by a persistent knocking on the front door. 'It's the police again, you see,' said Digby – wrongly, as Ant discovered when he answered it.

It was Bronya, eldest daughter of the newly widowed Carla. She looked straight past Ant at Digby, who jumped out of his chair as if jabbed with a stick. 'What do you want?' he demanded.

'To talk,' she said. 'I just want a quiet talk, that's all.'

'Does your mother know you're here?'

'Mr Frowse,' she said, with great dignity, 'I am not a child. And my mother is in no condition to concern herself with my whereabouts. But she has jumped to a conclusion about her husband's death that I think I should warn you about.'

'Huh!' said Ant, following her into the house. 'You think we need any warning from you? After the way you spoke to me yesterday? Accusing us of taking that packet that's gone missing.'

'That packet contained an extremely valuable gold necklace. And there can be no doubt that it has been stolen by someone on this estate. It was handed to a person here on Wednesday afternoon, who scribbled an illegible signature for it, and it has not been seen since. My mother believes that Rufus was out searching for it when he died. He was in his pyjamas, you know. He must have died during the night.'

'Which night?' asked Ant.

'That appears uncertain. We have to assume it was Thursday, but nobody seems to know where he was that day, so it might have been as long ago as Wednesday. The police have spent an hour or more trying to understand his movements on those days.'

'He was in pyjamas?' Ant was astonished. Then it became clearer to him. Of course, a wealthy plutocrat, idling his affluent way through the approach to Christmas, might well slob around the house all day in silk pyjamas and a cashmere dressing gown. 'All right for some,' he added cynically.

Bronya turned feline. If she'd had claws, his face might well have felt their points. 'What do you mean?' she hissed.

'I mean we live in different worlds, divided only by a

six-foot electric fence.'

Bronya turned back to Digby, who was standing stiffly beside the kitchen table, his face pale. 'Steady on, son,' he mumbled. 'Let her say what she came to say. Something about this gold trinket – am I right? So who signed for it? Was it a male or female?'

'Female. If the delivery man can be believed, which my mother is convinced he can.' She narrowed her eyes, as if in triumph. 'And it's her belief it was your wife.'

'Well, she's wrong. Rufus upset her badly by accusing her of having it. She told him days ago that she knew nothing at all about it.'

'She told you that?'

'She did.'

'So please fetch her now and let me ask her for myself.'

'She isn't here.'

'Where is she, then? Listen, you stupid man – my mother is convinced that this is obviously a motive for murder. If, as she suspects, it's established that Rufus was deliberately killed, you and your family will be the main suspects. The police have already found footprints in the woods, all kinds of evidence that somebody was there where he died. They will form a theory that you were hiding the necklace and my father found you doing it, and you killed him. Perhaps both of you together. Perhaps all *three* of you. That's what my mother believes is going to happen. I came, actually, to warn you.'

Ant tried to quell his pounding heart, blustering loudly, 'That's ridiculous. Nobody here's stolen anything. It'll turn up. One of your staff must know where it is. One of them might even have stolen it.'

Digby waved at him to stop. He was frowning, deep in thought. 'Does your mother know you've come here to warn us? Wouldn't it suit all of you better to just have us arrested and carted off, so you can come and demolish this house, as you've always wanted?'

The woman stood taller than ever, her broad shoulders seeming to expand sideways. She did not answer his first question. 'I am not like my mother,' she said. 'Nor am I like my sisters. They enjoy plotting and cheating and getting something over on people. They will make things far worse for you than you can imagine, now that Rufus isn't here to keep them in check. For myself, I prefer to keep everything clear and open.'

'Makes no sense,' Ant protested. 'You're no more concerned about us than your mother is. I think you're here to stir up more trouble, for your own reasons. I know your sort,' he finished, belligerently. He had squared up to her himself, closely matching her for height and width, so they looked like two bulls about to charge each other.

Bronya glanced at him speculatively. 'You know nothing,' she concluded. 'You are the least concerned – although my mother might not agree.'

'That's true enough.' Digby said, then chewed his lip for a moment, as if holding in words that might be best unspoken. 'I know you better than you think.'

'Nothing you know can do me any harm.'

'Believe it or not, my dear, I wish you no harm. If I have to take it that far, it'll be out of self-defence. So if we're throwing warnings at each other, then there you have it.

You get your mother to drop her crazy accusations, and I won't make any trouble for any of you.'

Again she narrowed her eyes, but to Ant's bemused gaze, she seemed to have softened a little. 'You overestimate my influence on my mother,' she said, with a grim smile. 'And none of us should forget Annika. My sister is a vixen.'

'And your mother is a she-wolf,' said Digby.

'Well, we're all Russians, after all,' said Bronya enigmatically, and took her leave without further comment.

Ant's heart continued to pound as he tried to grasp the significance of what had just happened. What had his father meant in those final minutes? What did he know about Bronya, and what did he really feel about her? There had been some sort of spark flashing between them, some consciousness that seemed to imply a shared knowledge. 'Why did she really come?' he bleated helplessly. 'At least explain that to me.'

'It's much better that you remain in ignorance,' said his father. 'In fact, your ignorance will save you, as I hope it will save your mother. There's nothing so dangerous as knowledge, at a time like this.'

'You've gone mad,' Ant said weakly. 'You're talking gibberish.'

'I can see it must seem that way. Well, so be it. Look, son, we've got to get through tomorrow as best we can. Nothing's going to kick off until that's over and done with. There's every chance your mother's going to come back in time to pull a few crackers with us. I'm not going to tell you everything's going to be all right, because that would insult your intelligence. But you'll be okay. In the long run, it might turn out to be just what you needed. It all depends on the despicable Carla.'

'I know it sounds childish,' said Ant, 'but all I really want is for my mother to come back.'

Thea's new friend was the man with the metal detector. Stephanie was in no doubt that these were the same slouching shoulders, the same long legs and grey jeans. Besides that, all doubt was removed when he carefully propped his strange device against the wall. 'This is Detective Sergeant Graham,' said Thea with a rueful smile. 'We knew each other slightly, some time back, as it happens. But he's not here as a policeman now. He's been having a fun time metal detecting all round the village, on his days off.'

'Gosh!' said Jessica. 'Fancy that.' She stared at his face. 'Stephanie spotted you, twice. Thought you were behaving suspiciously.'

'I thought you'd got a gun, the first time. Why were you doing it in the dark?' asked Stephanie.

'I got carried away, that's all,' he said, speaking for the first time. 'It's hard to stop, once you get going.'

Thea interrupted to offer him tea and make proper introductions. 'The big one is Jessica, my daughter, and the little one is Stephanie, my stepdaughter. Jessica's in the Manchester police, soon to be promoted to CID. And that's Hepzibah,' she added, indicating the spaniel who was in her basket licking her paws.

'And I'm Finch. Finch Graham – which I know is back to front. It should be the other way around. It causes all kinds of confusion.'

Jessica laughed. 'It's a nice name, all the same.'

Hearing an unfamiliar note in her stepsister's voice, Stephanie gave her a sharp look. She was facing the man, looking right into his eyes, her skin a slightly pinker shade than usual, her back very straight. And the man was looking back at her with the same sort of expression. It was as if an invisible membrane had wrapped itself around them, keeping everybody else at a distance.

'I want to know more about the metal detecting,' she nagged. 'How do you do it in the dark?'

'Simple – I've got a head torch. So when the thing beeps, I've got enough light to see what I'm digging up.' He was in his late twenties, with curly hair the colour of their kitchen table, a sort of dark ginger. 'But here I am, still at it, and no sign of anything. I'd just decided to pack it in when your mother accosted me.'

'No lovely Roman gold coins or amulets?' teased Jessica.

'Quite a lot of nails, maybe eighteenth century, a horseshoe and this.' He pulled a piece of square-shaped metal from his pocket. 'I think it's a shoe buckle, but it's very broken.'

'Well, that's better than nothing,' said Jessica kindly. 'Are you stopping for a mince pie?'

'You're not out searching for Beverley Frowse, then?' asked Thea incautiously.

Sergeant Graham was patently confused. 'Who?'

'Oh – I forgot. The police still don't know she's missing. Well, I've said it now. No need to phone Gladwin about it after all. You can tell her.'

Graham's confusion deepened. 'Er . . .' he said.

'You'll probably know there's been a body found on the Crossfield Estate,' said Jessica. 'Well, there's also a woman gone missing. She lives in the tied cottage there. Thea's friendly with the people in the cottage, and they told her about Beverley. They hadn't said anything to the police, last we heard, which makes it a bit awkward.'

The man took a slow breath. 'This is the first I've heard about any of it. I'm off duty, have been since Friday. Doesn't some multi-millionaire own that place? Got a helipad and security fences.'

'That's the one. And he's dead. They found him this morning. There's been trouble between him and his tenants for years now. Harassment and intimidation all the time. It's a wonder nobody's called the police before now.'

'And somebody's missing as well as him being dead? You'll be telling me next it was murder.' He paused. 'Although if that was so, they'd have called us all in. So it's natural causes, right?'

'Undecided, apparently. All down to the post-mortem, which won't be till Wednesday, most likely.'

'Christmas,' said Graham with a nod. 'Sounds pretty complicated, all the same. And you say you've been withholding information? What's DS Gladwin going to think about that?'

'She'll be grateful to me for not lumbering her with any more worries,' said Thea defensively.

'Maybe. But . . .' He scratched his head. 'You've told me now. I should probably get onto her. Can we sit down, and

163

you can go over it again.'

With a sigh, Thea did as asked. She rattled through the story while Stephanie and Jessica listened and added one or two extra points. Stephanie could tell that Thea was trying to make it sound as unsuspicious as she could. She said nothing about the phone call that Ant had told them about, where Beverley had referred to someone being dead. Jessica, more surprisingly, didn't mention it either.

'Okay – so we've got a grown woman, probably not just sick of peeling sprouts in spite of what you're trying to make me think, gone off on her own, leaving her hated landlord dead in the woods, a few yards from where they both live. That does look quite bad,' said DS Graham.

'Oh – and there was something about a missing parcel, which had some sort of jewellery in it. I suppose you should know about that. Maybe you'll be able to find it with your gadget. You really could discover some treasure, after all.'

The policeman glanced towards the hall where his detector stood. 'I'm not going to hold my breath,' he said.

He was draining his tea and preparing to go, when Thea's mobile starting jingling. Jessica picked it up. 'It's Drew,' she said, handing it to her mother.

Thea took the phone, but didn't leave the room. 'How's it going?' she asked.

There followed a one-sided conversation in which Thea said various things such as, 'Amazing!' and 'Really?' and 'You can say that again.' Drew was doing almost all the talking. Stephanie watched intensely, trying to ascertain whether the story was a generally positive one or not. It didn't sound as if the grandmother was proposing to join them for Christmas, at any rate. Nor did she get the impression that anything objectionable was being demanded of Thea. She laughed once or twice, and seemed quite relaxed. She ended by saying, 'That's great. Well done. See you when we see you, then. Mind how you go.'

'It's her husband,' Jessica explained in a whisper, while the conversation was under way. 'His father just died, and he's dashed up to County Durham to see his mum.'

'Bad timing,' sympathised Finch Graham. 'That's a hell of a way from here.'

'He thought it best to get it over with before Christmas. It's all rather complicated.'

'These things generally are.'

Thea finished the call and took a deep breath. 'Doesn't sound too bad. They've stopped at a service station for the loo and a snack. Timmy's fine. There was an enormous great dog at the house – a Malamute, of all things. Timmy thinks it's wonderful, apparently.'

Nobody had a quick answer to that. Stephanie experienced another pang of envy. 'What are they like?' she asked.

'They're huskies basically, I think. Lovely thick coat and uncertain tempers,' said Thea. 'Your grandmother's a braver woman than I am, to think she can handle something like that.'

'It'll be nice company for her, though, if she's just lost her husband,' said the young detective.

'Will she bring it here when she comes to visit?' asked Stephanie, imagining the scene with some trepidation.

'Not if I can help it. The dog would probably eat Hepzie.'

Graham got up. 'I'd better go. I've got to think what to do about this Crossfield business.' He looked at the three female faces with profound interest. 'I'm not sure whether to be grateful or annoyed about meeting you, and having all this dumped in my lap.' He fixed his gaze on Jessica. 'On the whole, I have to say I'm glad to have met you.'

'Me too,' she said. 'Come and see us again. I'm here for a couple more days.'

'And there's sure to be a whole lot of excitement still to come,' said Thea with a cheerful grin.

It took Stephanie some time to forgive her stepmother for that grin.

Chapter Twelve

Thea sat down on the sofa with a thump, and said, 'Well! How about that!'

'He was nice,' said Stephanie with a glance at Jessica. 'Don't you think?'

'Not sure about that hair,' said Jessica.

'It was providential, meeting him like that. I feel a huge sense of relief,' sighed Thea. 'It's all out of my hands now, and I can concentrate on Christmas like a good wife and mother.'

'Don't fool yourself. By this time tomorrow, you'll be desperate to know what's happening.'

'No, I won't. I give myself a bit longer than that. Maybe by the middle of Boxing Day I'll be feeling a bit curious.'

'What did Dad say exactly?' asked Stephanie. 'You didn't tell us all of it.'

'I pretty much did. He's okay, that's the main thing. And the roads aren't much worse than they were yesterday. He thinks they'll be here by eight. Which means I'd better get a move on. I haven't even lit the fire yet.'

'I'll get started on the potato cakes,' Jessica announced. 'I hope there's plenty of onions and cheese?'

'Don't use too many potatoes. We need them for tomorrow,' warned Thea. 'Aren't we supposed to fast on Christmas Eve, to leave room for the coming feast?'

'Onions? Cheese?'

'I really don't know. Go and see for yourself.'

Jessica went off humming to herself, while Stephanie retired to the sofa, with the dog as usual, and her beloved *Through the Looking-Glass*. Reading about the white knight and his inanities restored her to a better frame of mind. It was still the funniest piece of writing she could think of. The jokes were so fresh and unexpected. And it had all been written so long ago! It seemed like a kind of miracle to her – and certainly quite magical. Thea was kneeling in front of the woodburner, piling up sticks and rattling the vents. She stayed there watching the flames after the fire had become nicely established. Before long the smell of onions frying gently in butter came wafting through.

'Blimey – it's half past six!' Thea realised. 'I was off in a dream for a minute.'

Stephanie had finished the book and was half asleep. She had a feeling they'd lost quite a lot more than a minute. Dad and Timmy would be back before they knew it, and Christmas would really be only one sleep away.

'Ready!' called Jessica, and they all sat round the table with the golden-brown potato cakes in front of them.

'We always used to have baked beans with them,' Thea reminisced. 'When we were little. My father made them for Saturday lunch.'

'It was him who taught me how to do them, when I was about fourteen,' said Jessica. 'I do miss him.'

'Not another dead man to worry about,' begged Thea.

Mother and daughter met each other's eyes and burst into laughter. Stephanie stared. 'What's funny?' she asked.

'Oh, Steph – I'm sorry,' said Jessica, with a final giggle. 'It's just us. Take no notice. It's been quite a day for all of us. Let's change the subject. That policeman's nice, don't you think? Maybe he'll take us out metal detecting with him sometime.'

It was a transparently feeble attempt to improve Stephanie's mood. 'We already said that. And you'll have gone home before he comes again,' she said stiffly.

'That's where you're wrong, if I'm any judge,' said Thea. 'He'll be back on Boxing Day, I bet you. I wonder what he's said to Gladwin.'

'She's going to be pretty miffed at having her family Christmas interrupted,' said Jessica.

'Well, I hope she doesn't blame me,' said Thea.

Drew and Timmy were still an hour or so away, which gave Thea time to prepare mulled wine and mince pies to welcome the travellers home, as well as lighting candles

169

in the windows and the ritualistic stacking of the presents under the tree. Everybody had accumulated parcels under their beds or in cupboards, in preparation for Christmas Eve. This particular practice had been instigated by Thea, who had grown up with dogs prone to sniff out anything edible and attack the relevant parcel when nobody was looking. The children had strongly approved it, owing to the added excitement it produced.

The only interruption was an unexpected text from Gladwin. *Heard from DS Graham with your fresh info. Should probably be angry with you. Post-mortem to be done on Wednesday, so before that there isn't a lot we can do. No obvious signs of violence, but the medic isn't happy that it was a straightforward coronary, especially as the man was in pyjamas and it's December, and there's no hint of a reason why he would go out on his own like that. Expect I'll be seeing more of you next week.*

'Put it away,' urged Jessica. 'You said you wouldn't think about it again.'

'I know I did. I fully intend to try. But pyjamas – doesn't that change everything? Isn't it a bit sinister?'

'I don't see why. No—' Jessica held up a hand. 'Don't try to explain it to me. I don't want to know. The fire needs another log – and I'm going to bring my presents down.'

Stephanie could see that Thea wasn't ready to let it go. She kept reading the text and sucking her teeth. But she eventually gave up with a sigh.

Five o'clock on Christmas Eve saw the Frowses uncomfortably trying to find a way of getting through the coming evening.

Even Percy was subdued, licking his feet and sighing, after being given a very short walk to the end of the garden and back. Ant had taken him, and in the process had managed to glimpse the police gazebo standing on the further side of the fence. He reported back to his father the news that there was no remaining sign of police activity other than that. Digby had merely shrugged.

Ant had tried about twenty times to phone his mother, until finally flinging his device onto the sofa and snarling, 'She's doing it on purpose. It's not possible that she can't get to a phone. There's one in every pocket. All she has to do is go up to somebody in the street and ask to borrow theirs. Unless she's actually been kidnapped, it's got to be deliberate.'

'Don't be obtuse, son. She's hiding out. She knows if she switches the phone on, she can be tracked. She's scared.' Digby was oddly calm. 'But I've got one or two ideas about where she might be. We'll leave it a day and then I'll see if I'm right.'

'"Leave it a day"? Do you know what day it is tomorrow? She's never missed a Christmas. What about the damned goose and all those vegetables? Who's going to cook them?'

'Me, I presume. I can cook well enough if I have to. And Bev can have it warmed up when she comes home.' The elderly man tried to smile. 'Let me just see if I can find her on Tuesday. If I can't get her to come back, I can take her some sandwiches.'

It seemed to Ant that his father was wandering in his wits. He was talking utter nonsense, surely. He'd been strange ever since Bronya's visit, making less sense with every utterance. Now it was sounding as if he'd known more about his wife's disappearance than Ant had even begun to guess. 'If you know where she is, just tell me, and I'll go and fetch her. Now. What's to stop me?'

'You don't know *why* she's gone. You can't just force her back before she's ready. You could do a lot of harm that way. I told you before, the less you know, the better for you. Have patience, boy.'

Ant angrily repeated his question. 'Do you know why she's gone?'

Digby shook his head. 'Not for sure. But I know *her*. I know she'll have a good reason, and that she's got some trouble that she has to stay and sort out. She might think the police are looking for her, you see.'

'They probably are, after we told Thea.'

'Pity, that,' said Digby.

'Do you think she knows Blackwood's dead?' Ant's insides were cramping with panic. He couldn't put the next thought into words. Every time he tried to connect his mother's disappearance with the death of their landlord, his mind went foggy and his throat filled up. He clung to the forlorn hope that the timing would work in her favour. They'd managed to agree that Beverley had left home on Thursday, and Blackwood had not been seen by his family since Wednesday. Every time he went through it, Ant persuaded himself more strongly that there was no connection between the two events. But it was all so vague that he could not extract very much encouragement from his calculations. A nasty little voice insisted that logic quite strongly suggested that Beverley had gone off not very long after Rufus had died. There were any number of inescapable scenarios in which the two met fatally in the woods, all of which haunted Ant's imagination.

'Let's have a drink,' said Digby at last. 'We've got the port they gave you at the hotel. I could fancy a glass of port. And are there any mince pies? We've hardly had any food all day.'

Ant didn't move or reply. He had no appetite for food, and was wary of drinking in case he had to suddenly drive somewhere. 'I can't eat,' he groaned. 'I'm too agitated. Do you think Carla might have done it? Isn't it usually the spouse when there's a murder? Or he might have got entangled with that bloody fence and it electrocuted him. That would be a joke. Serve him right. Then it wouldn't be murder at all. Just a stupid accident.'

'We don't know the facts of it. Nobody does. It might yet turn out to be a perfectly ordinary heart attack. I tell you, son, we just have to hang on a day or so, and wait for a chance to do something for ourselves. The police are taking two days off, more than likely. We can put the jump on them. Don't panic, that's the main thing.'

'"Put the jump on them"? What the hell does that mean?'

'Forget it. Go and get the port, there's a good lad. I don't want to disturb the dog. He's missing your mum, poor old boy.'

'Maybe he could find her for us.' Ant was only half joking. Percy was an intelligent dog, who deserved a much less restricted life than he was allowed by the Blackwoods. Carla would go berserk if he ventured into their terrain and scared her precious Peke, so the Frowses had to take him along the road and onto the Monarch's Way every time he needed a run. There wasn't always time for more than a short excursion, which left the dog restless and bored.

Digby only snorted at this idea. He waited for his drink with obvious impatience. Ant finally got up and went to look for the bottle. It seemed wrong to open it without Beverley. The hotel manager had carelessly handed it over, as just one more gratuity for a long list of townspeople who gave sporadic paid help at busy times. The kitchen, gardens, bedrooms, car park and bar might all find themselves short of essential staff at unpredictable moments. Ant had only ever done gardening, apart from selling them their Christmas trees. He had been replacing one that had got damaged when Beverley had made the mysterious phone call. 'And say thanks to your mother,' the manager had added. 'She's been quite a help this year.' The implication had been that the port was meant for them both.

Ant told his father about this remark now. 'Don't drink all of it,' he said.

'What's she done for the hotel, then? I don't remember anything.'

'She made all those table decorations for the Rotary Club's Christmas bash, three weeks ago or more. The florist let them down, so Mum had to do it in a rush. She did a lovely job. You can't have forgotten.' The house had been fragrant with the holly and cloves and glue that had gone into the centrepieces. Beverley had added glittery little origami birds as a special touch, and the feedback had been glowing.

'Oh, yes,' said Digby absently. 'That seems a long time ago now.'

'Dad – do you really think you know where she is? Somewhere beginning with "Win"? That's got to be Winchcombe, hasn't it? Why would she be there?'

Digby shrank into his chair, shaking his head. 'I don't know for sure. Could be Winchcombe – most likely is. I wish you'd just stop going over it. Must be a hundred times by now. She was wrong to call you like she did, and say that about someone being dead. Can't imagine what she was thinking, saying that.'

'Why do I get the feeling you and she had some sort of plan, that hasn't gone the way you expected?'

'Stop moithering me, will you! You're twisting my words and making me say things I don't mean. Leave it, for God's sake. I'm telling you, I'll get to the bottom of it on Tuesday, when it's had a bit of time to settle. How many times do I have to tell you?'

Digby only said words like *moithering* when high emotion sent him back to his Lancashire roots. His first fifteen years had been spent in Manchester, where they said *snicket* and used a short *a* for *daft*. Ant understood that something had been going on behind his back; something that his parents had hatched and which involved the ultimate horror of sudden death. And yet, the idea was surely ludicrous, when he regarded it more closely. There had to be some simpler explanation – something to do with Christmas, perhaps – even a surprise present for himself. Straining his imagination, he arrived at a scenario whereby his mother had gone off to acquire an animal of some kind – Ant had always said he fancied keeping geese or pot-bellied pigs – and it had died. Perhaps she was in trouble because it was a valuable creature and her own carelessness had caused its death. Perhaps she'd let it onto the road and caused an accident. A *fatal* accident. It was starting to sound plausible inside his own head. Except for about twenty inexplicable details. Why keep up the secrecy? Why would she make that phone call? Why not get hold of another phone or find a charger for her own? How would she transport livestock in the family's small unreliable car? And hadn't there been a strong implication that the words *He's dead and I can't come home* referred to a human being? And all that before factoring in the bizarre conversation between his father and Bronya. He went through the chronology of events one more time, hoping to prove that there really couldn't be any connection between his mother and the death of Blackwood. It was impossible to believe that Beverley had loitered in the woods one evening in the dark, used fatal violence on their landlord and then dashed off to a hiding place without communicating with her husband and son.

'She's done something illegal, hasn't she?' he challenged his father. 'That's the only explanation that makes any sense at all.'

'I honestly don't know, son. And that's the last I'm going to say on the subject.' Digby drained his glass of port and defiantly poured another one.

Drew and Timmy made it home by eight-fifteen, when Stephanie was upstairs at the front window watching out for their headlights. They brought gusts of the outside world, disturbing the quiet and introducing topics that fitted awkwardly with the Christmas atmosphere. And yet none of the females in the family could resist asking endless questions, to which the males were more than happy to respond. An hour flew by, with them all flopped around the sitting room with the fire blazing up. Thea had made a rich, creamy soup from parsnips and onions and pieces of ham. 'Unorthodox but delicious,' said Drew approvingly.

'We'll be short of parsnips tomorrow,' Thea warned. 'But they do make wonderful soup.'

They then progressed to mulled wine and mince pies, as promised.

Jessica said little, watching the faces and trying to assess the implications of his father's death for Drew's marriage. Thea's own father had died a few years ago, leading to a slow but steady fracturing of the remaining family group. The siblings saw much less of each other than they had when the patriarch had organised get-togethers. His widow seemed only faintly interested in maintaining the Johnstones as a unit.

When invited to give a summary of the visit, Drew grimaced. 'She was completely different from how I remember her,' he began. 'She belongs to a choir which occupies half her time, volunteers all over the place, drives an electric car that cost a fortune and has a huge dog.'

'The dog's a monster,' said Timmy with a shudder. 'It chased me.'

'You shouldn't have run away,' said his father, with scant sympathy. 'It only wanted to play.'

'You told me that Tim thought it was wonderful, when you phoned,' Thea reminded him.

'He did at first. But it has an unreliable temper. I'm pretty sure it wouldn't have hurt him, all the same.'

'So your mother's all right?' said Thea. 'I mean, she doesn't sound prostrated with grief.'

Drew paused. 'No, she's not at all prostrated. I got the impression they'd been living very separate lives for quite some time. It turns out he got a hefty windfall from the PPI thing – got some agency to dig it all out, and ended up with nearly forty thousand. Claimed he was "financially naive" and had believed all the stories he was told about needing to be insured. Spent most of it on the car. My mother's gone astonishingly green, which is why she wants him to have a natural burial.'

Which got them onto the logistics of what was going to happen next. Drew, it turned out, had wasted no time in contacting a local green burial ground and fixing up a funeral for the coming Friday. 'He's having a cardboard coffin, and the choir are coming to sing at the graveside,' he added.

'In a snowstorm, most likely,' said Thea. 'Doesn't it snow all winter up there?'

'Not quite. We checked the long-term forecast and it looks reasonably mild all week.'

'And then what?'

'She wants to come and meet you and see Stephanie and mend bridges. She's pencilled in 4th January. And she's going to bring the dog.'

Timmy shuddered again, but Stephanie found herself

curious to meet the animal. It couldn't be entirely terrible if it had an old lady as an owner, she decided.

'How long is she proposing to stay?'

'Four days. Apparently there's a concert on the 9th she has to be there for, with a rehearsal the previous day.'

'Long way to come in an electric car,' said Jessica. 'Won't it run out of power before it gets halfway?'

'She's coming by train. We've got to meet her in Oxford, probably. She can get a direct line to there.'

Thea made a soft puffing sound of indignation, but said nothing. Stephanie was half asleep, her mind forming pictures of a strange grandmother setting stones on top of each other in an effort to mend a bridge, with a massive dog at her side.

'She sounds very organised,' said Jessica neutrally.

'She made Dad cut up logs,' said Timmy unexpectedly. 'She's got a big, fancy woodburner, twice the size of this one.'

'Are they green?' wondered Thea. 'I thought we weren't meant to burn things any more.'

'Apparently they're fine if they've got all the latest attachments to control the emissions. And I wasn't cutting the logs up, I was splitting them. It's actually very satisfying,' said Drew. 'She's got an acre of land, with lots of trees. She uses dead bits for firewood mostly, but sometimes there's a big branch to lop off . . .' he tailed away, suddenly aware that nobody really wanted to hear about his mother's fuel arrangements.

'An acre of land?' Thea echoed, picking up the only interesting detail. 'Maybe she should start her own burial ground, then?'

'I don't think so. Somebody's got two horses on it at the moment. There's quite a nice shelter in one corner.'

'You obviously got the guided tour. What about the house?'

'I think that's enough for this evening, don't you?' said Drew, noticing his somnolent children. 'It's probably going to be an early start tomorrow.'

'The later they go now, the longer they'll sleep in the morning,' said Thea optimistically. 'You do hear of kids bouncing on their parents' bed at 4 a.m.'

'Not these two. I've got them better trained than that.'

'And not me, either,' said Jessica. 'I always had to wait until seven. It was torture.'

'Well, the turkey should go in by nine. Otherwise I don't think I've got any deadlines,' said Thea. 'We can start on the presents after breakfast.'

Stephanie's eyes flew open. 'Presents! We haven't brought them down. And a mince pie for Santa.'

There ensued a flurry of activity, everyone producing parcels from hidden cupboards and corners, until the tree was swamped by them. Timmy had to be carried upstairs and undressed while more than half asleep. Everyone else soon followed, with the briefest of visits to the bathroom for teeth-brushing. 'It's good to have you home again,' mumbled Thea to Drew, as they both sank into oblivion.

Chapter Thirteen

Towards dawn, Stephanie had a succession of dramatic dreams. In the first, Ant's mother came to the door festooned with brambles and nettles and thistles, her face scratched and her hands bleeding. 'Help me!' she gasped, before collapsing in the sitting room and knocking over the Christmas tree. That was followed by one featuring a witch-like figure riding on a massive dog, which was chasing Timmy around a fallen tree in a field. Lastly, there was a lengthy episode in which she had to find a box containing Thea's Christmas present from Drew, which he had hidden and then forgotten where he put it. Only Stephanie could help, until Ant's beloved Percy appeared and started to dig under a hedge. A glint of bright silver wrapping paper had just become visible when she woke up.

Blearily she blinked at her father standing in the doorway, his arms full of peculiar shapes. 'Happy Christmas, kids!' he carolled. 'Don't tell me you're still asleep. It's nearly half past seven. Look – Santa Claus has been, as hoped. I found all this stuff by the fire downstairs.'

He carefully disentangled the two pairs of well-filled tights and gave one to each child. 'I hope I've got them right,' he said. 'Not that Santa seems to discriminate between the sexes so much these days.'

It felt wrong to Stephanie that he had had to wake them up. This had never happened before, and it made her think she must be getting old. The magic of the pre-dawn anticipation had been a crucial part of previous Christmas mornings. But Timmy had missed it too. He was as bemused as she was. 'Morning already?' he spluttered. 'Are you sure?'

'I think I am. Thea's not up yet, but Jessica's in the bathroom already. The sun's going to rise any moment now.'

'It's not till after eight, actually,' Timmy corrected. He knew about such things. But he was not trying to pick an argument. Instead his attention was diverted to the mysterious lumps and rattles of his Christmas stocking. 'It's heavy,' he said, his eyes widening.

'Well, just see what you've got, while I go and let the dog out,' said Drew. 'Don't eat all the chocolate at once.'

'How do you know there's chocolate?' demanded Timmy, alert for any hint that Santa might actually be a resident of their own home.

'I think I spotted it, about halfway down one leg.'

Stephanie was already pulling objects out of the tights. The stretchy nylon resisted as corners caught, and she tried not to make holes. First out was a wooden yo-yo, followed by something mounted on a cardboard rectangle. It was a strange puzzle set into a plastic frame, comprising moveable squares to create a picture. Delving further, she soon had a goodly pile of treasure on her duvet. Timmy, across the room, was yelping with delight every minute or two. It was unusual for them to be sharing a room, but Jessica's arrival made it necessary. Only three upstairs rooms contained beds, while the fourth, which was very small, was used as an emergency overflow only, with a folded bed kept in a cupboard. Timmy had begun to use it for his own overflowing collection of Pokémon figures and other things. He had instructed Jessica to be very careful when moving around his bedroom, because he had several delicate possessions sitting on almost every surface. 'Don't knock the orrery over, will you?' he begged her.

'The what?'

'It's a model of the solar system. I made it myself.'

'Wow! I promise I won't make any sudden movements,' she assured him.

Drew came back to inspect their stocking things, and then left them to get dressed and come downstairs. 'Nice smart clothes, remember,' he added. One of the aspects of childcare that he had always paid particular attention to was the way they were dressed. For this Thea had expressed considerable gratitude and relief, when first taking on her role as stepmother.

Jessica came into the kitchen, her phone in her hand.

'Snow forecast for Wednesday,' she informed them. 'Just as I'm supposed to be driving back to Manchester.'

'Hooray!' crowed Timmy. 'I like snow.'

'It should have been today, then we could have had a white Christmas,' said Stephanie. 'That never seems to happen.'

'You're right,' Jessica agreed. 'I don't think I can remember a single one.' The children had brought their stocking toys downstairs in cardboard boxes, and Jessica devoted herself to a thorough inspection of them, remarking that she thought a pair of tights was cheating, and she had only ever been allowed to hang up a handmade felt stocking that had been her father's. 'It only held about four things,' she said. 'And it had a hole in the toe.'

'Gosh – that old thing!' Thea exclaimed, overhearing this remark. 'Carl's mother made it in about nineteen sixty. I threw it away when you were fourteen.'

Stephanie digested this conversation with interest. Carl's mother must be Jessica's grandmother – the one that wasn't the person who she had met twice, when Dad and Thea had got married. 'Is she still alive?' she asked.

'Who? Carl's mother? Oh, yes. We've got the full set of grandmothers, in fact, even if we hardly see any of them.'

'Where does she live?' she asked Jessica. 'Your father's mother, I mean.'

'Oh, she's in a nursing home in Shrewsbury. I went to see her last month, actually. It's not terribly far from Manchester. Dad's father died ages ago, and she married a man called Stanley when she was seventy-five, and they went to live on the Welsh border. Then she got Alzheimer's. She usually knows who I am when I visit, but last time she thought I was one of her old schoolfriends. Somebody called Abigail.' She turned her attention to Thea. 'You've never been to see her, have you, Mum? She used to ask about you all the time.'

'I send her birthday and Christmas cards, and always put a letter in. Isn't that enough?'

'I would say not, actually. She lost one of her sons in a shocking accident. I remember her being in a dreadful state at his funeral.'

'So were we all. She hogged all the limelight, as if she was the only one entitled to any grief.'

'She didn't, Mum. It wasn't a competition.'

'Well, that's how it felt.'

'And what happened to Stanley?'

'Nothing. He's about ninety-two and fit as a flea, as they say.'

Both girls waited tensely, expecting Thea to defend herself further. Instead, she clapped her hands, and said 'Off you go, out of here. I'll come as well. We can have two rounds of presents, before I have to peel potatoes – right?'

'Let's get on with it, then,' said Drew, leading the way. He settled onto his knees beside the tree and reached at random for a parcel.

'Hey!' Thea objected. 'We've never done it like that,' referring to her years with Carl and Jessica. Drew had assumed it was perfectly acceptable for two or three people to open presents at the same time – wrongly, according to his second wife. Stephanie hurriedly put a hand on her father's arm and said, 'I think Thea's way is best.' She leant towards her young brother. 'It'll go more slowly like that, don't you think? It's horrible when everything's opened.'

'Wise child,' said Jessica, and Timmy nodded.

'Indeed,' said Drew, slightly rueful. Everyone silently acknowledged the ghostly presence of Karen, who had somehow become obscurely in the wrong for failing to enforce due present-opening discipline when she was alive. 'So, we start with the youngest, then. Let's find something for Tim first.'

'You'll be Santa, Dad,' said Timmy, handing his father the traditional hat. 'Find me one from an aunt.'

And thus another tradition was born. Drew unearthed a cube-shaped parcel wrapped with silver paper. 'To Timothy from Auntie Jocelyn,' he read.

'Good old Joss,' murmured Thea. 'She's always wanted more nephews and nieces.'

The present turned out to be a kit for making a model of the London Eye, with small pieces of metal. 'Wow,' said Jessica. 'Looks complicated.'

'Expensive,' added Thea with a quick grimace. Her younger sister was not particularly well-off, and if she spent this much on a step-nephew, what was she giving to her own children?

'Good start,' said Drew in a Santa Claus sort of voice.

'Now me,' said Stephanie.

She was handed her gift from Jessica – which was a bit higher up the ladder of likely value than Stephanie might have wished. It was much better to start with the small things and work upwards to the main event. She unwrapped it to find a denim rucksack decorated with embroidered motifs. She held it up dubiously. 'Great,' she said.

'Girls always need bags,' said Jessica. 'You'll be off travelling any time now, and this can be your day bag.'

'Travelling?' echoed Drew, as if worried that he'd missed something.

'She's joking,' said Thea. 'It's perfect for staying overnight with schoolmates, or visiting relations.'

'No,' said Stephanie. 'I'm going to use it for school. Thank you, Jessica. It's lovely.'

The round continued, followed by another one, with all five expressing delight. Thea then went back to the kitchen and applied herself to peeling potatoes. Stephanie drifted after her a few minutes later, and noticed a rather gloomy expression on Thea's face. Was she perhaps feeling sad about Carl, Stephanie wondered. It must be as hard for her as it was for Drew and his children, missing Karen. Carl had obviously been just as nice as her own mother. How strange, she mused, the way some people died when they were only forty and others lived to ninety-two. How uncertain it made everything seem, when you couldn't ever know which group you yourself might fall into.

'Are you thinking about Jessica's dad?' she asked warily.

Thea looked at her with a warm smile. 'Not really. Are you thinking about your mum?'

'A bit. It's sort of like they're watching us, don't you think?'

Sudden tears filled Thea's eyes, evidently startling her as much as they did Stephanie. 'Gosh – I didn't see that coming. You're right, though. They do feel closer, don't they? And they both loved Christmas, didn't they?'

Drew came into the kitchen, looking reproachful. 'I heard you. You're talking about dead people, aren't you? Give us a break – eh, Steph?' He grinned at his daughter, but the smile didn't look very genuine to Stephanie. The red hat with white fur trim struck her as ridiculous.

'We were feeling a bit sad,' she told Drew. 'In quite a nice way, really.'

'She started it,' Thea accused, with a sniff. 'Now go and play with your new toys while I baste the turkey. You'll make me forget some vital procedure if you stay in here talking.'

'I haven't got any new toys,' said Stephanie with dignity. 'How long are you going to be? We want to open more presents.'

'Five minutes.'

Over the next hour most of the parcels were unwrapped. It was all over far too quickly, and even with the big meal still to come, there was a growing sense of the best being over already. Stephanie's main present had been a lavish chess set with onyx pieces and board. She had started to learn to play over a year earlier, and was proving to be more than capable of plotting moves and grasping the big picture. 'Who's going to play with me?' she demanded.

'Who do you think?' said Drew, who was less than averagely competent at the game. 'You'll have to get the school to start a club.'

'I think there is one already, but they're all Year Nine and above. I told you that before.' But she was deeply happy to be the owner of such a handsome set. It made her feel almost adult and determined to become an excellent player.

The next thing was the complex task of bringing the kitchen table into the living room. Drew and Jessica took an end each, and by twisting and tilting it, they got it through the two doorways. A gleaming white damask tablecloth was produced, and the cutlery laid out. Jessica disappeared, only to return holding a creation made of pine cones, baubles, beads, ribbons and gold-sprayed evergreens. A red candle stuck up from the middle of it.

'Your centrepiece!' Stephanie cried. 'It's fabulous!'

Everybody clustered round to admire it, repositioning glasses, mats and tablespoons to accommodate it. The candle was lit, and the table deemed ready for the ceremonial presentation of the turkey, along with plates, bowls and dishes containing all the necessary accoutrements. Thea wiped the sweat from her brow, and let Drew take over the carving.

As with the presents, so with the food. It was all gone in no time, with the unsightly wreckage stacked uncomfortably on all the kitchen worktops. 'I'll need that table back again before long,' said Thea.

'Shouldn't somebody be taking the dog out?' Jessica asked.

'Feel free,' invited her mother. 'After you've done the washing-up, of course.'

'I love you too,' said Jessica.

At Crossfield, Ant and Digby were making very little effort to celebrate Christmas. Everything felt wrong. They could barely even be civil to each other, with the undercurrents and anxieties making them both sharp-tempered. Poor Percy found the situation increasingly worrying. Nothing was going as usual. His devoted mistress was absent for much too long. People came and went, leaving the atmosphere even worse than before. He hadn't had a decent walk for days, and when he tried to encourage Ant to play a ball game with him, the response was chilling. And he had a sore foot. Nobody had noticed that he was constantly licking at it, to the point where pink skin was now showing through. He'd scarcely noticed when the damage had first been done, but now it was getting more painful every day.

Ant was impossibly restless, roaming the house like a small child searching for his mother. He went into her bedroom, with the vague idea of finding a clue as to her whereabouts. Standing by the bed, he tried to form a telepathic link with her. *Where are you, Mum?* he thought, forming the words silently on his lips. *What have you gone and done?*

Something was different in the room, he slowly realised. There was a gap where there shouldn't be one. Seconds later he was downstairs again, confronting his father. 'Aldebaran's ashes have gone!' he shouted. 'What's happened to them?'

Digby blinked up at him from his customary chair. 'What? What do you mean, gone?'

'They're not there. The shelf is empty. They've *gone*.'

'Never. They never have.'

'Go and see for yourself. You're telling me you don't know where they are?'

'I haven't the faintest idea where they are. I haven't touched them, if that's what you mean. Your mother must have moved them to somewhere else. Maybe she found them upsetting, sitting there like that.' The elderly man was thinking more quickly now. 'That'll be it. She'll have put them in a cupboard somewhere. They won't have *gone*, as you put it. We went to too much trouble to get them for that to happen.'

It was true that there had been a wealth of paperwork, expense and argument before they could take possession of Ant's sister's remains. They had been transported across the Atlantic by special courier and submitted to intense scrutiny by the British customs people. There had even been an article in the newspaper about the whole exercise, when Beverley decided to make the matter public in an attempt to highlight the insane levels of bureaucracy.

'I'll find them if so,' said Ant, who proceeded to ransack every cupboard in the house. Twenty minutes later he reported that they were definitely nowhere on the premises.

'Well, it's a mystery to me,' said Digby crossly. 'Now can we have something Christmassy, do you think? I got you this, look.' He thrust a badly wrapped parcel into his son's hands.

'Oh! I nearly forgot. Hang on a minute.' He went to the slightly crooked Christmas tree that had been part of his own stock, and sifted through the modest pile of parcels at its foot. 'Here,' he announced finally, proffering a small item wrapped in sparkly gold paper.

Each man unwrapped his present with an air of going

191

through a wholly irrelevant ritual. 'Hope it's not a gold necklace,' Digby muttered.

'Very funny.' Ant was holding up a cellophane pack containing a pair of trousers that appeared to be old-fashioned moleskins. 'Great, Dad! Thanks very much. Just what I was needing.'

'That's good. There's more, look.' There were two T-shirts still inside the wrapping, one blue and one black. 'Should be the right size.'

Ant held them up against himself. 'Perfect,' he said. Then he watched his father picking carefully at his own present, intent on keeping the paper from getting torn. It was a family joke the way Digby still kept paper of every sort to be used again. 'I can't help it,' he would say. 'My mother drilled it into us from infancy.'

Finally, a leather pouch was revealed, and from inside that Digby extracted a penknife made of something dark brown and a large compass in a silver case. 'I got them in a junk shop in Cirencester,' Ant said. 'The knife's made of Bakelite. It's very unusual.'

Digby opened the knife and inspected the blade with his thumb. 'Nice and sharp,' he approved. Then he examined the compass. 'For when I go yomping about on the wolds, I suppose? Lovely case.'

'It's solid silver. Nineteen-o-six, according to the hallmark.'

'Beautiful. Thanks, son.' He seemed genuinely moved, blinking rapidly and shaking his head. 'Very thoughtful. You know I've got a thing about Bakelite.'

'I do.' Digby's collection of unlikely objects made of the

early form of plastic was arranged on a shelf in his bedroom, along with old radios made of the same material. When Ant listened to young Timmy Slocombe talking about his Pokémon and other accumulations, he realised that some men just never quite grew up.

'Let's have some more of that port, then,' Digby said after a few moments. 'It was intended to be drunk, after all. What time do you think we should eat? We'll have to cook that goose, if it's not to go to waste.'

Ant groaned. 'It's already too late to have it ready for lunchtime. It'll have to be dinner. Say six o'clock. We can have ham and eggs or something now – a sort of brunch.' He eyed the remaining parcels under the tree. 'Are we going to open any more of them?'

'Best not. If I remember rightly, goose has to be done slowly. It'll be in a cookbook somewhere. I know we did one a few years back, and it was disappointingly tough.'

'That was about twelve years ago now. Deb was still here.'

'Tastes a lot better than turkey, even so. Lovely skin, if you get it right.'

'You can find some instructions on the Internet, I suppose. We might not have all the right ingredients, though. They're sure to say garlic and fancy spices.'

'Could be your mother ran off just to get out of having to cook a goose,' joked Digby. 'I know she wasn't looking forward to it.'

'I think she expected you to do it, all along.' Ant knew better than to take his father seriously, or offer any sort of argument or reproach for his flippancy. But inwardly he winced at what felt like a lack of concern over something that he personally was finding very worrying indeed. The disappearance of his sister's ashes had compounded the mystery tenfold, as well as deepening his dread. If Beverley had taken them with her, that could all too easily mean that she never intended to come back.

It was late in the afternoon when they finally attempted to eat the goose. It was at least thoroughly cooked and much less tough than Ant had expected. He was, he had to admit, hungry. The past hour had been filled with tantalising smells that his empty stomach had yearned for with increasing urgency. He realised that he had half believed his father's assurances that Beverley would come walking in sometime during Christmas Day, with a supremely rational explanation of where she'd been. But darkness fell on a household that still only contained two men and a dog.

Chapter Fourteen

Mid-afternoon found the Slocombe family amid a sea of wrapping paper and new possessions. Thea had issued each child with a cardboard box to put their presents in. Jessica had a big canvas bag for hers, while Drew and Thea were making piles on the sofa. Thea was starting to think she should phone her mother, who was spending Christmas with Jocelyn, her youngest daughter. Everything had run smoothly all day, the two different sets of expectations and habits combining without much friction. And then Jessica spoilt it.

'I wonder how your friends in the cottage are getting on,' she said unthinkingly to Thea, thereby opening a box worthy of Pandora.

'Poor Ant,' sighed Stephanie, making it worse. 'He

must be awfully worried.'

'It's ever so sweet of you to think of him,' Jessica told her. 'Not many people your age worry about others the way you do. Kids are generally completely self-absorbed. I know I was.'

'What's the matter with him?' Drew asked, looking from face to face.

'Ah,' said Jessica. 'Sorry. We weren't going to bring that subject up until tomorrow. I forgot.'

'So why is my daughter so sweetly worrying about him and why should I not know about it?' He was addressing his wife, under no illusion that the answer lay with anyone but her.

'It's a long story. There's been a lot of trouble over at Crossfield since you went off the day before yesterday. A world of woe, you might say.'

'I honestly hadn't given them a thought until now,' Jessica claimed, as if that made any difference.

'I have, a bit,' Stephanie admitted. 'I was wondering if Mrs Frowse has come back. And I was a bit sad for the Russian lady, even if she is rather nasty.'

'You're too good for this world,' said Jessica. 'Drew – you've bred a saint.'

'It's just the way we brought her up,' said the proud father, momentarily diverted from the main issue. 'She watched me arranging funerals for weeping families from a very early age. It made her realise that sad feelings are normal and nothing to be scared about.'

'Hmm,' said Jessica, tilting her head sceptically. 'Or maybe it's just her natural character, and nothing to do with you at all.'

'Can I humbly suggest that we do not raise the matter again until tomorrow?' begged Thea. 'We all agree that Stephanie has very fine sensibilities, that put us all to shame. Let's leave it at that.'

'Suits me,' said Drew, with a little frown of irritation.

Stephanie was powerfully affected by this exchange, taking it to heart and brooding over it for the rest of the day. There had been no hint of mockery in it, or any criticism that she could discern. It was pleasing, on the whole, to have such close attention for a few minutes. It made her feel more substantial, more of a *person*. At Drew's acceptance of Thea's edict, she sighed with relief and returned her gaze to Timmy, who was sitting with a good-sized box on his lap. 'What's that?' she asked him.

'A game.' He frowned. 'Something to do with trains. It's from Jessica. You saw me open it before lunch.'

'Oh, yes. I forgot.'

'We can play it later,' said Jessica. 'A friend of mine in Manchester's got it, and it's really good. It takes a while to set it up and get the hang of the rules, but it's not too complicated, compared to some.'

Timmy nodded. 'I do like games. Thank you very much.'

'We can play it in a little while,' said Thea, who had been sitting with her dog, watching them all. 'If we're not too sleepy after stuffing ourselves with turkey. At least you lot can – five's an awkward number for most games.'

'Why? Where are you going to be?' It could have been any one of them asking this startled question, but in fact it was Drew.

'Here, of course. I never said I was going anywhere, did I?' The fact that they had all assumed that that was what she had meant was alarming in itself. It made Stephanie sad on Thea's behalf, that they all thought she was so unreliable, so anxious to be somewhere else. But it was still true; even the way she sat gave the impression that she was about to jump up and leave them. The way she was obviously thinking about other things even when talking and laughing with Drew and Jessica made her seem perpetually detached.

The moment was quickly over, and a small amount of tidying up was accomplished. The game was postponed until after they'd had some salad and cake, which was entirely surplus to requirements, but somehow expected.

'But first we all have to go outside for a bit,' Thea ordered. 'If only for the sake of the dog.' To Stephanie's surprise, there was wholesale enthusiasm for this plan, despite a cold breeze and cloudy skies.

'Can I take my drone?' Timmy asked, picking the new toy out of his box.

'Is it a real one?' asked Drew. 'Who gave you that?'

'It was in his stocking,' said Thea. 'It's not very high-tech, but it looks like fun. You wind it up, and then let it go. Let's see it, Tim.'

The child handed it over, and she read the notes on the packaging. '"Soars twenty feet into the air. Only to be used outdoors." Sounds great. We can all have a go.'

When they gathered in the lane outside, the same loud Christmas music was coming from Mr Shipley's house over the way as they had heard the day before. 'Isn't that the same carol as yesterday?' asked Jessica. 'Is he just playing it all on a loop, or what?'

Thea paused to listen more closely. 'It's odd that he's there at all. I distinctly remember him saying he was going to London for the whole week.'

'Maybe it's done by remote control, to make burglars think he's at home,' Jessica suggested.

'Not very likely. I don't think he's very high-tech. All he does is leave the landing light on when he goes away.'

Drew and Timmy were striding down towards the field, chatting earnestly. 'Look at them!' marvelled Thea. 'That trip to his mother's seems to have done wonders for their bonding.'

Stephanie was trying to peer up Mr Shipley's driveway to see if she could detect any life in the house. She liked their neighbour, who was a middle-aged bachelor with old-fashioned manners. He had taken the trouble to talk to her about books and local history more than once, treating her like a grown-up and asking her opinion. When his sister died and Dad did the funeral, they had grown even closer. One of their conversations had dwelt with remarkable frankness on the merits of burial over cremation, with particular reference to environmental considerations.

'Could we invite him to come for a drink, like we did that other time?' she asked Thea.

'Oh! That was Easter, wasn't it? Didn't he stay for the meal as well?'

'He could come and have some cake.'

'It's much too short notice, Steph,' said Jessica. 'And what's he going to think? That you'd forgotten all about him until now, probably. Or you had a sudden surge of Christmas spirit at the last minute. If he's lonely or bored, he might not want you to know about it. And some people really prefer to forget the whole thing.'

'Oh,' said Stephanie, trying to imagine herself into such a person's shoes. 'I can't see his car, anyway. He usually leaves it in front of the garage. He told me he's got too many boxes and stuff to get the car in. So probably he's not there, after all.'

'So what's with the music?' wondered Thea.

'That's a mystery,' shrugged Jessica, trotting after the menfolk. 'Hey, you two, wait for us.'

In the field, Stephanie was reminded again of the metal detector man who turned out to be a handsome young police detective. 'Let's go down into the next field and see if we can find some treasure,' she said, and began running across the short grass with Hepzie flying after her. None of the human beings seemed inclined to follow, so she slowed down, but kept on in the same direction. 'He was just here,' she muttered to herself, arriving at the foot of a towering oak tree. Idly she scuffed her boots back and forth in the slowly decomposing leaves shed by the tree. It appeared to her to be a singularly improbable spot in which to bury stolen jewels, or whatever it was Finch Graham had been searching for. All the same, the idea of hidden gold was magical enough to fire her enthusiasm. 'Nothing here,' she soon concluded, and began to work her way along the hedge, before rejoining the others. Timmy's drone was proving to be something of a disappointment, apparently. It wasn't powered by batteries, but an old-fashioned clockwork mechanism that seemed slightly babyish to Stephanie. She watched an abortive launch in which it leapt to a height of about ten feet and then instantly flopped back to the ground.

'You're supposed to wind it up,' came Thea's voice across the open field.

The next attempt was far more successful, the little grey gadget whirring high overhead for at least twenty seconds. Everybody cheered.

Jessica began walking over to meet Stephanie. 'Find anything?' she called.

'No. It was a silly place to look, anyway.'

They drew closer, until normal conversation became possible. 'I don't expect he stayed here for long. My mum found him up in the village somewhere, didn't she? Presumably he was just trying different places at random. I wonder if he got proper permission?'

'He was here on Friday as well, remember. Here in the field, I mean. He must have thought he'd find something. Enough to make him come back again.'

'Probably just got carried away. Isn't that what he said? They tell me it's addictive – like gambling. You keep thinking you'll miss something if you don't just try for a few more minutes. And it's all very Roman around here. Maybe he thought there was ancient treasure to find, as well.'

'What's this?' came Thea's voice behind them. 'I thought we weren't supposed to be thinking about that.'

'What?' said Jessica.

'Gold jewellery and dead men in the woods, and people

who are our friends getting into trouble.'

'We weren't talking about any of that. It comes under the heading of banned topics of conversation.'

'Drew can't hear me. Anyway, the day's almost over now. You must admit I did a good job. I think I deserve a star.'

'You just did what about five million other women have done, all across the country.'

'Ungrateful brat,' said Thea.

'That's probably what the five million other women are thinking – and saying – at this very moment, as well.'

'I'm grateful,' said Stephanie brightly.

'Careful,' Jessica warned her. 'Even you can go too far in the sainthood stakes.'

Thea laughed. 'Oh well – it's been nice, whatever you say. And right after breakfast tomorrow I'm going to go back to being my old self, and might well start with a phone call to Antares Frowse.'

To her own surprise, Stephanie felt like cheering. Then she visualised the scene back indoors, with the underlying friction between all the adults, and the unresolved issues floating around, and she felt a powerful desire to stay outdoors a bit longer. 'Can I see if I can find Mr Shipley?' she asked Drew.

'What? Why? Where do you think he is?'

'He's probably at home, although his car isn't in the drive. I could go and knock on his door. I want to tell him about my new chess set.'

'No, love. I don't think so. Not by yourself.'

'Timmy can come with me, then.'

But Timmy didn't want to. He had toys he had not yet

examined, and besides that he was tired. Stephanie began to feel mulish. 'It's just across the road. You could hear me if I shouted.'

Thea intervened. 'She's been worrying about him since yesterday, spending Christmas by himself. We don't know for sure, of course, that he did. He might easily have been invited to be with people somewhere.'

'The music's still playing,' Jessica pointed out. 'Which is a bit odd, when you think about it.'

'Just go quickly, then. We'll give you fifteen minutes to do your bit of Christian charity,' Drew decided. 'After that, we'll come looking for you.'

'We're meant to be playing more games, don't forget,' said Thea, with a glint of determination in her eye. Games were starting to feel like more of a duty than a pleasure to them all.

Stephanie crossed the road, still in an obstinate frame of mind. She had been out in the village by herself numerous times. She knew the paths and shortcuts, and how to avoid being mown down by traffic. She and Hepzie were familiar to all the permanent residents. She enjoyed solitary strolls around the fields, like a child from a much earlier time. It helped her to think, which was something she needed to do at this moment.

With deliberate disobedience, she checked for any watching relative, and then turned to the left, avoiding Mr Shipley's house altogether. She was going to go down to the houses by the church, and look at their decorations through their uncurtained windows. It wasn't yet quite dark outside, but people would have turned their lights on indoors. It was always fascinating to peer in at this time of day. If she gave herself ten minutes, before finally seeking out Mr Shipley, all would be well.

The fading light gave everything a dreamy atmosphere, and it was great to be out of the house, wearing a woolly hat and scarf and not seeing another human being. She could pretend it was two hundred years ago, when a girl her age would be either working, or acting as an assistant teacher in a small local school. Before education was compulsory, when most people could barely read, she assumed she would have been one of the clever ones, with parents who valued learning. Before Queen Victoria; before electricity or cars or indoor lavatories – it was all deeply fascinating, and barely credible. At the big school, the history teacher had instantly become Stephanie's favourite. They had been taken on a trip to Cirencester to look at Roman stuff, but that paled in comparison with the project they had done on local industry. Two centuries ago there had been needle-making in Chalford, and weaving everywhere. It was all done by hand, in poor light, for hardly any money. Girls of Stephanie's age were an important part of the workforce. They had very little free time, and scarcely any luxuries. With all the talk of giving up fossil fuels and not using plastic any more, she made the inevitable connection to those pre-industrial days, finding the idea of going back to something similar more than a little enticing.

Drew had understood and partly agreed. After all, his funerals were more or less the same as they'd been in the 1820s. 'And how wonderful if everyone put their phones away,' he'd joked.

That had made her think again. What if there were no more planes or computers or washing machines or meat? All things she had heard listed as no longer acceptable. 'That's all a bit too extreme for me,' said Dad, when she voiced her worries. 'And one thing's for sure – you can never go back. Whatever happens, it won't be the same as it's been before.'

Another person who had encouraged such thoughts was Ant. He was naturally inclined to a simple life, wearing the same clothes for years and waging war on plastic, but even he had a phone and a van and cheerfully ate meat. He talked it all through with her in a straightforward way that she found reassuring and informative. 'If we gave up meat, there'd be no cows or sheep or pigs, except possibly in a few children's zoos. That might be okay, of course. But at least the facts need to be faced.'

Thea was far less satisfactory. 'Gosh, when I was your age all I ever thought about was fighting with Jocelyn and who my best friend should be. I did like history at school, I suppose, although it was mostly about the American Civil War and the development of medicine. That went on for years – all four of us did those same topics.'

None of which meant anything to Stephanie. Her stepmother spared little thought for the issues of the day, and consistently advised Stephanie to have confidence that everything would turn out perfectly fine. 'They're always changing their minds about when the end of the world will be,' she laughed. 'You can't take these things seriously.'

It made a degree of sense, Stephanie supposed, and Thea

had many virtues that balanced her tendency to flippancy. She did, after all, get personally involved in the search for murderers, often very bravely. Dad loved her and she made him happier than he would have been otherwise. Now it was their friends affected by a nasty mystery, and Thea could be trusted to march in and see what she could do to help.

So it was only reasonable to assume that nothing would be different this time. Ant's mother was a nice lady, who had given Stephanie and Timmy some delicious fruit cake a few weeks ago. The occasion had been a winter bazaar in Chipping Campden, at which Beverley had been running a stall, selling bags of fudge, jars of chutney, home-made gift tags and many other products. Everything was her own work. The whole family had been there, eating the first mince pies of the season and buying presents from the well-stocked stalls. Hepzie had not been allowed in and was in the car outside. 'Bring her round to our house tomorrow and I'll give her a nice beef bone,' said Beverley. 'Percy can easily spare it.'

But they hadn't followed up on her invitation. Drew had been too busy, and Thea hadn't been in the mood. It was raining, and she persuaded herself the whole thing had not been meant seriously. 'You have to phone her and say we're not coming,' Stephanie had urged. 'It's rude otherwise.'

'She didn't say a time, did she? Not even morning or afternoon. It's Sunday. People don't want visitors on a Sunday.'

When Beverley had phoned at two o'clock to ask if they were coming, Thea had been severely wrong-footed. 'Oh,

Lord – sorry,' she had spluttered. 'I don't think we can make it after all. The kids haven't done their homework, and we've already been out with the dog half the morning.'

Beverley took it well, but Stephanie could see that Thea felt guilty. And quite right too, she thought. As it turned out, that was probably weighing on Thea's conscience enough to make her want to find Beverley now she was missing, and make sure she was all right.

She realised she had walked further than intended, while her mind whirred on autopilot. She had passed the church and turned right, down a small lane that was home to the little old Quaker meeting house. She ought not to go any further. There were a few houses beyond the meeting house, and then a field, but she didn't know their occupants. She should turn back to the big cherry tree beside the row of houses with the lighted windows. It was time she got home. Even Thea might worry a bit about an eleven-year-old girl being out longer than the allotted fifteen minutes, without even the dog for company. She was going to skip the Mr Shipley plan and tell them he hadn't been at home.

She began to feel rather brave, even intrepid, at having such freedom in a world full of paranoia. Teachers had endlessly repeated 'Be safe' as a mantra, all her life. The children tolerated it, chafing under the yoke of overprotection while ignorant of what real freedom might entail. Stories from the past where people aged six or seven walked two miles to school and back, or jumped on and off London buses any time they liked, were sheer fantasy to Stephanie's generation. They were told repeatedly that there was danger everywhere, in all guises. There was a universal belief that determined abductors lurked behind every hedge, waiting to snatch an unwary passing child.

Not a single car went past, and she could hear no human voices, although she could see people moving inside one or two of the houses. In a topsy-turvy way, she felt the outdoors was a cosy, appealing place to be. The darkening sky felt friendly, the magic of Christmas Day an ever-present delight. She had no need of a dog or small brother to defend her, even if either had been anything of a fighter. Why would they need to fight anyway? Nothing was going to happen to arouse any hostility. That was a message that Thea could take credit for. All her murders had been resolved, explained and efficiently dealt with. The motives for killing were evident – greed, fear, social pressure, unhinged ideas. None of those held any threat for children. Even thinking about all this gave her no cause for anxiety. Then a voice from behind her said, 'Hello? Is that my friend Stephanie?'

She jumped, but only slightly, and turned round to see the very man she was meant to be seeking – their neighbour, Mr Shipley, was coming from the small lane she had just traversed herself.

'Were you behind me just now?' she asked, with a little frown.

'I was, to tell you the truth. I thought you might need someone at your back. Like a guardian angel, if that isn't too presumptuous.'

She gave it some thought. 'It sounds quite nice, actually. Where's your car?' she wondered.

'Oh – it's fallen ill, the silly thing. I left it with the garage on Friday and have been stranded ever since.'

'Oh dear. That sounds horrible. You can't have had a very nice Christmas.'

He smiled in the dim light, a few front teeth shining white. 'Not as much as you have, I'm sure. It's a time for children, after all.'

'Is it? You mean the presents and all that?'

He took a deep breath, and looked over at the church. She could sense a sort of sermon coming on, and found herself oddly eager to hear it. This, she dimly realised, was what had been missing from the day all along. Mr Shipley did not disappoint. 'More that it's a time to celebrate the mystery of birth. Not just the birth of Jesus, but *every* new child. I mean, it's extraordinary, don't you think? Where do those new souls come from? All those different personalities and talents and eccentricities. They just *arrive* from somewhere. I think that's the real message of Christmas.'

Stephanie felt a small thrill that a grown man should be discussing where babies came from with her. It was very slightly scary, in fact. 'Oh,' she said.

'Well, I probably haven't explained it very well. And it's probably not what I should be saying to you, either. I can't guarantee that I've got the orthodox theology of it right. In fact, I obviously haven't. You're supposed to focus on the Word made flesh, in just that one instance. In my own heretical view, the same goes for every instance of a new birth. Every single human being embodies the Word, if you ask me. That's the Quaker line. I am something of an old Quaker, when it comes down to it.'

'The Word?' Stephanie queried, starting to feel that she was being exceptionally privileged to hear Mr Shipley's views. It was, after all, something she had been hankering for.

'The line is "There is that of God in everyone." That's the modern version, anyhow. In the Gospel of St John, he calls it "The Word", which is vague but nice, don't you think? Covers a multitude of spiritual stuff. But it's a bit exclusive, if you ask me, giving it all to just one man. That's my main point. Christmas should be reminding us that every single person is worthy of dignity and value and respect, and all those things. Instead, we all just eat too much, and sing carols without attending to their words, and buy more plastic rubbish that nobody really wants.' He sighed.

'It *is* a mystery about babies,' she agreed. 'Where they come from. And where we go to at the end,' she added, thinking of Drew and funerals and her mother. 'My mother died, you know,' she said, with a sense that this was central to what they were really talking about.

'And for that discussion, we really ought to wait for Easter,' he said gently. 'Meanwhile, enjoy yourself, my dear. It's what she would have wanted.'

For once, Stephanie felt that this was absolutely true, and not just something people said. 'Thank you, and have a happy Christmas as well. Oh – and do you play chess?'

He laughed. 'Like most people, I know the moves, but can't claim any great skill at it. Why?'

'Well, I got a lovely chess set for Christmas from Dad and Thea. Now I need somebody to play with.'

'I'd be more than happy to give it a try. In fact, it would please me inordinately to refresh my mind in that way. I shall be here until next weekend. Perhaps we ought to make a date now?'

'Well, we've got visitors until Friday morning. What about Friday afternoon?'

'Perfect,' he said. 'And now you should get home. Your people might be worrying about you.'

With a bounce in her step, humming 'Hark the Herald Angels Sing' to herself, she returned home, and walked in through the unlocked front door.

It was suddenly half past six and Timmy was drooping. 'It was rather a short night,' said Thea. 'Although they both slept like logs – didn't you have to wake them up for their stockings?'

'I did,' said Drew. 'But we'll have to keep them going for a while longer. They'll wake at some unearthly hour tomorrow otherwise.'

'Which wouldn't really matter, would it?' Thea had never calculated hours of sleep, even when her own child had been small. There had been no regular nap times, and no hesitation about taking little Jessica out in an evening, if that suited her own wishes. Drew's anxieties about bedtimes and adequate sleep and imaginary social rules only irritated her. 'People sleep when they're tired,' she insisted. 'It's not something to obsess about.'

'I'm not a bit tired,' said Stephanie.

In any event, Timmy's exhaustion overrode all discussion and he sank into a deep sleep on the sitting-room sofa. 'We'll wake him up in an hour or so, give him some food and put him to bed properly,' said Thea, which seemed to satisfy Drew.

It was time for a summing-up of the day. Stephanie began by thanking the adults for her presents – again. 'I love my chess set, and Mr Shipley's going to play it with me on Friday,' she said. 'He says he'll be more than happy to.'

'Here or there?' asked Thea. 'I mean – his place or yours?' She giggled.

'I don't know.' Stephanie was aware that both Jessica and Drew were entirely unamused at the line that made Thea laugh. 'It'd be quieter in his house, I suppose.'

'We've all had a lovely day,' Drew asserted, a few minutes later. 'It's been an excellent team effort, don't you think?'

'Absolutely,' agreed Jessica. 'Although I suspect I didn't pull my weight as much as I should have.'

'You were excused on account of being the honoured guest,' said Drew.

'You did quite a lot of washing-up,' Thea acknowledged. 'And entertained the children.'

There was relative silence for a minute or two as everybody looked back over the day. 'We forgot to take photos,' said Jessica, but nobody seemed to find that of much importance.

'There's still quite a lot of food to be eaten,' Thea remarked lazily. 'Anybody feel like some cold Christmas pudding? Or I could put it in the microwave for a minute. There's brandy butter and cream to go with it.'

'No thanks,' said Stephanie.

'We can have it tomorrow,' said Drew.

'I could manage a small amount now,' said Jessica, who

had always been fond of her food, puddings in particular.

'We're running out of logs,' said Thea. 'And the fire's going to go out in a minute. It's down to a few ashes.' There was only one log left in the basket, so Drew had to go out to the shed at the back and collect some more.

'It really has been a fabulous day,' sighed Jessica. 'Thanks, Mum.' Stephanie made confirmatory noises.

'Well, it's only once a year, I suppose,' said Thea, evidently unaware of the import of her words. Stephanie was glad her father wasn't there to hear them. It often seemed as if she, Stephanie, grasped the ironic undercurrents of what her stepmother said, while Drew took them all too seriously.

'You don't mean it,' said Jessica, switching to anger in a heartbeat. 'You can't possibly be as horrible as you make yourself sound.'

Thea was genuinely surprised. 'What did I say? How am I different from about ninety-five per cent of women in the country? I might be a bit more honest, that's all.'

Drew came in with a basket full of logs and by mutual consent, the conversation was suspended. But the air was still full of it. 'What?' he said.

'Nothing,' Stephanie quickly told him. 'Can we watch a film now?'

'If we must,' said Drew. 'Although I was hoping to just do nothing for a bit.'

Stephanie knew that there was no such thing as doing nothing. You talked, or read, or did a bit of tidying. Even if you just sat still, you were thinking. She also knew that neither of her parents – meaning Drew and Thea – were capable of inactivity for more than about a minute. Nobody argued with him, but the atmosphere was restive.

'Did you ever phone your mother?' Drew asked Thea a moment later. 'Weren't you supposed to do it this morning?'

'I did, at about half past eleven. She was in the middle of doing something crucial in Jocelyn's kitchen, so it only lasted half a minute. Maybe you ought to phone yours.'

'I don't think so.' He frowned. 'That would be weird after all the years of not. What would I say? She didn't give us any presents. She never used to like Christmas much.'

'Another one of the ninety-five per cent,' muttered Jessica.

'What?'

'Oh – Thea says there are very few women who do like it. Too much work, I suppose. All that cooking.'

'Either that, or they're left all on their own to make the best of a pork pie and a silly hat,' said Thea.

Stephanie began to discern a theme, which sent her thoughts flying to Mrs Frowse, who had gone off to be by herself on Christmas Day, in spite of having a perfectly good husband, son and dog willing to spend it with her. The world seemed to be full of unhappy women, wishing the whole thing would hurry up and be over for another year, whether they had families or not. It made her wonder how it would be for her when she grew up. 'I think I'll go to a hotel in Spain for Christmas when I'm grown up,' she announced. 'Or Australia.'

'Can I come?' said Timmy, who had woken up without anybody noticing.

'You won't want to. You'll have a wife who'll do all the cooking for you, and five children.' It was Jessica who gave him this unsolicited prediction, like a fortune-teller. 'And they'll all want you right there, so they can tell you how much they love you.'

'Pooh,' said the little boy, going rather pink at this appealing picture.

'That's right,' said Drew, a trifle too heartily.

'It *was* lovely, though,' Stephanie insisted. 'All the presents and turkey and crackers.' She leant over the cardboard box at her side, full of her new things, and then looked up with a wide smile. 'I can't wait for Tim to get his fish tank.' Drew and Thea had given him a promissory note for a tank for tropical fish, with all the trimmings. 'We couldn't get it in advance,' Drew had explained. 'There'd be nowhere to hide it all. And this way you can choose exactly what you want.'

'First thing on Wednesday, we'll go and get it,' he said now.

'I don't think they open again until the New Year,' Thea cautioned. 'And don't forget we've got Damien coming.'

Somehow she made it sound like something to dread, every time she mentioned the upcoming visit. For herself, Stephanie was very much looking forward to meeting little Kim and getting to know a new set of step-relations. It would prolong the Christmassy atmosphere, or so she hoped. 'Next week is fine,' said Timmy with a very grown-up display of patience. 'I've got loads of other things to be going on with.' The prospect of the new fish was definitely exciting, and Stephanie could see that her brother was learning that anticipation was well over half the enjoyment when it came to any kind of pleasure.

'Good boy,' said Thea.

'I don't know how you got so lucky with these kids,' said Jessica.

'Mostly good management, actually,' Thea corrected her. She was never one to let credit for anything slip away into other hands. 'Although I agree it was lucky I met Drew when I did. Just down the road from here,' she added reminiscently.

Stephanie took that to mean that her stepmother had no regrets, which was definitely reassuring.

But the day had not quite ended, and the harmony couldn't last. Afterwards Stephanie could not decide whose fault it had been, or how it might have been averted. Jessica had been harbouring an annoyance with her mother that seemed uncalled for. Thea was, as usual, chafing against the responsibilities of the coming days, and both women knew there was still a lot they had not told Drew about events over at the Crossfield Estate. That, Stephanie suspected, was the real issue. All three female members of the family had become involved in a sudden death that was very likely to develop into a murder enquiry within a few days. Drew never approved of Thea's activities in that direction, and he never liked it when Gladwin made contact. When it happened again, he was not going to be pleased. And knowing that put them all on edge.

It began innocently. Thea had simply switched on her phone and glanced at the screen. 'Expecting a call?' asked

Drew, with no hint of irritation.

'I thought my mother might get back to me. She hasn't thanked me for the jumper I gave her.'

'Bad example,' he smiled. 'But tomorrow's soon enough, surely?'

'She's really checking to see if there's anything from Gladwin,' said Jessica – which was, Stephanie concluded, definitely a piece of mischief, even if it didn't sound like it at the time.

'Oh?' said Drew, still perfectly relaxed.

'Well, not really,' Thea defended herself. 'At least – I *have* been wondering whether anything else has happened.'

'Else?' He was now more alert.

'We'll tell you about it tomorrow, okay?'

It was too late. Stephanie closed her eyes, already grieving for the wrecked atmosphere. All three of the adults seemed to be impelled to fight, for absolutely no reason. There must be some horrible aspect of human nature that came to the surface whether you chose it or not. She thought of Mr Shipley saying there was that of God in everyone. There was also obviously that of the devil as well.

'What is there to tell?' he persisted.

'There's a police investigation into the death of Rufus Blackwood,' said Thea, with a sheepish expression.

Drew gave her an exasperated look. 'And that's the reason you turned the phone on? Aren't we enough for you?' The question went deep and true. It was a most searching and accurate question that needed an answer which treated it seriously.

'That's not it, exactly,' Thea began. Then she squared up to the three faces before her. 'Well, if you put it in those words, I suppose the truth is that you're not, no. I love you all and I love all this Christmas happiness and I want everything to be warm and safe and contented. But there has to be more to life. I can't help it.'

'That's all fine. I've no problem with that. But on *Christmas Day*? That's just not reasonable.'

'He's right, Ma.' Jessica's voice contained real anger. 'If you felt like that, why did you ever marry him?'

Stephanie put her hands over her ears and shrieked. 'No! Stop it!' It was her worst fear, that something like this would erupt and spoil the day. The best of it was already over, of course. Once the presents were opened, there was no more magical anticipation. But they could at least enjoy the aftermath in peace – couldn't they?

'Don't shout,' said Timmy in a very small voice. 'What's the matter?'

'Nothing. Nothing.' Thea got up and went to hug him. 'It's all my fault for looking at my phone. Just shows, doesn't it, what beastly things they are. I'm very sorry, Tim. Don't get upset, either of you. It's time for a drink and a bit of cake or something. Then you two can go to bed and tomorrow we'll tidy up and eat cold turkey. Is everybody happy now?'

Jessica forced a smile that convinced nobody, and got up from her place on the floor. 'I'll go and make us some coffee,' she said.

Stephanie slowly expelled the air she'd been holding onto, still hearing echoes of her own outburst. It had certainly had a good effect. The real shock had been Jessica's words, taking the whole conversation into unbearably deep waters. *Why did you ever marry him?* It carried ghastly implications that Thea and Dad might get *un*married, and what would become of them all then?

Before they drifted off to sleep, Stephanie suddenly asked Timmy, 'So what's she really like? Our new grandmother, I mean.'

He turned towards her in the faint light coming from the landing, 'What?'

'You heard me.'

Timmy lay flat on his back, and stared at the ceiling, happy to be invited to share his impressions. 'Well, she's a bit like a person from a Roald Dahl book. Knobbly fingers and bushy eyebrows. But her nose is just like Dad's, and she does that thing with her knees the same as him.'

Stephanie knew exactly what he meant. All her life she had watched her father gently strumming an inaudible tune on first one knee then the other, whenever he was sitting down. It was maddening for anybody in the same room and everybody tried to stop him from doing it. Only Thea seemed to find it appealing. 'At least it's better than humming,' she often said.

'Really?' Stephanie was highly intrigued by this proof of family likeness. 'That's amazing.'

'She was quite scared of seeing us, you know,' Timmy elaborated. 'And sad about Grandad or Grandpa, or whatever we're meant to call him.'

'It probably doesn't matter, now he's dead,' said Stephanie. 'Go on.'

'She hardly looked at Dad at all when we first got there. Picked me up and squeezed me as if I was about three, and said I looked just like her husband.' He grimaced at the memory. 'That was horrible.'

Stephanie examined her brother's face with interest. His colouring was as fair as hers, except for his eyes, which were light brown, while hers were blue. The shape of his head was different, too – longer and narrower. She remembered how people had commented on how unlike his mother he was, when he was little. 'Oh,' she said.

Timmy hadn't finished. 'And then she let the dog attack me. The house was cold – all the windows were open. I think she was trying to get rid of the smell.'

'Smell?'

'I think there was a problem with drains or something,' he said vaguely. 'And there's an awful old cat that pees everywhere.'

None of this fitted at all with the picture Stephanie had gained so far. 'She sounds awful. Is she really *old* then?'

Timmy shrugged. 'Quite. But she can move about all right, and isn't deaf or anything. And she's strong – the dog can't pull her over and she throws great hunks of wood about. She might be a bit mad. But she laughed when Dad went round shutting the windows and said she should light the fire.'

'That's when he had to cut the logs, is it?'

'No, he did that after lunch. She made us cottage pie with carrots and cabbage. It wasn't too bad, actually.'

'What did they talk about?'

'Funerals mostly. Then they sent me upstairs to look at Dad's old books, and I suppose they talked grown-up stuff while I was out of the room. Dad looked funny when I came down again. He didn't say anything much, and she went to do things in the kitchen. She's got a big sitting room, much bigger than the one here. She said they knocked a wall down, and made two rooms into one.' He paused as if speculating about the possibilities. 'Couldn't do that here,' he concluded.

'What's so great about a big room?'

'Nothing, really,' he agreed.

'I still don't get why they never saw each other for all this long time. I mean – didn't they *like* each other?'

Timmy had no answer to this, to Stephanie's frustration. She knew if she had gone instead, she'd have discovered much more about the family history. 'Oh, well,' she said. 'I suppose I'll see for myself when she comes here.'

'She won't like Thea,' said Tim suddenly. 'That's for sure.'

'Why not?'

'They're too much like each other.' He seemed surprised at his own words. 'I can't explain exactly, but they *are*.'

Stephanie gave a fleeting acknowledgement of the two senses of the word 'like'. Did you like things that were like each other? Did being alike imply a liking? Not according to her little brother. 'That should be interesting, then,' was all she said. 'But I expect you've got it wrong. You're only nine, after all.'

Downstairs, they had put a Christmas CD on, and

the carols came wafting up the stairs. Stephanie tried to convince herself that the day had been as good as anybody could reasonably hope. There were no raised voices, everything seemingly restored to harmony.

'I'm really looking forward to my fish,' said Timmy before sliding into a deep and happy sleep.

At midnight, as a tragic conclusion to two local families' Christmases, there was a collision on the A44, not four miles from Broad Campden. In one car there were three young men, the flower of Blockley youth, driving home in a southerly direction after a happy day spent with relatives near Stratford. Not one of them was under the influence of alcohol. Two of them died. In the other was a woman aged sixty-five, transporting three teenage grandchildren back to their families in Evesham, after a happy day spent with relatives near Oxford. She had consumed almost a whole bottle of Cava and a glass of brandy. All three grandchildren died.

The coincidences were legion. In each car, the dead youngsters were related, and in both cases the driver survived. And, as was to eventually be revealed, there were distant familial connections between the two sets of people. They were all descended from a single Victorian businessman, down diverse branches of the family tree. It was calculated that they were fourth cousins to each other. This was to make the story additionally poignant in the newspapers over the coming weeks.

Such an accident placed great strain on the depleted police pathology department. The precise cause of death had to be established as soon as possible. Five post-mortems had to be performed as a matter of urgency. This meant that the already-queued-up body of Mr Rufus Blackwood had to be dealt with quickly. On Boxing Day, in fact.

Chapter Fifteen

Boxing Day started even earlier than Christmas Day had done. Both children were awake by seven, and Timmy was fiddling with one of his stocking toys that he had taken to bed with him. Stephanie experienced an uneasy mixture of irrepressible interest in what was happening to the Frowse family and apprehension as to how things were standing between Thea and Drew.

'What's Boxing Day really *for*?' Timmy asked, over breakfast.

'Nobody seems too sure about that,' Drew told him. 'Fox hunting. Delivering charitable goodies to the peasants – in boxes, I suppose.'

'But no boxing matches,' smiled Thea. 'Not that I know of, anyway.'

'And no proper fox hunts, any more. Just pretend ones,' added Jessica.

'People go for long walks, and write thank-you letters,' Thea remembered. 'Or they did when I was little.'

'We can send texts,' said Stephanie. 'I want to tell Auntie Jocelyn how much I like the tights.'

'And my kit,' added Timmy. 'My kit's awesome.'

Which inevitably led to the production of mobile phones by Jessica and Thea, and the day was set in a pattern that was to persist, with minor variations, until dark.

It began when Gladwin called Thea at nine-fifteen. 'I heard from DS Graham,' she said. 'I gather you've been withholding information from me.'

'You mean about Beverley Frowse being missing? Yes. Sorry. It was rather awkward, you see.'

'Skip the excuses. We're past all that.'

'Are we?'

'You haven't heard the news, then?'

Anybody but Thea would have said *What news?* But instead, she saved time by saying, 'Almost certainly not.'

'Nasty accident on the A44. Our Blackwood man's PM is happening as we speak, accordingly. Results expected in a couple of hours, with any luck. All systems go, if they show it was homicide – which we assume they will.'

'Oh.'

'Are you going to be available today? This little matter of the Frowse woman scarpering is very much of interest, and without you, we wouldn't know about it. And now we're done with Christmas, it's going to be all hands to the pump. Or something. Probably.'

'I expect I am available,' said Thea, glancing round the room. Everyone was there, frankly listening. Drew gave a groan. 'You realise that if it is murder, whoever did it might be in Australia by now.'

'We'll know who to blame, then, if that happens. If it turns out to be Mrs Frowse, at least.'

'Thanks. But gosh, Sonia – it's going to make a huge story if he *was* murdered. The man knew Alan Sugar and Pippa Middleton and all sorts of celebrities. He was really somebody.'

'So it seems. I keep imagining the funeral.' Despite being a detective superintendent, Gladwin was seldom able to stay stern or solemn for very long. And Thea Slocombe was skilled at arousing her more frivolous side.

'Which isn't going to take place in our little burial ground, is it?' Thea laughed. 'I think Stephanie was already hoping it would be.'

'I've got to go. I'll keep you posted. Don't go anywhere, will you.'

Thea ended the call and looked up. 'She told me not to go anywhere,' she said. 'That nice Finch boy has really got things going.'

'You can't blame him,' Jessica protested.

'I wasn't, really. Oh – there's been some sort of accident not far from here. In the night, I presume. People must have died, because the pathologist has had to go in to do the post-mortems. At least, I think that's what she meant.'

Drew cleared his throat. 'Why don't you just slow

down and explain it all to me? I seem to have missed a lot more than I realised. Stephanie's hoping for a burial? Pippa Middleton's got something to do with it? And who in the world is the "nice Finch boy"?'

Jessica went first. 'We met him on Sunday. He's a detective sergeant. Finch Graham.'

'How did you come to meet him?'

Thea spoke up. 'I found him wandering around the village with a metal detector. Looking for treasure, apparently. He found some nails and an old shoe buckle. I already knew him by sight, from one of my house-sits, and I suppose he knew who I was, though he didn't exactly say so.'

'And?' prompted Drew.

'And I brought him back here and we got talking about Blackwood being dead, because he was off duty and hadn't heard about it, and we said a bit too much about the Frowses, and now he's told it to Gladwin, and she's not best pleased.'

'We knew he would,' Jessica pointed out. 'We rather hoped it would happen, didn't we?'

'Losing me,' Drew interrupted. 'It sounds as if you practically adopted him after five minutes' acquaintance.'

'He was instantly dazzled by my lovely daughter, and when they discovered they were both in the police, it all just started to flow. So to speak. It's not exactly surprising, considering we'd just come back from hearing all their troubles from the Frowse men. We were already involved. It's not as if we're just ordinary members of the public having a gossip.'

'More's the pity,' said Drew with a sigh. He hesitated

as a new thought struck him. 'Was Stephanie with you when all this was happening?' He gave his daughter a worried look.

'Obviously she was. So what? She hasn't been upset about it. She's used to people dying, after all.'

'But not when they've been *murdered*,' he shouted. 'She's been shielded from anything like that, ever since—'

'Ever since her mother was attacked. Yes, I know. I get that. But this is – different. Tell him, Steph,' Thea appealed.

'I *am* a bit upset about Ant and his mother,' Stephanie admitted slowly. 'It's horrible for them. But it's been horrible for ages, with that beastly landlord, so now he's dead, it might be better. Because we're sure it wasn't them who killed him. Aren't we?' She threw it back at Thea.

'I certainly hope so. We'll probably know a lot better by the end of today. It's all still very unsure at the moment. The man might still have just died of heart failure or something.'

'So now tell me what you expect to happen today,' Drew went on, more and more like a magistrate or a counsel for the prosecution.

'I have no idea, except that I want to speak to Ant, and I want to hear the results of the post-mortem. After that, it's completely unknown territory.'

'Right.' Having it presented to him like that, Drew could find no reasonable grounds for objection. It was apparent to everyone that he wished passionately to stay out of the whole business, as he had more or less successfully done with nearly all of Thea's previous adventures. He managed to conveniently overlook the fact that it had been a murder, less than half a mile from where they now lived, that had originally brought him and Thea together.

'Isn't there an exotic Russian wife?' he remembered now. 'Or widow, I should say.'

'There is, and two equally exotic daughters. Three, in fact, but one of them seems to be out of the picture for the moment.'

'Anything else?'

'I don't think so. You don't want every detail, do you? I've told you the basics.'

'Don't forget the missing package,' said Jessica. 'The one Andrew told us about on Friday.'

'Oh, I don't expect it's relevant,' said Thea.

'Remind me anyway,' ordered Drew.

'It's just that the Blackwood man was accusing Beverley of stealing his registered parcel with some jewellery in it. It was just the latest in a whole string of rows between the landlord and the Frowses. We must have told you before that the Blackwoods have been terrible landlords, with harassment and intimidation going on for years. Just look at that ghastly fence.'

'I don't think I've seen it,' said Drew mildly. 'But I heard about it.'

'They found him only a few feet away from it,' said Jessica. 'From what we could gather.'

Drew snorted. 'He wouldn't be stupid enough to let his own fence kill him – would he?'

'I doubt if it's powerful enough to kill anybody. That wouldn't be legal. Although . . .' Jessica grew thoughtful. 'Now you mention it, it's an idea.'

229

Ant and Digby, unlike the Slocombes, were in no hurry to get up for Boxing Day. It was shortly after ten-thirty when they were forced to pay attention to somebody banging on their front door.

Ant opened it, holding Percy back, to find three women standing there. 'Good morning. This is quite a visitation,' he said. The dog's hackles were standing vertically on his neck.

Carla and her two daughters surged forward. 'What do you call this, then?' she shrilled. 'How do you explain this?' She brandished something chunky and yellow in his face.

'You found your necklace. Congratulations.' His voice shook, despite all his efforts. Something bad was happening. Percy had known all along.

'*You* stole it. You or your ludicrous mother. And I'm calling the police right now. Bronya, Annika, one of you – where's your phone?'

It was a staged melodrama, performed by people who should by rights be piled on a sofa weeping for their lost husband and stepfather. The action was progressing into the Frowses' living room, whether they liked it or not. The shorter of the sisters produced a phone. Digby was standing in the middle of the room, blank confusion on his face.

'It's Boxing Day,' Ant reminded the Russian trio. 'If you dial 999 for a lost-and-found necklace, they won't be very pleased.'

'You found it,' said Digby. 'That's good, isn't it?'

'Hidden in *your* garden. Under one of *your* piles of rubbish.'

'My goodness! Really? How did you come to track it down there, as a matter of interest?' asked Digby.

'Annika has a metal detector. She used that. She was certain you had it, so she went in search of it.' Carla was shrill, her face rigid with rage, her emotions barely under control.

Digby had clicked into one of his more familiar roles. He stood easily, the picture of unconcern. 'Well, that's quite amazing,' he said, throwing an admiring look at Annika. 'Out of all these hundreds of acres, she managed to locate the thing on the first attempt on a totally groundless suspicion. Miraculous.'

Ant was far less relaxed than his father. The invasion of his home, the loud female voices, the fact of Rufus Blackwood's death all combined to make his head swim. More than that, he was transfixed by the sight of the necklace, still dangling from Carla's hand. It was chunky and tasteless and any fool could see was worth umpteen thousand pounds.

Annika replied with a vicious snarl. 'She knew you'd stolen it. She said so all along.'

Digby turned his calm gaze onto Bronya, and a little smile lifted the corners of his mouth. Ant watched as he gave her a tiny nod, but was at a loss as to what it signified. 'She knew no such thing,' Digby contradicted the woman. 'Let's try this for a hypothesis. What your hysterical mother knew was that she herself had intercepted the wretched delivery man, signed for the package and hatched a plot to incriminate me and my family in its theft. I dare say you knew all about it yourself. And I dare go on to suggest that you were so impressed by the idea that you extended it to the point where it became a motive for murder. Or am I running ahead too quickly for you?'

Carla, not unlike Ant, was having trouble in following the logic. 'Motive for murder?' she screamed. 'Don't talk to me about motive for murder. You've been wanting us all dead for years. Admit it.'

'And vice versa, I imagine,' Digby riposted, with a little circular wave of his hand. 'None of us has lost any love for the other side. But wanting anybody dead is putting it a little too strongly for us English peasants. I think you'll find it's more of a Russian thing.'

Bronya had not uttered a word. Now she addressed her sister. 'Annika, I don't believe you can sustain the story about finding the necklace in the way you claim. It might have been sensible of you to consult me first, before putting your plan into action.'

Digby, Ant and Carla took varying lengths of time to absorb these words. Was it, Ant wondered, as great a betrayal as it sounded? Had one of the threesome astonishingly defected to the other camp, without warning? Or had there been warning in that little nod she'd been given by Digby?

'C-consult you?' stammered Annika, who was perhaps the slowest of them all.

'Bronya? You little bitch – what are you saying?' screamed Carla. 'These people *stole* my husband's gift to me. They stole it before he could even wrap it up. And he knew it. And now they've killed him. Annika—'

'We did not steal it,' Ant interrupted loudly. 'If you

ask me, the shock of your husband's death has unhinged you.'

'It's very strange to be out metal detecting in somebody's garden so early on Boxing Day, you know,' said Digby, evidently wishing to prolong the confusion. *Even for a Russian*, was the unspoken implication.

Annika had still not perceived that the game was lost. 'I couldn't sleep. I was so angry and puzzled. So I got up, and decided I should search the premises of our family of tenants, who live like tinkers.'

'Gypsies,' said Carla. 'Filthy Gypsies. In Russia, the Gypsies have been eradicated long ago.'

All three women spoke excellent English, but the overtone of something foreign never quite went away.

'You'd like us to be eradicated, I know,' said Digby.

'And I believe the correct term is "Roma",' said Ant, suddenly enjoying himself.

'Whatever you call them, they're all criminals – like you,' said Annika. 'And we have the evidence to prove it.' Bronya sighed and rolled her eyes. She plainly thought both mother and sister were beyond stupid. For her and Digby, somehow the matter was already settled.

'We are not criminals. We did not take your gold and we did not kill your husband. I think you'll find you have to look closer to home for the perpetrator of both crimes,' said Digby.

'Be quiet!' Carla thundered, her contralto voice dropping even lower. 'As Annika says, there will be evidence. We have cameras recording everything you do. I am going back to the house now, to view the recordings from the camera over our gate. I will discover one of you two, or your mother, in the act of hiding my property. Everything will be there as evidence.'

Annika made a strange sound in her throat. 'Camera?' she said.

Bronya sighed again. 'You forgot the camera, didn't you?' she said. 'You are by far the biggest fool I've ever met, you know. Mother's going to find a nice clear piece of film showing you leading us here, half an hour ago, pretending to find the necklace with your idiotic device.'

'Right,' nodded Annika uncertainly. 'That's right.'

'But it won't show anything else, will it? Not you moving around the junkyard out there, digging up one thing after another, until finally you magically discover the necklace itself. None of that will be there, because none of it happened.'

'There's an awful lot of metal out there,' said Digby. 'That thing would have beeped its clever little head off, once you started swinging it about in our private property.'

Annika fell silent, and Digby confronted Carla. 'I'm afraid you have rather a lot to talk over between yourselves,' he said, with devastating kindness. 'The good news is that you've got your jewellery back. Small consolation, I'm sure, in the much greater loss of your husband – but even so.' This time when he turned to Bronya, Ant observed a definite wink.

Carla tossed her head in a tragic attempt at dignity. 'Come along, girls. We're leaving now.'

'You two go ahead,' said Bronya. 'I don't think you'll be needing me.'

Annika revived at this. 'Yes – you stay away, now you've done your worst. You disgusting *traitor*. You've always envied me, done all you can to make me look stupid, treated everything as a competition. Ask Olga – she'll say the same.'

'I didn't have to make you look stupid, Anny. You just *are* stupid. And our precious mother is about to find out just how very, very stupid that is.'

Carla was ageing as they watched. She had shrunk in stature, her anger festering as she fought against accepting that it belonged rightfully to her own offspring. But she had not entirely lost her grip. She gave Bronya a final questioning look. 'Why are you staying behind? What do you have to say to these men?'

'Nothing for you to worry about. You go back to the house now. I'll see you in a while.'

When mother and daughter were safely out of earshot, Bronya sat down at the kitchen table, and faced father and son squarely. 'Mrs Frowse,' she began without preliminaries. 'Where is she? There hasn't been a sign of her for days now, has there? The car has been gone since Thursday, to my certain knowledge. In fact, she and my stepfather both went missing at very much the same time. I want you to understand that I'm not making any accusations – merely stating the undeniable facts. And wondering what you yourselves make of it.'

Ant felt the ground caving in beneath his feet. 'Whose side are you on?' he demanded. 'One minute you're sticking up for us against your own family, and now you're saying my mother must have murdered

Blackwood. What does it all mean?'

She gave a rueful smile. 'I told you before. I like to keep everything clear and honest. Not always possible, I admit. We all have our shameful secrets, after all. But as far as possible, I think we should face the truth. That business with the necklace – I was doing nothing more than saving time. If Annika had gone to the police with that ludicrous accusation, they would quickly have seen it for what it was. It would have angered them and thrown suspicion onto us as a family. Do you see? It would have tainted the water, and cast doubt on our probity. I couldn't let that happen. As it is, my mother will ensure that the necklace is removed entirely from the picture. Except,' she held up a finger, 'except that it was the cause of a strong disagreement between your mother and Rufus. To that extent, it could be useful.'

'You're saying you have every intention of stitching up my wife for the killing of your stepfather,' said Digby. 'Or have I got that altogether wrong?'

'I'm stating obvious facts, that's all.'

'And what about certain facts that I have knowledge of?'

'Ah – now we get to it.' She leant forward. 'Tell me – what are these facts?'

'I'm saying no more. It's obvious that you inherited your sister's share of the brains, and a bit more. Too clever for me, I shouldn't wonder. Let's wait and see, shall we? For all we know, the old man just expired quietly from his heart trouble. Maybe the famous pacemaker wasn't as wonderful as he thought. Maybe they won't find any signs of foul play, after all.'

'A consummation devoutly to be wished for,' said Bronya, to the perplexity of both men.

'Just go home, dear,' said Digby wearily. 'We've played enough games for one day, and it's barely even coffee time.'

She left them then, and five minutes later, Ant texted Thea Slocombe.

Trouble with Carla and Co. Necklace found. Everything utterly confused. Can I call you?

Chapter Sixteen

There was a strong sense of hanging about waiting for things to happen, back in Broad Campden. The weather was chilly but fairly bright, and Jessica kept saying they were wasting the fresh air.

'We could play my new train game,' said Timmy hopefully. 'We should have done it yesterday, but I fell asleep.'

'We can't embark on it now,' said Thea. 'Games are for afternoons. It's a law.'

'It's not,' said Timmy, uncertainly. 'Is it?'

Jessica disappeared for twenty minutes, saying she had to catch up with some of her friends and thank them for gifts she had brought with her. Thea busied herself with housework. 'I've got to tidy away all this wrapping paper and other rubbish,' she insisted. 'And I suppose you'll be waiting for something for lunch.'

'I'll do that,' said Drew, without conviction.

'No, you won't. But you can go and wash up the breakfast things, and some more pans. We didn't finish them all yesterday.'

Everyone attended to their varied activities for ten minutes, and then Thea evidently had an idea.

'I wonder if we ought to ask Mr Shipley over, as Stephanie suggested. Now we know for sure he's here, it seems a bit mean not to,' she said.

'Oh, yes!' Stephanie endorsed the idea enthusiastically.

'Really?' Drew asked Thea. 'That's not what you said yesterday.'

'I know. But he's been nice to Steph, and he is our neighbour, after all.'

'True. I've never really known what we're supposed to do about neighbours. My father always said they were God's way of making us behave ourselves. He didn't mean it nicely. He thought the ideal was not to have neighbours at all.' Then he said, 'Are you sure you'll even be here at lunchtime? I thought we were all on standby for a summons from your friendly detective lady.'

'You and Timmy can entertain him by yourselves, then,' she flipped back at him. Then she softened. 'I imagine we'll be here for some lunch, whatever happens.'

'Can I have that in writing?'

'Oh, Drew, stop it,' Thea sighed. 'There's no reason to get agitated about it. It was just an idle thought. He can come for tea, or evening drinks – or leave it a few days. I just thought perhaps he might be feeling unloved.

I expect he usually went to his sister, and now she's died, there isn't anybody. Not as far as we know, anyway.'

'Or he might be revelling in the peace and quiet,' said Jessica. 'If he was that miserable, he could have asked us to go over there.'

'All five of us?' said Drew. 'I don't think so. He'll have seen we've got a strange car outside.'

'You're overthinking it,' said Thea to her daughter. 'And why should you care anyway?'

Before Jessica could reply, Drew interceded. 'No need to get tetchy, anybody. We've agreed that we can't make any plans until we've heard from Ms Gladwin. We've all got things we can be getting on with, and if we choose to be neighbourly, we can ask Mr Shipley over when we have a better idea of what we're doing. Is that okay with everyone?'

'Absolutely,' said Thea, throwing him one of those smiles that made Stephanie's heart swell with relief.

'Time for some more drink, if you ask me,' said Drew. 'It is still technically Christmas, after all. How about some sherry?'

'Lovely,' said Thea with a laugh. 'Wonderfully decadent. And don't you say anything about driving, either,' she warned her daughter, lightly. 'Whatever happens next, we can do it on foot.'

'I wasn't going to say a word,' said Jessica.

Then Ant's text came through, and the air thickened again. 'They found the necklace,' Thea reported. 'He wants to talk to me.'

'Nobody's stopping you,' said Drew.

'No rush,' said Thea, sipping her sherry. 'Let's just wait for Gladwin. I've had enough of being caught between those two.'

It seemed to Stephanie that she was not the only one who made very little sense of this remark.

It was twenty past eleven when Ant's phone jingled. Before he knew it, his mother's voice was in his ear. 'Happy Christmas, a bit late,' she said. 'Are you all right, both of you?'

'Of course we're not all right,' he shouted back at her. 'We thought you were dead.'

'No, you didn't. Don't be silly. Anyway, I'm coming back this afternoon. You'll have to tell your father.'

'Tell him yourself. He's right here.'

'No, no,' she said quickly. 'I've only got a minute. Less than a minute. I don't want to talk to him.'

Digby was flapping at him from his chair, pushing Percy aside so he could get up. Ant didn't know what to say. 'Whose phone are you using?' he asked his mother.

'Winnie's. I'm in her guest house in Oxford. I told you that on Friday.'

'Your phone cut out. I thought you were saying Winchcombe. Who the hell is Winnie?'

'My old friend from school. She's really called Janet, but we always knew her as Winnie.'

'I wish you'd stop sounding so *normal*. Everybody thinks you killed Blackwood.' But the line had gone dead before he could be sure she'd heard him. Digby gave a snort, half frustrated, half amused.

Ant's mind was whirling helplessly, like a toy car lying on its back, wheels still spinning. His parents' marriage suddenly seemed to be at the heart of this whole mystery. Had Beverley gone off because Digby had said or done something she couldn't tolerate? He had noticed that she was getting increasingly tetchy with him as he got older and slower. 'I'm going to call her back,' he said. 'I've got the number now.'

'She won't answer,' said his father, with a fatalistic sigh. 'What did she say to you?'

'She's coming home this afternoon. And she's staying with somebody called Winnie. Or Janet. I have no idea who that is.'

'Yes, you do. She came to visit when you were about nine. Stayed nearly a week and drove us all mad. She's a throwback to the seventies, all feminism and short hair and big shoes.'

'I don't remember that at all.'

'Typical,' said Digby. 'Though I would never have guessed that's where she'd gone, I have to admit. I thought she'd be in Winchcombe with her sister. That's where I was going to start looking if she didn't come back.'

'Auntie Laura? Isn't she about a hundred by now? Is she even still *alive*?'

'She'd be ninety-one. She was twenty-two when Bev was born. Half-sister, of course. Not much good as a relative, but that's the only place I could think of starting with "Win". Not many wits left, last I heard, poor old Laura.'

'Why wouldn't Mum speak to you?'

Digby shrugged. 'She'd said it all to you already. Why

did you have to say that about Blackwood? That wasn't very bright, was it?'

'Wasn't it? Why not?'

'If you can't work it out for yourself, I can't explain it to you.'

Ant's confusion deepened even further. It was beginning to look as if his father had some specific agenda, to which everyone around him was failing to conform. Including Ant himself. 'Sounds as if nobody's doing what you want them to,' he said crossly.

'That's just about the size of it,' said Digby.

'I'm taking the dog out,' Ant decided. 'I need to have a think.'

The morning was typical of December. The sun might be relatively high in the sky, but it was faint behind misty clouds. The temperature was close to freezing. The bare trees looked dead and slightly threatening where they marked the line of the Monarch's Way, up over the hill towards Broad Campden. But their dormancy would be short-lived. Already, with the passing of the shortest day, their sap would be stirring, the buds rapidly swelling, even now, in midwinter. There would be snowdrops in another two or three weeks, and he had seen the little green daffodil shoots nosing through the grass in their scruffy garden. Beverley had planted two hundred bulbs, nearly twenty years ago now, when she had been happy to live in the cottage, tied as it was to Digby's job. Since then it had come to feel less and less as if it was theirs – the landlord so clearly determined to dispose of them, and probably pull the whole building down the moment they were gone.

Ant spent several minutes reproaching himself for wilful

blindness to the state of his parents' marriage. Suddenly everything came into focus, and the full extent of the unravelling became impossible to ignore any longer. The separate bedrooms, the absence of anything resembling conversation. Beverley's refusal to discuss their meals, to plan a holiday, share in any outings – it all pointed to a loss of affection – even perhaps an active dislike. For the hundredth time he reran his mother's Saturday phone call and came to the startling conclusion that she could have said *He's dead to me and I can't come home*. There had been a crackle on the line, a noisy street competing for his attention. Could she have been talking about Digby all along?

The only things his parents really had in common were grief for Aldebaran and animosity towards the Blackwoods. And, he supposed, his own welfare. He wondered whether he was actually doing them any good by hanging around and behaving like a teenager. He was in his thirties, for heaven's sake! When anyone hinted that it was high time he set up home on his own, he experienced a panic that he struggled to conceal from himself. 'Can't afford it, mate,' he would say lightly. But to himself he insisted that his parents could never function without him. They would be at the mercy of Rufus and Carla, trapped inside that dreadful fence, harassed and intimidated. 'And the dog would miss me,' he might add. The dog was mostly his, but Beverley loved it as much as he did, and Percy himself was very fond of Digby. It would be a cruel violence to either remove him, or leave home without him. He watched now as the lithe brown body cantered along the track, delighted to be having the first real freedom of the day. Percy was a most excellent dog, obedient and undemanding. His parentage was something vaguely gun dog – some retriever in there and a dash of setter, perhaps. He'd come from a rescue, a few months old, and nobody could say what his forbears were. 'He was in a dustbin,' the Frowses were told.

But now something drastic was happening, right under his nose, and he was at a total loss to understand it. Everything had changed. His mother had abandoned him and his father on Christmas Day, to go to a distant friend who had not been mentioned for at least ten years. The landlord was dead, and his wife was in danger of losing her wits, thanks to the bizarre games her daughters were playing. Had one of those women killed Rufus, for fairly obvious reasons to do with financial gain? He tried to think back, to remember whether he had seen a strange car arriving, or heard strange voices at any time between Wednesday and Friday. The big house was within earshot of their cottage, but with no direct line of sight. Cars came and went along their fork of the driveway, and the Frowses did their best to ignore them. Beverley had, a year or two ago, found herself obsessively monitoring all the traffic, until she realised how unhealthy that was. 'Why should I care about his life?' she asked herself aloud. 'He doesn't care about mine.'

'Quite right,' said Digby.

They could not ignore the airborne visitors, however. The noise of a helicopter landing a hundred yards away was enough to drown all conversation and set the dog barking wildly. The very fact of a helipad made the whole family furious. It was ostentation of the most sickening kind. It was a signal from the Blackwoods that they were not just rich, they were *hugely* rich. They were the aristocracy of the Cotswolds, with money to burn, and nothing could stop them.

'We owe it to the workers of the world to bring them down to earth,' said Digby once. And he made even more of an effort to strew messy objects around the garden, and let the grass grow shaggy. 'We'll be the thorn in their sides, the clouts in their coffee, the mote in their eye, if it kills us,' he added.

'Let's hope it doesn't come to that,' Ant had laughed. For himself, he could see that the Blackwoods were an outrage, but he never took it quite as personally as his parents did. But now Blackwood was dead in very mysterious circumstances, and there were police people swarming about. Everything was in flux, and Ant could not work out where solid ground might lie. The phone call from his mother had not answered any of the important questions. His father's reactions had been peculiar from the start. The behaviour of Carla and her daughters was beyond bizarre as well. 'Well, Perce, old son, we're surely going to remember this Christmas, whatever happens next. Don't you think?' He muttered the words aloud, confident that nobody would hear him on this exposed upland in the heart of England. An England that accommodated more than its share of super-rich characters and émigrés from just about everywhere. People who operated under entirely different rules from those of the sentimentally English John Major or even Jeremy Corbyn. They were both essentially naive politicians who followed rules and assumptions from their grandparents' day, and let menials from lower down the ladder handle the complexities of the incomprehensible present.

The dog glanced over his shoulder, hearing his master's voice. He knew there was something odd going on, with the mistress absent and the walk routine disrupted. His dinner had been outrageously late the previous evening, and as far as he could tell no food at all had been consumed on this day so far. His feet were sore. There were strange smells inside and outside the house, and the terrifying wire fence might have something to do with it. Percy had touched it once and had never forgotten the appalling result. His nose still throbbed at the memory

Ant was sorely tempted to keep walking until he came out on the Broad Campden road, opposite the pub. From there it was about three minutes to the Slocombe house, where the very clever Thea lived. Hadn't she plainly said she wanted to help with the mystery of Beverley's disappearance? Should he not tell her that there'd been a phone call and there was no obvious cause for concern? The sad fact was that there was nobody else in Ant's life to whom he might confide any of these thoughts. No wise friends or elderly relatives, and, tragically, no sister. Aldebaran had been his best friend as he grew up, his protector and guide. She had explained the world to him, and accepted his limitations as of no importance. She knew he would never venture far from the Cotswolds, never train for a profession or create anything lasting. And she loved him anyway. Thea Slocombe was no substitute for Aldebaran but she was certainly the next best thing.

In addition to that, Ant had been quietly but instantly

smitten by Jessica Osborne. Not that anybody had noticed, nor would they be very interested if they had. She lived somewhere miles away and probably had a partner already. She would never give him a second glance. Women seldom did, for some reason. But this added element in an already disastrously complicated Christmas was almost a final straw. Everything was happening at once, and poor Ant Frowse, who only wanted to be a gardener and handyman, found it all too much.

He did not go into Broad Campden, but turned round at the gate that had been lying off its hinges in the hedge for years now. He liked the sad, abandoned sight of it, a patch of untidiness in the all-too-neat Cotswolds. He would often give it a quick pat when he was walking that way. Leaving it behind him, he headed back under the watery sun and was home fifteen minutes later.

At much the same time, Detective Superintendent Gladwin was knocking on the Slocombes' door, the post-mortem on Mr Blackwood having already been accomplished and a report having been transmitted to all interested parties. Thea told Stephanie and Tim to stay in the kitchen, while she led Gladwin into the living room, which smelt of woodsmoke and candles.

'He died of electrocution,' the detective said, after very few preliminaries. 'And because he was at too great a distance from the electric fence for it to have been an accident, we have to assume it was a deliberate act of homicide. A relevant factor is his pacemaker, which was badly damaged by the electric current that passed through him.'

Jessica had resolved to detach herself from any conversation between Thea and Gladwin, but she quickly changed her mind when she realised the detective had not come alone. DS Finch Graham was at her side. And there was no denying the fascination of the case. 'How?' she demanded. 'How do you electrocute someone, using their own fence?'

'That's what a team of officers is trying to establish as we speak. There's a junction box thingy very close to where he was found, and it would not be impossible, apparently, to divert the current and send it through a human body.' She sighed. 'We did it in physics, a hundred years ago, and I can't remember any of the details. All I can relate it to is the electric chair in America, and *The Green Mile*. It helps if the person's wet, and if you connect to vital organs.'

'One person surely couldn't do it on their own,' said Thea. 'How would you keep your victim still?'

'Bash him on the head, I suppose,' said Gladwin. 'But there might well have been more than one attacker.'

Thea was thinking about Digby and his clever games with the keypad electronics at the gate across the track up to his house. Would that qualify him to operate a diversion of current from the fence as well? 'It sounds awfully dangerous,' she said.

'It was a fairly high voltage, and it stopped his heart, thanks mainly to the pacemaker,' said Gladwin. 'The pathologist found minor burn marks on the skin, which confirmed it as electrocution.'

'Are you saying that anyone could have died if they touched that fence?' Thea was loudly indignant.

'No, not at all. You'd have to be soaking wet, and holding it for at least a minute, preferably against a vital organ. Otherwise it's just a nasty jolt.'

'But was the Blackwood man wet?' Jessica wondered.

'He might have been. Hard to tell, given he was lying outside for two days or more before anyone found him.'

Thea was quick to jump on this. 'That long?'

'Or thereabouts. Could have been a bit more, but not much less. You know how it goes. It's impossible to pin the time of death down closer than that.'

'But it's got to have been premeditated,' said Jessica. 'Wouldn't the killer need cables and stuff?'

'I haven't got that far yet. Presumably one cable, a couple of those clips they use, and maybe a bit of sticky tape. Not the sort of thing you'd carry around with you. I don't think anyone's going to argue that it was a spur-of-the-moment attack.'

'Doesn't that sound like some business thing, then? Somebody with a grudge, wanting revenge? Catching him when he's relaxed in the run-up to Christmas, luring him into the woods somehow?' Thea's mind was working fast. It seemed to matter a lot that no suspicion would fall onto the Frowses. But even as she spoke, she could hear a voice saying, *Yes, but Ant and his parents had a massive grudge against Blackwood.*

Jessica and Finch were sitting together on a window seat that was very seldom used. Mostly it was stacked high with magazines, toys, work in progress, so there was never any room to sit on it. The window looked onto a thick hedge at the side of the house. They were facing each other awkwardly, with a gap of a foot or more between them, but the message was clear that they had opted to withdraw from the main conversation.

'What did you bring him for?' Thea asked Gladwin in a whisper. 'You won't need any more metal detecting now they've found Blackwood's missing necklace.'

'Pardon?' Gladwin blinked in puzzlement.

'You know – the gold necklace that Blackwood was accusing Beverley of taking. They found it, apparently.' She clamped her mouth shut, wondering if she'd been a complete fool to mention it. 'I got a text a little while ago, from Ant. I haven't spoken to him today,' she added defensively. 'It's not as if Finch was actually searching for that, was he?' she finished weakly.

Gladwin looked over to the detective sergeant. 'Have you any idea what she's talking about? Because I haven't.'

'Come on,' Thea urged her. 'Somebody must have told you. That was the whole reason why Beverley went off when she did – or so they think. Back on Wednesday or Thursday, or whenever it was. Blackwood accused Bev of taking it.'

'Gold necklace?' Gladwin was still showing every sign of confusion.

'Nobody told you?' Thea concluded. 'Well, fancy that. Cock-up on the communication front, because I seem to recall that Carla reported it to the police.'

'Does it matter?'

'Who knows? I haven't seen it. And now they've found it, so I suppose it was just a red herring all along.'

'What's the latest on that car crash?' Jessica called

from the far side of the room.

'Five fatalities, all needing the pathologist. Everything got shifted up to make time for it.' Gladwin was clearly pained by the accident.

Thea did a rapid automatic survey of the people she held most dear. No – none of them could possibly have been on the A44 on Christmas night. '*Five?*' she echoed. 'How terrible. The poor things.'

'It hardly bears thinking about,' nodded Gladwin. 'Except of course I've got to, because it's my job. And now I've got to figure out who killed our famous local plutocrat with an electric cable.'

'And it's still only Boxing Day,' said Finch from across the room.

Jessica giggled briefly, but the others did not react.

'I'm going over to Crossfield now, to see where things stand. We've got people there already, of course,' said Gladwin. 'Any chance of a coffee first? I missed breakfast.'

Thea got up and looked at Finch. 'You want one as well, do you?'

'If it's no trouble. Thanks.'

In the kitchen, Stephanie and Timmy were sitting at the table doing nothing. There was no sign of Drew. It was obvious that Thea had interrupted a conversation that the children did not want her to know about. 'What are you two plotting?' she asked. 'You look terribly guilty.'

'They're going to arrest Ant, aren't they?' Stephanie burst out. 'They think he killed that horrible man.'

'Whatever gave you that idea? Were you listening to us in the sitting room?' She realised it would not have been difficult for the children to hear what had been said. The doors had both been open and nobody had thought it necessary to lower their voice.

'Some of it,' Stephanie admitted.

'Well, you heard wrong. If you ask me, it's far more likely to have been Mr Blackwood's wife, or some businessperson he's cheated or bullied – something like that. The man's incredibly rich, and rich people nearly always have enemies. It's probably bad news for Ant and his parents, as well, though. If the estate's sold, there'll be even more pressure on them to move out.' This thought had only just struck her and she paused to examine it. 'So that would give them the opposite of a motive, don't you think?'

Timmy was looking very unsure about the whole conversation. His friendship with the Frowses focused mainly on the dog. Stephanie, however, was keeping up admirably. 'But they do hate him. Everybody knows they do. And where is Mrs Frowse? How could she just disappear and leave them on Christmas Day? Poor Ant!' She sniffed back a flurry of sympathetic tears.

'Hey, Steph! Don't get upset. It'll turn out all right, you see. And it's not such a big deal about Christmas when you're a grown-up. I don't suppose they minded as much as all that. They know Beverley's okay, because she phoned them on Saturday. At worst, she'll have had a bit of a funny turn and decided she needed to get away. A sort of panic attack, probably.' Thea was convincing herself rather more successfully than she was convincing the child. 'I bet you that's all it was.'

Stephanie sniffed again. 'Are you going out now?'

'Me? No – this is strictly police business. I'd only be in the way. But we could walk over there this afternoon, maybe, when things have settled down a bit. I'll text Ant and see if he'd like that, shall I?'

'Okay,' Stephanie nodded. 'And Timmy?'

'Of course. Timmy's Percy's best friend, after all. And he missed out the last time.' Their Christmas Eve visit to the Frowses seemed a long time ago now, as did Drew's epic trip to see his mother. Everywhere she looked, Thea saw loose ends and unfinished business. Drew's mother, especially. 'Where's Dad?' she asked, then. She had assumed that Drew would be in the kitchen as well.

'In the office, I think,' said Stephanie.

The implication was that he was sulking, hiding away from Gladwin because he did not approve of her presence in his house. But there was no sense in trying to placate him yet, since Thea was highly likely to compound her misdeeds further before the day was done. Stephanie was right, of course, in her assumption that at least one of the Frowse family was liable to be taken in for questioning now that it was established that Blackwood had been murdered. Thea wasn't sure why she had been so slow to grasp that herself. Her momentary relief at realising it would probably work against them to have the man dead had quickly evaporated. They hated him quite strongly enough to override such a consideration.

And Beverley Frowse hated him worst of all.

Only a few minutes after Gladwin and Graham left, Thea

thought better of her judgement on Drew, and went to find him. He might be wanting some coffee, even if he was disinclined to speak to her. She tapped lightly on his office door and opened it without waiting for a reply.

He was sitting at his desk, writing on a pad of old-fashioned notepaper. 'Gosh – is that Basildon Bond?' she laughed. 'Where did that come from?'

'I think Karen gave it to me about fifteen years ago. Or rather, perhaps somebody gave it to both of us as a wedding present. It was in a big blue box with a ribbon attached to one corner. Most of it's still left, as well as about two dozen blue envelopes.'

'And you've kept it ever since.' It made her feel fond of him, for some reason.

'It's not the sort of thing you can just throw away. It's excellent quality. I rather wish I was using a fountain pen, to do it justice.'

'You're a dinosaur. The only forty-year-old in the land to write a proper letter by hand.'

'I expect I am. I don't know why I'm doing it, to be honest. And I won't be forty for a long time yet.'

'It can only be a letter to your mother,' she realised. 'Better than an email, easier than a phone call. I get it.'

'Do you?' He looked up at her for the first time. 'Thank goodness for that.'

'Do you want to tell me what you're saying to her? Do you think I should put a note in as well?' She thought about it for a moment. 'I should, of course. Do I call her "Mother" or "Sandra"?

'She doesn't like Sandra much. Her friends – and my

father – call her Sandy. I think you'll have to ask her, not me.'

'Tell me more about her. I feel stupid, hardly knowing a thing about my own mother-in-law.'

Drew sat back in the chair and nibbled his pen. 'Well, let's see . . . She was born in nineteen fifty and worked in a racing stable before she was married. Some of her horses won big races. She always followed the Grand National and all the rest of them, on the telly when I was little. I never liked horses myself.'

'Was your father horsey as well?'

'Not so much. He preferred mechanical things. But they followed the hunt on Boxing Day every year. On foot, not horseback. They never actually owned a horse of their own, which I think my mother still resents to this day.'

'Boxing Day's today,' said Thea, superfluously.

'Yes, I know. That's why I'm writing, partly. I was just saying I remember how it was thirty years ago – although I haven't put the bit where I refused to go with them, when I was about twelve, because I said the hunt was cruel and barbaric and outdated and morally unacceptable. She probably hasn't forgotten, which means it's probably daft of me to mention it.'

'Tricky,' said Thea. 'But your side came up trumps in the end. The whole thing's banned now.'

'There'll be people out there today, dragging a pretend fox about and letting their horses and hounds rush about over the wolds, much the same as before. The hope is, of course, that they'll accidentally stumble on a real one, and accidentally let the hounds go after it.'

'You think?' Thea had never given the topic much thought. 'I get the impression this is going to be quite a long letter, then. Do you want some coffee to fortify you while you write it? Lunch is in about an hour. Leftovers. Including the uneaten Christmas pudding, which isn't going to be very nice.'

'It's bringing an awful lot of stuff back,' he said, ignoring the inconsequential food talk. 'Most of it makes me feel horribly guilty. My mother up there, waiting for his funeral all over Christmas. It's all wrong. What was I thinking, letting it carry on for so long?'

'You've been busy with your own life. It seems to me it was up to them to make the first move. Where were they when Karen died? And before that – when you needed help with the kids? I know it's not all on one side, but nobody could doubt that they were the pig-headed ones.' She went to him and cuddled his head against her front. 'If you ask me, you did what you had to, to survive. I know I've never heard the full story, but it's obvious that they were pretty rubbish parents.'

'Don't say that.' His voice was muffled. 'They probably did their best. It goes back generations, if you start looking for blame.'

'Well, I think people can learn to do things better.'

'Which is why I'm writing to her now. I want to do things better.' He gave her a tragic look. 'It's about Timmy, you see. I woke up this morning and it hit me. If I don't watch myself, I'll end up doing to him what my father did to me.'

She kissed the top of his head. 'Timmy's going to be fine,' she assured him. 'From here on, we're going to make darn sure he is.'

He grabbed her tightly and squeezed. 'I love you, Thea Slocombe,' he said. 'And I absolutely don't deserve you.'

'That could go two ways,' she laughed. 'Some people might wonder what you did to deserve such a terrible wife.'

'Some people don't know what they're talking about,' said Drew.

Over lunch, Jessica talked about Finch Graham. 'He was telling me a bit more about the metal detecting. It's been a hobby of his for years, and he's got really good at spotting likely places where stuff might be hidden. He liked to think he'd find stolen goods out in that field, but really he'd heard a whisper that there might be some Roman hoards still to discover. There must be quite a few villas that haven't been unearthed yet, even round here.'

'I doubt that,' said Thea. 'The whole area's been gone over minutely in the last century or so. More than anywhere else in Britain, probably.'

'Even so, it would be easy to miss a small one. And even easier to miss a stash of buried coins or jewellery. Think about it – in the first place, the person hiding them would use a secret place, not close to a road or buildings. Maybe near a big tree, so he could find it again. Then the tree blows down, and brambles and nettles grow all over it, and new baby trees spring up and eventually it's a real little wood, and nobody thinks of it as having been open ground at one time. All this rewilding that's going on shows how quickly a patch of land can change. It's all very exciting,' she finished with a sigh.

Stephanie and Timmy were both following this with wide-open eyes. 'I want a metal detector,' said Timmy. 'I'm going to find some treasure with it.'

Jessica beamed at him. 'So am I,' she said.

Drew was inattentive, eating quickly. 'Dad?' Timmy said. 'Can I have a metal detector for my birthday?'

Drew looked up in confusion. 'Birthday? That's not till September. You've only just had Christmas. And I'm not sure they're suitable for children, are they?' He looked at Thea and Jessica for enlightenment.

'Finch might let you go with him sometime, when he's using his,' Jessica told Tim.

Stephanie had been watching Drew and Thea since before lunch. Something nice had happened; they were being all lovey-dovey, like they'd been a year ago, before Thea started getting bored. It was probably just Christmas, she concluded. The presents and the food and the candles had all conspired to make everybody happy, after all. And now it was almost over, the cold meat and stodgy rewarmed pudding's faint echoes of the wonderful Christmas lunch – but the *niceness* of it, not just the meal but the whole day – were lingering on. She tried to think of a better word – 'warm', perhaps. 'Loving' seemed a bit strong, but 'affectionate' wasn't strong enough. Dad was distracted, but not in a worried way. He was looking at Timmy as if he was really glad to have him. And Jessica was being mushy about the Finch person.

Only Thea was making her uneasy. Even now, when she was smiling at Dad, and putting her hand on his shoulder when she went to get something from the fridge, there was something unreliable about her. She never let you forget that there was a world just outside their front door where strange and scary things were happening. There was always a mystery of some sort, always a reason to go out and involve herself in other's people's trouble. Stephanie herself was torn between that unsettling lure of the outside and the comfort and contentment of a person's own home. Timmy, she suspected, was essentially a stay-at-home sort of person, like Dad.

Her thoughts rambled along these lines while the meal came to an end and Drew hurried back to his office. She began to sort everybody she knew into one category or the other, until at some point she drew the surprising analogy between burial and cremation. Her father was a burial person – wanting to stay snug and secure in the same grave for ever. Thea, on the other hand, would want her ashes scattered to the four winds, free to float away in all directions. Not surprising, then, that Dad had become an undertaker specialising in burials. He probably had the site for his own grave already secretly decided. But Stephanie, once she gave it some serious thought, rather imagined she might prefer the other option.

'I suppose I'd better think about what we're going to feed Damien,' said Thea. 'They'll be here tomorrow. We'll have to put the cot up, and tidy away anything that Kim might break or hurt herself with.'

'What time are they due?' asked Jessica. 'I could stay and see them if it's not too late.'

'Mid-afternoon. You won't get home till after dark if you do that.'

'So? I'm not scared of the dark. It's motorway practically

the whole way back. I've never even seen Kim. She's my cousin – she should know who I am.'

The prospect of suddenly exchanging Jessica for a new set of step-relatives gave Stephanie pause. The house would become full and noisy, and she would have to spend two more nights sharing her room with Timmy. She wondered how her father was feeling about it. He had never met these people, either. It seemed a rather rude intrusion to turn up right after Christmas and expect food and hospitality. From things Thea had said, she wasn't even sure that Damien was very nice.

'Please yourself,' Thea said. 'For myself, I can't help thinking – roll on Friday.'

'You're awful,' Jessica told her. 'I guess I should think myself lucky you let me come and stay.'

'Don't give me that,' said Thea, who never let a remark like that pass unchallenged. 'You can come any time you like.'

'She'll want to come quite often, so she can see her new friend Finch,' said Stephanie, instantly feeling that it wasn't a very tactful thing to say. Jessica gave her a playful smack, but said nothing to contradict her.

'That'll be nice,' said Thea placidly. She looked at the clock. 'Don't the days go fast at this time of year? It feels as though it's only light for five minutes.'

'Horrible,' agreed Jessica.

'Can we play games after lunch?' asked Timmy, who had been sitting quietly assembling a jigsaw on one corner of the table.

'I thought we were all going to walk over to Crossfield,'

said Jessica, with a face that made no secret of the fact that she found the idea of playing games a fairly unappealing prospect.

'I should phone them first,' said Thea.

'Blimey!' called Digby from just outside the front door. 'Come and listen to this. Is it what I think it is?' Female shrieks could be clearly heard, emanating from the big house. 'Are they killing each other, or what?'

Ant had no answer; fights between women were entirely outside his experience. Or any fights, come to that. In this particular corner of the Cotswolds, disputes were almost never settled by physical combat.

'Wouldn't mind if they did, come to think of it,' his father went on with a sardonic grin. 'Serve them right.' In spite of his sense that it was beneath them both, Ant had joined his father outside and both were listening intently. The shrieks were getting louder, if anything. 'Am I right in thinking they're coming this way?' Digby wondered, looking suddenly less amused. 'Bar the door, son. We don't want them in here again, do we? They might break things.'

Ant made no move to obey, rightly assuming the remark was not meant seriously. 'They won't come here,' he said.

'You can't be sure. Why would they take their battle outside?' He cocked an ear. 'You're right, though. They're not getting any closer. I think it's only two of them – Bronya must have had the sense to stay out of it.'

'It's her fault for stirring everything up and landing her sister in trouble,' Ant reminded him. 'Are there any servants around, I wonder? They'll probably call the police, if so.'

'Don't call them servants,' Digby objected. 'They're *staff*.' It was an exchange they'd had before. Digby insisted that *servants* was a derogatory word, which Ant couldn't see at all. 'I expect one or two have stayed on over the holiday. Somebody has to make the beds.'

'One of them could have killed Rufus, then.' Ant wondered why he hadn't thought of that sooner.

'Very likely,' said Digby abstractedly. 'I always thought that woman who does the cooking looked a bit dubious.' The team of employees whose purpose was to ensure the smooth running of the house were shadowy figures to the Frowse family. None of them ever engaged in conversation, and there were regular new faces seen in the distance, arriving or departing. Digby had focused on the cook because she had been there a long time, and was sometimes to be observed in the kitchen garden that was visible from his bedroom window.

After another minute or two Ant went into the kitchen, deliberately clattering crockery to cover the female voices. He found it increasingly unsettling that grown women should so forget themselves as to make such a noise. The sounds he heard were not screams of pain, but of rage. There were words, shouted at full pitch. There were *oh, oh, ohs* as if to indicate grief, betrayal, disbelief.

Digby came back in soon afterwards. 'I think they're *chasing* each other round the yard out there, yelling and screaming. That Carla is like a grizzly bear. She's off her head, if you ask me.'

'They can't go on much longer, surely? We might have to do something,' Ant said, with a worried frown.

'Not us. I did wonder whether they're in view of any of the cameras. It'd make a very entertaining film, if so.'

'They've stopped,' Ant realised. Everything outside had gone suddenly quiet. 'And I need you to stop, as well. You're treating it all as a joke, when it seems to me we should probably be feeling seriously scared.'

'It won't be long now, son. Once your mother gets back we'll get a better idea of what comes next.'

'You think?'

'I do,' the man nodded with a certainty that Ant felt wholly unjustified.

Chapter Seventeen

What came next was another visit from the police, who issued a request that the two men refrain from leaving the house until further notice. There had been fresh developments, and formal interviews were imminent. 'On Boxing Day?' queried Ant in disbelief. 'I thought nothing was going to happen before tomorrow?'

'There's a fresh forensic team examining the scene,' they were told. 'Please stay well away from the area.'

'You'll be telling the Blackwood people the same thing, I assume?' said Digby.

The policeman looked severely down his nose and gave no reply to this.

'Bound to be,' said Ant quickly, fearful that his father was intent on alienating the forces of the law – which could do no good whatsoever.

When the officer had gone, Digby blew out his cheeks. 'Bloody nuisance. Your mother's going to walk right into the middle of all this, just when we thought we had the day to ourselves.'

There it was again – the implication that his parents understood a whole lot more than he did. 'What does *that* mean?' Ant shouted. 'Why does it feel as if everything's been happening behind my back?'

'Calm down, there's a good chap. Shouting doesn't help anything.' Digby gave a rueful snort. 'I wonder what they'll find over at the mansion. For all we know, Carla's run off leaving both daughters dead on the floor.'

'Not Bronya. She's kept out of it. She might even have called the police herself, for all we know.'

'Don't talk rubbish. She's got more sense than that. Still – I don't like it, not knowing what this fresh evidence might be. Best thing we can do is keep our heads down and co-operate for all we're worth. Salt of the earth, remember – that's us. Hard done by, but bearing it meekly, because they're the lords and we're the peasants. They've only got to look at that bloody fence to understand how we've been expected to live. That's our line – best you remember that. Looks to me as if they've worked out that our friend Rufus did not die accidentally. That's shocking news – right? Got to be some Mafia-style character got the wrong side of the man. All that wheeler-dealing he did, making money hand over fist, bound to upset some people along the way. Isn't that right?' Digby looked hard at his bewildered son. 'Isn't it?' he repeated with some force.

'Er . . . I guess so, yes. But they never said it was murder, did they? Aren't you jumping the gun a bit?'

'Could be,' Digby acknowledged. 'Trust me to make two and two equal five, eh? Silly old sausage, getting all ahead of myself. So, we just sit tight and wait and see, that's the best thing. And if your mother shows up, don't you rush in with a whole lot of half-baked ideas. Let's just give her time to settle down again first.'

'You think she intends to settle down? That's not how she sounded to me.'

Digby wriggled his shoulders. 'We'll have to see, won't we? She'll be surprised we made such a fine job of that goose.'

There was something rather pathetic in this, to Ant's eyes. His father was clutching at straws, trying to salvage something that Ant had not until then understood was probably beyond repair. Something had happened over recent days, right under his nose, and he had been blissfully unaware of it. There had to have been clues he had missed, comments he had overlooked. But perhaps it had all been so gradual that the final straw had been some tiny word or event that nobody could be expected to notice. And perhaps it was all entirely separate from the death of Rufus Blackwood. Perhaps there was absolutely no connection at all.

Still he had two burning questions to ask his mother, and nothing was going to stop him confronting her with them, the moment she came home.

'She has a bit of explaining to do,' he said mildly. 'Assuming she really does come back.'

'Oh, she'll come back. She won't be able to help herself. Never was much good on her own, you know. Talks a blue streak about being her own woman and wanting her independence, but mostly she lets other people make the running. She's broken all records this time, staying out all this long while.' The bravado was evidently boosting Digby's self-esteem, as he convinced himself of the truth of his own words. He was not going to lie down without a struggle.

Again, Ant found himself wondering about his parents' marriage in more detail than he had done for years. Maybe he never had thought about it as he did now, when it might be too late. Digby was not speaking fondly of his wife – more like sarcastically, and definitely critically. Ant could not remember any real demonstrations of affection in either direction, since he was about ten. When Digby had given up the farm work, Beverley had made some rules concerning the running of the house. Obvious things like making him do some of the shopping and cleaning, and learning how to work the washing machine. As far as Ant could see, there had been very little friction as a result. 'You do *want* her back, don't you?' he asked, rather shakily. It felt like a moment in which most of his lifelong assumptions could find themselves shaken and even destroyed.

He could see his father wavering between a careless dismissal of such a question, and a rare moment of honest reply. 'That's a bit of a facer,' he said, putting on a mock accent, as he so often did. 'As they used to say,' he added. But then, when Ant said nothing, he gave a defeated sort of sigh and said, 'She went off me years ago, you know.

Never forgave me for something I said in about nineteen ninety-one, and since then everything's been pretty much my fault. I should have earned more money, so we could have bought a place to live before it was too late. I should have listened to her better, and understood her feelings without having to be told everything twenty times. All the usual stuff that comes with being married, in a nutshell. The thing is – your mother *cares* about everything a lot more than I do. It doesn't bother me so much that we've got a dirty great fence all round us. At least . . .' He tailed off, shaking his head.

'You care every bit as much as Mum does,' Ant corrected him. 'It's probably more humiliating for you than it is for any of us. You used to *work* here. You were the *manager*, for God's sake. Then a new bloke moves in, who never knew you in those days, and who thinks you're just a poverty-stricken tinker who's determined to embarrass him. On top of that, he does his best to make our lives difficult in any number of nasty little ways. And the final straw is when he marries some Russian psychopath who gets him to turn the whole property into Fort Knox.'

'All right. But I never got into direct battles with him, unlike your mother. It's still a pretty good place to live, compared to what we'd have ever managed to find somewhere else. The rent here is laughable, thanks to the decrepit state of the house. We've got space, fresh air, good friends. I don't care what you say, I think I've been a lot more contented than your mother has – until now.'

'So what changed?'

'No single thing, that I can see. Just attitudes hardening,

the state of the house getting to the point when it's going to fall down if something isn't done soon. Next time the rent's assessed, we're going to have to put in a proper report, and push for some serious repairs. Or we would have had to. That's all changed now, as well, of course.'

'Probably for the worse.'

'That remains to be seen,' said Digby, looking at the floor, as if searching for some sign of the future.

'I don't think you've got out of that chair more than four times in three days,' said Ant suddenly losing patience. 'You've even stayed there to eat. You'll get old before your time if you go on like that.'

'Can't see there's much to get up for. Time enough for action when the police come bothering us again. I've got all I need right here.' Digby had one of his massive American Civil War histories on the floor beside him, as well as two smaller ones. He dipped into them in some sort of rotation that Ant found incomprehensible.

'Don't you think we ought to be trying to work out what it'll mean for us, that Blackwood's dead? Carla's going to be the owner of the estate now, presumably. She'll pull every string she can to get us thrown out. I wouldn't put it past her to set us on fire one dark night. For a start, I bet she'll try and poison poor old Percy.' He was thinking aloud, letting himself get more and more agitated as the implications got darker. 'She's got to be the one who killed Rufus, don't you think?' he went on, visualising Carla's volatile behaviour, not just that day but ever since she'd come to live at Crossfield. 'She seems completely unhinged to me.'

Digby merely nodded slowly and said, 'Could be. If they lock her up, the place'll most likely be sold.'

This was such a leap into the unknown that Ant shuddered. 'Are we sure Rufus hasn't got some offspring somewhere? Would they inherit if Carla was in gaol?'

Digby roused himself slightly. 'He was married before Carla, wasn't he?'

'Don't ask me. You're the one who spends half his time on the Internet.'

'I never saw a sign of any other Blackwoods. But I wasn't looking very hard. I'm more interested in where his money comes from. Mind you, if there were sons or daughters, they'd probably be shareholders or directors or something, and their names would pop up automatically. Which they didn't.'

'The police'll be having a rummage for all that. They always think the family's top of the suspect list when there's a murder.'

'Except when there's a tenant family who clearly hates the landlord's guts,' said Digby.

'And who've got some mystery of their own, concerning their missing wife and mother.'

'Could be,' said Digby again.

'Don't you *care*?' his son burst out angrily. 'Why are you being so limp about it? Lethargic, even. It's not like you.'

'Just keeping my head down, son, same as you should be doing. Don't rock any boats or attract any attention. It's generally the best way when things get a bit unnecessary.'

'But I haven't played a single game all Christmas,' Timmy was whining. 'Why can't we do it now? It says it only takes an hour and a bit. There'll be time to do other things as well.'

So the train game was finally being set up, and everybody but Thea was valiantly trying to follow the convoluted rules. Timmy was winning, and Jessica was finding the whole thing exasperating. 'This tunnel business is insane,' she grumbled. 'And I don't see how anybody could ever get to Scotland or Ireland.'

'It probably gets clearer after a few times,' said Drew. 'It's always confusing the first time you play something new.'

'Don't tell me I've got to go through this again,' Jessica pleaded.

'Not if you don't want to. It's not compulsory.' This was a line Drew used quite often, and it always made Stephanie smile. There was something so elegantly reproachful in it, putting the emphasis on the other person's unreasonable objections to doing something. In recent months she had come to appreciate nuances in the English language that gave her real pleasure. At the same time, it made her realise how near impossible it would be to properly master another language. The classes they had been given in French in their first term were so basic as to be infantile. But, as the teacher insisted, you had to start somewhere.

'No, it's not compulsory,' she repeated, catching her father's eye and grinning.

'Oh, you two,' sighed Jessica, significantly increasing Stephanie's delight.

Thea was wandering in and out, showing no signs of being gainfully employed. She had paused to watch the game for a moment, and heard this exchange. 'They read each other's minds,' she said. 'You get used to it.'

Timmy was shaking his dice and plotting his next move, but he did not miss what was going on around him. He looked from sister to father and back, and gave a little shake of his head. 'You don't really,' he told his stepmother.

By an obvious lucky fluke, Timmy won the game, and the grown-ups suddenly got all hyperactive. Timmy was contentedly sifting through his box of new things on the big chair by the fireplace. Stephanie was cuddled with Hepzie on the sofa, also assessing her acquisitions. Then Thea spoke. 'Did I mention that I had a card from Lucy Sinclair? The woman I house-sat for in Hampnett two years ago?'

Drew and Jessica both looked at her in confusion. 'So?' said Jessica.

'She's moved to Northleach, which is hardly any distance from where she was before. It was a converted barn and she had some land as well. Now she's in a small house in a street.'

'This card – it must have had a letter in it as well,' Drew noted. 'And isn't she the woman who phoned for you last summer, when you were in that Barnsley house?'

'Right,' said Thea, waiting for the next question.

'And now she wants you to house-sit for her again,' said Drew with certainty. 'I can hear it in your voice. And you've waited until now to mention it.'

Everybody held their breath. Stephanie silently repeated to herself, *It's all right, it doesn't matter, it's not a big disaster*. Because why did it feel as if it was very bad news?

'It's not definite,' said Thea. 'But she's got to go and have an operation at some point. Her back's got something wrong with it. And she probably took some of her animals with her, so they'll need looking after, though she doesn't actually say that.'

'Is she the one with the rabbits?' Timmy asked. 'When Mrs Gladwin helped you feed the baby ones?'

It was a familiar story, one of the less grisly ones in Thea's repertoire. Even so a rabbit had died by violence. 'That's the one,' she said. 'Fancy you remembering.'

'I've never heard of Northleach,' said Jessica.

'It's an old wool town. Made a fortune out of sheep. Enclosures, peasants' revolts – all that stuff. Absolutely steeped in history, in fact.' Thea spoke with relish.

Drew sighed, and then smiled ruefully. 'So now you've broached the subject, I suppose I'm meant to get used to the idea for a bit, and then when it happens, not raise any objections?'

'Something like that,' said Thea.

Chapter Eighteen

Everything was happening at once at the Old Stables. Thea phoned to announce that she was walking over; the police showed up in force with a new SOCO team; and Beverley came home.

Ant had found himself yearning increasingly for the return of his mother. Without her Digby seemed like a different man, unpredictable and unsettling. Random new suspicions kept occurring to him. Was there another person involved somewhere? That didn't strike him as at all probable. Living in a group of three nearly always meant that one person was at a distance from the other two, whose relationship was the dominant one. But in the case of the Frowses, it was not apparent who this third person was. If forced to say, he would suggest that he and his mother formed the central bond, with Digby further away from either of them. His father had taken outside work when the fruit farm was dismantled, often being out for ten hours or more in the summer. His expertise with trees came in useful, as well as a skill at building drystone walls and erecting fences. But the work had dwindled over the years, and now much of the equipment required for these tasks lay unused around the front garden of their house, along with his car-boot sale stock and other junk. When Aldebaran died, Digby had stayed upstairs for two days demanding to be left alone. When Beverley ranted about the Blackwoods, he would nod and say something sarcastic or mocking about them, but never suggested any action. His modest computer skills enabled them to circumvent the keypad on the gate, which Ant found deliciously enjoyable, while Beverley was even more ecstatic. Digby had refused to explain exactly how it was done, and from that point on, began to experiment with other technologies on the reconditioned laptop that Ant had got for him. 'I'm a silver surfer now,' he would say.

He would announce numerous arcane discoveries he had made thanks to Google – but he never ventured into the shark-infested waters of Facebook or Twitter.

'I just wish she'd come home,' Ant said, almost involuntarily. 'This has gone on long enough.'

And then she did, five minutes before Thea and Stephanie Slocombe came through the gate, and yet another police car followed them up the driveway.

In the event, all five of the Slocombes had set out for the

walk along Monarch's Way. 'Surely we can't all descend on the Frowses?' Jessica objected. 'You didn't say that when you phoned them.'

'I thought maybe just me and Stephanie would go the whole way. The rest of you could circle back through Chipping Campden, if you've got the energy,' said Thea.

'How far is it?'

'Probably three miles. No more than that, unless you get lost.'

'That's a lot for Timmy.'

'He's nine, not three. He could walk twice that and barely notice.'

Stephanie was proud to have been selected for the main purpose of the walk, even though it was fairly obvious all along that it would be her. She knew Ant and Percy better than anyone, after meeting up with them on several strolls along the footpaths. The young man and his dog would be out in all weathers, at most times of day, simply walking for the sake of it, as far as she could tell. 'The dog likes a good run,' was the answer she got when she made a comment to this effect. 'And he likes to meet other dogs, like your Hepzie.'

'I'm desperate to see if Beverley's back,' said Thea, trying to hurry things along. 'And find out what the police have been saying.'

Jessica made a sort of throat-clearing noise, before saying, 'It is a murder investigation, remember. It might get a bit nasty.'

Stephanie knew that this was a coded way of saying that Jessica didn't think a child should be exposed to such situations. She smiled up at her stepsister. 'It's okay,' she said. 'I've seen lots of dead people, you know. That sort of thing doesn't bother me.'

Thea took her hand and gave it a funny little shake. 'That's my girl,' she said. 'Though this time's rather different from anything you've come across before.'

Jessica pulled a funny face. 'I thought *I* was your girl,' she said, in a silly voice.

'You don't really want to come. You're having a holiday from police stuff,' said Thea. 'And besides, it's completely outside your patch.'

Jessica gave a little laugh. 'Nobody says "patch" any more. You're hopelessly out of date.'

'They do on the telly,' Thea argued. 'I don't believe you.'

'It comes to us all,' said Drew from behind them. 'Don't try to get between Thea and Stephanie, if you know what's good for you. They're going to make a formidable team in another few years.'

Stephanie's feeling of pride burgeoned even more. They were treating her almost like a grown-up, taking her seriously and obviously pleased with her. She gripped Thea's hand, pretending it was because they were walking on slippery stones where the footpath climbed upwards, and looked around for the spaniel. 'Hey, Hepzie!' she called. 'Run!'

The dog needed no encouragement. She began to fly across the adjacent field, long black ears flapping. 'Lucky there aren't any sheep,' said Jessica, who was the only one apparently feeling less than joyous.

'Did you know that this footpath is more than six hundred miles long?' Timmy offered, after a short silence.

'It zigzags a lot, you see, because it's much less than that from Worcester to Brighton, which are the two ends.'

'That's amazing,' said Jessica, sounding as if she really meant it.

'It's because the King was escaping, in the Civil War, and he had to keep going off course to hide,' said Stephanie. She looked around her. At first glance, there were very few obvious hiding places, but then small banks as well as walls and hedges came into focus as ideal shelters. The land tipped and buckled, forming dips and creases where a person could lie down and become invisible. She connected it with the missing Beverley, as well as the possible presence of buried Roman treasure and suddenly saw the entire landscape with new eyes. 'I expect there were more trees here then,' she said.

'Probably not,' Thea corrected her. 'They'd been felling most of the English oaks for a long time by then. And don't forget this was an area with huge numbers of sheep. You don't get trees in sheep country. They eat all the baby saplings as fast as they pop up.'

'And they made coffins out of the elm trees,' said Drew, reminding them of what he did for a living. 'Lovely straight trunks, you see. I heard that they're coming back at last. Won't that be nice?'

Stephanie had an agreeable sense that everything connected. Charles I and Beverley Frowse, English oaks, sheep, old estates, dogs and death – they all danced around in her mind, joining up in a strangely coherent picture. Thea had often commented on how there was not a single inch of Britain that had not been walked on by people over thousands of years. 'And a lot of it will have the bones of the dead lying down there as well,' she usually added. Battles, old burial sites, family members interred close to the homestead – layers of dead people forming part of the very ground they walked on. But probably not up here on this particular wold, she decided. Just dead sheep and birds would be decomposing out here.

It was an idle conversation, with little emotional heft. The wind was slight but very cold. She remembered that Dad had said something about snow. It felt quite cold enough for it. 'Are those snow clouds?' she asked, pointing ahead, where the sky was very grey.

'Could be,' said Drew. 'I forget what the forecast said now.'

'Something about a light covering tomorrow. Maybe I should move my car,' said Jessica. 'At least as far as the church.'

'If it really snows, Damien won't be able to come,' said Thea hopefully. 'Please God, let it snow.'

'Don't be so nasty!' Stephanie protested. 'I want to see Kim.'

'Kim and Tim!' said Drew. 'I only just realised. Like people from a storybook.'

'It should be Tim and Kim because I'm older,' said his son.

'Timmy and Kimmy sounds even better,' said Stephanie.

They had almost reached the road, where they would divide into two groups, according to Thea's plan. The ground sloped downhill, providing better shelter from the cold wind. They had not seen a single person. 'Why is it so deserted?' asked Jessica.

'It's usually like this in winter. The tourists mostly go for better weather, even the walkers, and the second-homers are enjoying their log fires and mulled wine,' said Drew. 'You know what – I forgot to take you to see the burial field. It's very different from when you were last here.'

'Have we got time now?'

He looked dubious. 'Not really. Not unless we go back the way we came, and down the other road.'

'It's just a field, Dad,' said Timmy, who did not at all share his father's and sister's relish for graves. 'And it's windy on the footpath. It might be better if we go the way Thea said.'

'I have to say you're right,' Drew agreed. 'Sorry, Jess. Next time, eh?'

The parting of the ways was upon them. 'You'll be back before us,' said Thea. 'Put the kettle on. If we're later than five, you can start making something with the cold turkey.'

Drew looked alarmed. 'What sort of something?'

'Cut it into little bits and fry it up with onion and tinned tomatoes. Jessica can help, if that's too difficult for you.' Drew's cooking abilities were famously minimal, and yet he had managed to keep himself and two children alive for years when Karen was too ill to do it, and after she died. 'We'll have rice with it, but don't start it until we're back.'

'You'll take the dog presumably?'

'Of course,' she said.

As Thea and Stephanie rounded the bend before the entrance to Crossfield, they could see three or four vehicles

281

parked along the edge of the driveway, between the road and the gate up to the big house. 'Looks as if the police are still here,' said Thea in some surprise.

'I wonder why.'

'They'll be pressured into finding every scrap of evidence, now they know for sure it was murder. Gladwin's probably here. Better put Hepzie on the lead. They won't like it if she gets in their way.'

Stephanie caught the dog and attached her to the lead. 'Where are we going?' she asked.

'Better start with Ant and Digby, I suppose. They can bring us up to date, and it was them we came to see, after all.'

'And we shouldn't intrude on police work,' said Stephanie, feeling very grown up.

'That's right,' said Thea with evident regret.

The electric gate was partly open, and when Thea pushed it, it shifted quite easily. 'They've disconnected the electrics,' she realised. 'Mrs Blackwood won't like that. Though I suppose she's got other things to worry about.'

Stephanie had never seen Mrs Blackwood, but had heard plenty about her from Ant. She privately thought it very likely that she had killed her husband in a fit of rage. But the whole business of the murder was still very confusing. 'How exactly did Mr Blackwood die?' she asked Thea now, as they walked the hundred yards or so up to the cottage.

'I probably shouldn't tell you. I'm not really meant to know. It'll all be made public soon enough, I expect.'

'We haven't been very good detectives, have we? Not like you usually are. We haven't actually *done* anything.

And we don't know very much, either.'

'We know he was wearing pyjamas when he died.'

'Oh.' Stephanie wasn't sure that this was a pertinent detail. 'And a dressing gown?'

'Probably, at this time of year.'

A car came up behind them and hooted. It turned out to be Gladwin, obviously heading for the cottage as well. She put her head out of the window, her expression stern. 'Not a good time to be visiting,' she said.

'Oh? Why not?' asked Thea.

'We're here to arrest Mrs Frowse,' came the stunning reply. 'I'm told she arrived home five minutes ago.'

Chapter Nineteen

Ant had the presence of mind to ask his two questions almost before his mother was out of her car. He paused only to check that she was not damaged in any way, mentally as well as physically. She appeared drawn, apprehensive even, but perfectly steady. 'What did you mean when you said "He's dead and I can't come home"?' he burst out. 'That's what you said to me on the phone.'

She shook her head in puzzlement. 'What? What are you talking about? Where's your father? What are all those cars doing in the driveway?'

'You said those words. You must remember. What did you mean? Who was dead? It's important.' He wanted to shake the answer out of her.

'Oh. Is that what you thought I said? I was talking about

284

Digby. "He's dead to me" is what I said, or something like it. It was quite a bad line. You must have heard it wrong.'

Ant fell silent, running the phone call through his head yet again. 'No,' he decided. 'I didn't hear it wrong.'

'You've been thinking I killed someone?' She looked back at the police activity in the woods. 'That I killed Rufus Blackwood, in fact?' The smile that went with these words made Ant even more terrified than he was already.

'I've got another question,' he went on hurriedly. Digby was standing in the doorway, waiting for them to join him. And there was a strong sense of events closing in, leaving no time to spare. 'Why did you take Aldebaran's ashes with you?'

'Ah!' Beverley stepped back to her car. 'They're quite safe – I strapped them into the passenger seat.'

'But why . . . ?'

'I didn't want your father to have them,' she said simply.

Which only left two more minutes for Digby and Beverley to confront each other, with a minimal exchange of words. Those they did utter were gibberish to Ant.

'I saw you,' said his mother. 'I came back on Thursday and saw you.'

Digby did not flinch. 'Whatever you think you saw, you got it wrong,' he said.

'Nobody's ever going to convince me of that.'

'So what do you think happens now? There's trouble, whichever way you look at it.'

'Visitors,' said Ant, pointing down at the gate.

Although they kept well out of the way, Thea and Stephanie

did not go home despite the knowledge that they were intruding on matters that were none of their business. They saw Gladwin supervising the arrest of Beverley Frowse, and taking her away in the back of the police car. 'We're taking you in for questioning,' the senior detective intoned. 'With regard to the unlawful killing of Mr Rufus Blackwood.'

Ant and Digby stood at the gate watching the departing vehicle with blank faces. Percy came out to rub noses with Hepzie, both dogs subdued and watchful.

Ant belatedly took notice of them and beckoned. 'You'd better come in,' he said. 'We might need some distraction.'

'I hope you're going to tell us everything,' said Thea. 'This has got to be a mistake, surely?'

'There's hardly anything to tell. We only spoke to her for a minute before you got here. And you saw what happened then.'

'So where has she been? What was she doing?'

'She was at her friend Winnie's,' said Ant. 'Which will be very easy to prove. The police really are wasting their time, you know. If they're looking for a murderer, they'd be better off concentrating on me and my dad. At least we were right here. My mother was miles away.'

'Steady on, lad,' said Digby. 'Don't go confessing to something you haven't done.'

Ant blinked, and then laughed awkwardly. 'Th-that isn't what I meant,' he stammered.

'No. Well,' said his father repressively. He turned to Thea. 'They'd be better off interrogating Carla and those daughters of hers. They'd soon find out that things are a lot more complicated than they think.'

'Really?' said Thea. 'I suppose they'll be doing that anyway.'

Digby was suddenly much more active than he had been for days, pacing around the kitchen, watched worriedly by Percy. He was muttering, more to himself than the other people in the room. 'Makes no sense. Why do they think she came back, if she'd killed bloody Blackwood? Arresting her is ludicrous.'

'The way they see it, they want to know why she went off like she did if she *didn't* kill him,' said Ant.

'And how do they think she did it, then? With a crowbar or what?'

Thea spoke before fully engaging her brain. 'Oh, no. He was electrocuted. It mucked up his pacemaker, apparently.'

Digby stopped his pacing and dropped his jaw. 'You can't be serious,' he gasped. 'So the careless bugger must have got himself tangled up in his own fence, then.'

Ant spoke at much the same moment. 'That's right – it must have been the fence. The old fool was so sure the medics had fixed his heart trouble once and for all – when all the time it just took a few volts . . . so why are they so sure it was murder?'

'Something the pathologist found in this morning's post-mortem,' said Thea, belatedly trying not to say too much.

'Have you spoken to the police, then?' Ant was now the sharper of the two men, Digby still open-mouthed and speechless. 'Are they telling you what they're thinking?'

Thea was plainly embarrassed. 'We're friends, you see, me and Gladwin. And she knows I'm matey with you as well, so it seemed to make sense for her to come to me . . .'

'You're a spy,' interrupted Digby angrily. 'What the hell have you told her? Is it down to you that they've arrested Beverley?'

'Um . . . well, in a way, I suppose. But they'd have found out anyway, of course.'

'Found out what?'

'That she'd been missing since before Christmas.'

'How?' Digby shouted. 'How would they? Nobody else knew about that. Not a single soul. We don't talk about our private business to anybody.' He turned on his son. 'You've been blabbing to this woman, haven't you?'

'You were right here as well,' Thea pointed out. 'You heard everything he said.'

'And I knew at the time he was an idiot.' The man's rage, which did not come naturally to him, was rapidly subsiding. 'Well, it's done now,' he groaned. He looked across the room to where Stephanie was loitering by the door. 'And what are you doing bringing this little one into all this mess?' he finished, with another flare of aggression.

Stephanie was unsettled by Digby's angry words, but not especially alarmed. She trusted him to calm down quickly and return to his usual affable self. Anybody would be cross in his situation. The police thought Beverley had killed the Blackwood man and had taken her off to prison. She and Thea were wrong to be there at all – a point which Digby had been trying to make, she suspected. And he was probably right that Thea had interfered when she shouldn't have done.

And now there was this new information about

electrocution. That was the bit Thea had refrained from telling her, only a little while ago. She had an image of jagged forked lightning stabbing into the man, his hair on end and eyes staring. How could anybody deliberately arrange for that to happen?

'We should probably go, then,' said Thea. 'I'm sure everything's going to work out all right. Gladwin's a good detective. She won't charge Beverley without rock-solid evidence.'

'We hope,' said Ant. 'If that's right about electrocution, I still can't see that they can be sure it wasn't an accident.'

Thea averted her gaze, with a little shake of her head. 'I never was much good at physics,' she said.

'What happened about that jewellery thing?' Stephanie asked, out of the blue. 'Did you tell Thea that somebody found it? Where was it?'

'Oh, yes,' said Ant quickly. 'That's got nothing to do with all this other stuff. One of Mrs B's daughters had it all the time.'

'Really?' Thea was obviously intrigued. 'They had the decency to come and tell you that, did they?'

'Not exactly,' said Ant uncomfortably. 'But it's not relevant – take my word for it.'

'Yes, you do that,' echoed Digby. He gave Stephanie a rueful look. 'Best not to ask too many questions, pet. You never know where they might lead.'

'Oh,' said Stephanie, feeling a quiver of alarm.

'Come on, then,' said Thea, gathering child and dog, and opening the front door. 'We'll get out of your way. But I hope we can get together again soon, and patch up any differences.'

'Differences!' snorted Digby, waving them away.

'What a mess this place is,' Thea muttered, as they crossed the junk-filled garden. 'Look at it!' There was a rusty wheelbarrow not far from her, containing a car battery and a roll of wire. Next to it was a buckled sheet of galvanised iron and a garden fork with a broken handle. 'It all needs to go to the tip, if you ask me.' She kicked at a dented metal bucket that stood close to her foot. It fell over, despite being full of water, with a dirty sponge at the bottom.

Stephanie scrutinised every item, including the bucket and its spilled contents. 'I expect some of it's useful,' she said vaguely.

'I doubt it. Looks like complete rubbish to me. Engines, old lawnmowers, chunks of oily metal – you'd have to have a proper workshop to make anything of this lot.'

'Mm,' said Stephanie, still examining the various objects with close attention.

They trailed back along the footpath, each feeling far from cheerful. Stephanie went over the accusation that Thea was a spy, and could see how it might seem that way. In fact, it could even be true that the police would never have arrested Beverley if Thea hadn't told the young Finch Graham about the woman being missing. She had worked out without being told that he had passed the information on to his senior officer. Very little of the whole business had been conducted out of her hearing, anyhow. Much of the time, Thea and Jessica seemed to forget that she was there, paying close attention.

'It can't have been Mrs Frowse who killed him, can it?' she asked, after a few minutes.

Thea replied quite readily, apparently uttering thoughts she'd just been mulling over. 'It's hard to see anybody deliberately rigging up some sort of lethal device, and then connecting him to it and killing him. He wouldn't just keep still, would he? I mean – he was outside, in his pyjamas. It might work if some maniac doctor decided to do it in his surgery somehow, but this just seems ludicrous.'

Stephanie concentrated on the idea of the electric fence being the real murderer. Her first term at the big school had introduced her to the wonders of physics, with some basic experiments with electricity the high point so far. She had drawn diagrams and learnt new terms such as 'resistance' and 'voltage' and 'conductor'. She knew that water helped the current to flow, and that human skin was providentially resistant to electricity. Gold, silver, copper and aluminium were all good conductors, especially when cold. She knew that 'earthing' was important, and along the way had been shown how to change an electric plug. She had found the whole subject fascinating, as had most of the rest of the class.

Thea was thinking along different lines, evidently. 'It could have been one of the staff, of course. They'd have the opportunity and probably the means. And there's likely to be plenty of motive as well. Blackwood doesn't seem to have been the greatest employer, if his treatment of the Frowses is anything to go by.'

'Mm,' said Stephanie. 'I wonder if he had bare feet?'

'What?'

'I think it makes the current stronger if you're not wearing shoes. And if you're wet, of course.'

'I expect he had some warm, fleecy slippers on.'

They walked another hundred yards, the power of their thoughts slowing them to a crawl. Then Stephanie stopped dead. 'We've got to go back,' she said. 'Or phone Mrs Gladwin. Or *something*.'

'What do you mean?'

'The car battery,' she said urgently. 'They did it with the car battery.'

Chapter Twenty

Thea insisted that they should carry on home, and talk it over calmly before taking any action. But now they proceeded at a trot, arriving in Broad Campden barely ten minutes later. Stephanie kept trying to describe the process. 'There are terminals, you see. And if you lie a piece of metal across them, and then hold that against someone's heart, they're likely to die.'

'Okay, but—' Thea floundered, ignorant of more than the absolute basics. 'Are you really sure that's right?'

'We can check it on the Internet.'

'But Steph – if you're right, that looks terribly bad for Digby. Or Ant.'

'Yes, I know,' said Stephanie. 'But if it's the truth . . .'

'The truth can be terrible,' said Thea softly. 'I just wish

you didn't have to learn that so young.'

Stephanie's impatience was almost painful. She wanted to confirm her theory and assure herself that she wasn't being stupid. She remembered Timmy talking about the film *The Green Mile* which he had been outrageously allowed to watch at his friend Oliver's house. He had talked about it obsessively for days afterwards, mostly to his sister, giving her a graphic description of the electrocution scene. Something about a wet sponge having to go on the top of the victim's head, and the sadistic prison officer not providing it, so the whole thing would hurt more and take longer. Timmy had found it both terrifying and fascinating. 'Hurry up,' she urged her stepmother. 'We're almost home now.'

'What's the rush?' puffed Thea. 'I can't go any faster.'

Stephanie couldn't properly explain. It felt as if the ideas that were filling her mind would either evaporate or somehow overflow. She had to capture them calmly, organise them just as she'd been taught to write up her science experiments. There were so many potential obstacles – her father, the police and Digby himself. All or any of them might just laugh at her and dismiss everything she had to say.

But then they were in the house at last. Everything was calm and normal, and it seemed almost violent to burst in as they did, and start gabbling about Beverley and police and electrocution. Thea was of little help. Random comments emerged from her with no logical thread until Jessica physically gripped her shoulders and made her stop.

Drew was irritable. 'We've only just got back ourselves,'

he said. 'We're all tired out. Can't we just have a bit of peace for a while?'

It was much as Stephanie had feared. Thea had made it worse, behaving more like a child than a grown-up. She went over to Timmy, and sat with him in the window seat, leaving the adults to settle down, watching each face anxiously.

When salvation finally came, it was from another source entirely. The doorbell rang and there was Detective Sergeant Finch Graham, looking boyishly apprehensive. 'DS Gladwin sent me,' he said. 'I'm to ask you a few questions.'

'Who? Me?' Thea asked foolishly.

'Who else?' sighed Drew. 'Take him into the office, why don't you?'

They were gone for only a few minutes when Thea reappeared and told Stephanie she should join them. 'He wants to hear it from you,' said Thea. 'The stuff about electrodes or whatever it is.'

Stephanie sat down on a chair reserved for people arranging a funeral, while the detective took Drew's place. Thea was next to her. Carefully she presented her theory, waiting for Finch to make notes as she went. At last he looked up at her. 'That's incredibly clever,' he said. 'I'm enormously impressed.' Then he deflated her again. 'But I don't think it'll do, you know. The problem is, you could turn almost anything into a lethal weapon if you really want to. Knitting needles, belts, lavatory cleaner, you name it. And as well as that, you can push a person under a train or off a roof or into a river. And you can make all those things look like an accident, with good planning.'

'But—' Stephanie had no idea what to say. She had been so *certain*.

Thea was indignant. 'I thought you were going to take her seriously,' she protested. 'Now you've just made her feel silly.'

'I'm sorry,' he said. 'And I promise you it isn't silly at all. We will have a look at those things you're telling me about, of course. But without any actual evidence, they're just bits of junk in a front yard.'

'If they're still there,' said Thea darkly.

'You'll tell Mrs Gladwin, though, won't you?' begged Stephanie, with a hazy notion that a female listener might give the theory more credence. After all, her stepmother showed signs of believing her. Another thought struck her. 'And if they've been moved and hidden away, that's a sort of evidence as well – isn't it?'

'It would be suspicious, I agree,' said the detective.

'Did you ask Thea the questions?' Stephanie enquired, wondering at the brevity of the interview. 'The ones you came with?'

'It was really just the one.'

'And I didn't know the answer,' Thea admitted. 'I've been pretty useless, in fact.'

Finch Graham tapped his teeth for a moment. 'There are a whole lot of connections we haven't worked out, you see. Along with some findings at the scene.'

'Which he won't tell us about,' Thea said to Stephanie.

'Well, it wasn't Mrs Frowse,' said Stephanie firmly. 'You should let her go back to her family. Percy's missing her.'

The return to ordinary family life felt terribly wrong to Stephanie, but she did her best to go along with it. After all, it was still Christmas, and she had failed hopelessly as a detective, so she ought to try and forget the whole murder business.

Timmy was sifting through his new toys in the sitting room, taking them out of the big cardboard box they'd gone into as he unwrapped them, and putting them in piles. 'Wow, Tim! Look at all those new things!' said Thea.

'Lots of them were in my stocking.' He fingered a puzzle in which you had to move small squares in a frame to make a picture. 'I like this one. Stephanie's got one the same – except it's a different picture.'

'I had those when I was small. I didn't know you could still get them.' Thea was careful to preserve the myth of Santa for another year or two, where Timmy was concerned. One of her ploys was to find unusual items that harked back to an earlier kind of childhood.

Stephanie was inclined to be impatient with all this after the events of the afternoon. She felt superior to Timmy in his artificially preserved innocence, including his determination to believe in Santa Claus. She knew that deep down he was perfectly aware that adult human beings supplied the contents of his stocking, but he still enjoyed the pretence, and wouldn't hear any suggestion that it was false. It produced a tension in her that was uncomfortable. She snatched at the puzzle toy, and examined it, holding it away from her brother. 'Mine's better,' she said nastily.

'Hey!' protested Timmy. 'Give it back.'

'Let me have a go on it first.' She started shifting the little squares, sliding them around each other, but always finding the bottom of the picture stubbornly returning to one side, and the corners refusing to co-operate. Within two minutes she had thrown it back at Timmy in frustration. He took it and deftly arranged it into the finished picture in forty seconds flat.

'Easy,' he said. 'You have to push them the opposite way to what you want, sometimes. You need to think about the gaps,' he tried to explain.

'I have a feeling it's true that boys are better at this sort of thing,' said Thea. 'Although my brother was always hopeless at jigsaws.'

'I am as well,' said Stephanie crossly. 'And I bet Mrs Gladwin is, too.'

'She probably is,' Thea agreed. 'Although she seems to work by some sort of lucky intuition, much of the time. She can't possibly really think Beverley killed that man, can she?'

Timmy looked up questioningly. 'Does she?' he said.

'They arrested her,' Stephanie informed him.

'I don't get it at all,' Thea went on, not really talking to the children so much as speaking her thoughts aloud. 'If the man was electrocuted, why do they think it was done deliberately? Isn't it always an accident?'

'Not if it's the electric chair,' said Timmy.

'What do you know about that? It's much too gruesome for you.' Thea looked mildly concerned.

When the small boy explained about *The Green Mile*, Drew also took notice. There followed a pointless bit of bickering about the dependability of Oliver's parents.

298

'It's a very odd investigation,' mused Jessica, interrupting. 'I mean – surely the two Frowse men must be the main candidates for killing the landlord bloke? They hated him. He made their lives a misery. With him dead, the place will probably be sold, and a new person would be sure to be an improvement.'

'Not at all,' said Thea. 'That's wrong in about ten different ways. For a start, it's Carla who they really hate. Rufus was an idiot, too rich for his own sanity, but not really malicious like her. Plus those terrible daughters, who float around causing trouble and taking up space. *Plus*, if the estate gets sold again, there could well be ructions for the tenants. It would make Carla even more determined to eradicate them. Beverley talks big, arming herself with all the relevant legal protections, but they're really very vulnerable. Nobody would speak up for them if it came to the crunch. They'd have to pay for a barrister or something – which they couldn't hope to do.'

Stephanie was following this closely, wondering why Thea was making it all so complicated. 'You should just ask Mrs Gladwin to tell you what evidence they've found,' she said. 'Isn't that the simplest way?'

'She wouldn't tell me. Not while she's still right in the middle of it all.'

Jessica made an impatient tutting noise. 'I wish I'd been there,' she said. 'She might have told me something – one police officer to another.'

'I doubt it. She sees you more as my daughter than any kind of colleague,' said Thea. 'And I suppose we'll know soon enough. It's not really as if we're personally involved, is it? I like the Frowses, and would do anything I could to help them feel more secure – but this is way beyond anything I can offer them. Beverley going off like that is very mysterious, let's face it. It looks bad. I'm not surprised she's top of the list of suspects, even if Stephanie's so certain she didn't do it.'

'They called you a spy,' Stephanie reminded Thea, who seemed to be going back on earlier remarks.

'Yes, I know. They were upset, quite understandably.' She spoke to Jessica, 'Young Mr Graham passed everything I said directly to Gladwin, needless to say.'

'Of course he did. That's his job. And don't pretend you didn't know he would, all along.'

'It didn't occur to me that her husband and son would find out, though.'

'Oh well, that's a minor detail. From the little I've managed to glean about the whole set-up, it looks pretty likely to have been the wife anyway – whatever you might think. Or possibly one of the exotic Russian daughters. They might even have dreamt it up as a way of disposing of the Frowses, once and for all. If it's a frame-up it could still work out as they want it to. Who says the widow's going to sell up, anyway? Why would she?'

'As a way of disposing of the Frowses?' Thea echoed, on a rising note of incredulity. 'Kill her own husband and frame Digby and Ant for it? That's ludicrous.'

'I don't think it is,' Jessica shrugged. 'You say the man was in pyjamas. Doesn't that suggest something domestic? Going out like that, with her going along as well – some sort of argument. Then forgetting about the fence, or switching it to high power or something. She might have pushed him into it, or made him hold something lethal, by mistake. Then she panicked and left him there dead.'

Stephanie and Thea both stared at her. 'Are you sure you want to join the CID?' Thea asked. 'Because I have to say I'm not at all convinced that you're quite right for it. Can you honestly imagine anything like that happening?'

'Why not? What's wrong with it?'

'It just doesn't ring true. These people are multi-millionaires. They've got *staff*. They don't conduct their marital fights in public. And nobody dies from being pushed against an electric fence. It would have to be planned down to the last detail – which we have to assume it was, because Gladwin doesn't appear to have found any glaring evidence.'

'She might have done. We really don't have much idea about that.'

Both women went quiet, the mystery too much for them. Stephanie was sitting very still on the sofa, with Timmy on the floor beside her. He had stopped listening to the conversation some time ago. Drew was in the kitchen for some reason. The spaniel was on Stephanie's lap, gently licking her front feet.

'What did you say was for supper?' Timmy asked idly. 'I'm hungry.'

'Leftovers,' Thea told him briefly. 'I'll start making something in a minute.'

But then her phone warbled and she was yet again distracted. It was Ant, to nobody's great surprise. 'I know this is an awful cheek, especially after what Dad said to you, but do you think you could come and fetch Percy and hang onto him until all this business is over?'

'Why? Where are you going to be?'

'That's just it. We have no idea. It seems more than likely we'll have to go in for questioning sooner or later. Dad thinks they're quite capable of turning up at 5 a.m. and carting us off. And then there's Carla and the others. She was in such a crazy state today, we're actually a bit scared as to what she might do. Annika's as bad. Worse, even. We just thought it would be less of a worry if we knew he was being looked after.'

'Well . . .' Thea tried to catch Drew's eye, and assess his likely reaction. 'I've got my brother coming tomorrow, with a small child. Percy's awfully *big*.'

Only then did it become clear to Stephanie and Timmy what was being asked. 'Yes!' shouted Timmy. 'Whatever it is, the answer is yes.'

'I heard that,' laughed Ant. 'Seems I've got at least one supporter.'

By a rapid connection, Stephanie recalled the probability that her new-found grandmother was threatening to turn up with a dog far larger than Percy, sometime soon. This would be good practice. She nodded wildly at Thea.

'Drew?' Thea asked.

'I appear to be outnumbered,' he said. 'I just hope you haven't agreed to adopt a grizzly bear.'

'It looks as if we'll cope somehow,' she told Ant. 'Did you say I had to come and collect him?'

'If that's not too much to ask. If you get him settled with his dinner and bed and everything, he's more likely to be acclimatised by bedtime. Though I can't promise what he'll do in the night. He's never been away from here at night before.'

'I'll come right away, then. Timmy can come with me.'

She had ended the call before Drew could say, 'No, I don't think so.'

'You don't think what?' she frowned at him. 'I've said we'll do it now.'

'Not that – whatever it is exactly. I'd rather you didn't take Timmy over there, that's all.'

'We're only looking after their dog for a day or two. I need someone to hold him while I'm driving. I don't know what he's like in a car. He might think I'm abducting him.'

'Take Jessica, then.'

'Oh, no – he'll get mud and hair all over me. I only brought one jumper.'

'Can I go, Dad?' Stephanie asked, in a tone she reserved for him alone. 'I'm fairly muddy already and Percy likes me.'

'He likes me as well,' muttered Timmy mutinously.

'Just providing you don't let Thea get embroiled in any more murder stuff. Straight there, collect the dog and straight back, right? I'll give you twenty-five minutes. And that's generous.'

'Don't you love it when he's masterful!' giggled Jessica.

It felt very weird to be back at Crossfield again, this time in a car, with darkness falling. 'How many times is this, in the past week?' wondered Thea. 'I've lost count.'

'Do you think Finch will tell Mrs Gladwin about my ideas?' Stephanie asked wistfully. 'Or does he just think

I'm a silly little child?'

'I think he's bound to tell someone, but it might not be her. There's a whole team of them, don't forget. It's not at all silly, either. It's rather brilliant, actually.'

'Just wrong.' Stephanie gave a deep sigh.

'The thing is, the police don't work in the sort of way ordinary people expect. It depends entirely on evidence. They quite often know who's done a crime, but unless they can prove it, they're not allowed to arrest them or charge them. It's fair enough, in theory. Otherwise there'd be scope for all sorts of corruption. Guesswork, or taking revenge on somebody, or just cutting corners and not doing the job properly. Do you see?'

'But they have to write down everything people tell them, don't they? Because some of it might turn out to be evidence after all.'

'That's exactly right,' said Thea.

Ant heard them coming and met them at the door, holding Percy by the collar. 'I'd better put his lead on,' he said. 'But I can't find it for the moment.'

'We left the car down by the gate, just in case,' said Thea awkwardly. 'I mean – in case it's working again. I wasn't sure what to expect.' She faltered a few more apologetic phrases, unpleasantly aware of the antagonism she had aroused only an hour or two earlier.

Ant shrugged it all away and went to look again for the dog lead. Thea followed him into the house, but Stephanie was compelled irresistibly to have another look at the contents of the old wheelbarrow, unsure whether or not she hoped they would have disappeared.

It was all still there. She picked up the strip of copper, which she had at first taken to be wire. In fact it was flatter and wider than that, at least two feet long. She could vividly imagine it being placed across the terminals of the car battery and extended to make contact with the naked skin of the murder victim's chest. Except of course, he would have to co-operate by keeping still, unless a second person held him down. And the killer would have to wear some sort of protection against receiving a painful shock himself. Gloves, perhaps.

Digby was all of a sudden standing beside her. She met his eyes, still holding the copper. 'What are you up to, then?' he asked, in a friendly voice.

She should have been more afraid, she thought afterwards. Instead, she simply said, 'This reminds me of a lesson we did at school – in physics. There's everything you need here to give somebody a big electric shock. The sponge in the bucket as well.'

'What an amazingly clever little girl!'

It was not Digby who spoke, but some other person, standing at the gate between the garden and the drive. The fading light showed only a fair-headed woman. She moved towards them. 'You've met your match, my friend. Foiled by a schoolgirl. How will you abide the humiliation?'

'Bronya,' breathed Digby. 'What are you doing here?'

'Trying to gather the courage to face my deplorable mother and sister, if you really want to know. But first I thought it might be wise to check how things are with you. I never expected to catch you being challenged by a ten-year-old detective.'

'I'm eleven, not ten,' said Stephanie. Nothing was making any sense, but that hardly mattered. It was almost unbearably exciting to think she was right at the heart of something crucially important. 'And I've already told the police there's this battery and things here.'

'Looks bad for poor Mr Frowse, doesn't it?'

'Looks worse for you, ducky,' Digby snapped back. 'You're not going to lay this on me.'

'What's going on?' Thea's voice came loud and clear from the house. 'Stephanie? What are you doing?'

Stephanie remembered Drew's deadline, and wondered how angry he would be when they failed to meet it. Because fail they would. Nobody was going anywhere now.

She didn't have to say anything. Thea ran down the garden, obviously scared. 'Who's this?' she demanded, staring at Bronya.

'I could ask you the same thing,' said the young woman calmly. Stephanie realised that she looked rather like Jessica. The same fleshy shoulders and creamy skin.

'Everyone's trying to fit me up as the murderer,' said Digby, with a little laugh. 'If that's the right word. When I can tell you for certain that this lady here is the real criminal. Not that there's likely to be much proof against either of us.'

They all just stood there, as Ant came slowly to join them, pulling Percy behind him. 'What's wrong with his foot?' Stephanie asked, seeing the dog was limping.

'He's been licking it for days,' said Ant. 'I don't suppose it's anything much.'

'Let's see,' said Thea, taking Percy back to the light of

the open door. She bent the front leg back to inspect the underside of the foot. The dog whined when she touched it. 'There's a nasty big blister on it,' she reported. 'It must be really sore.'

Ant joined her, bending over the foot. 'That's a burn,' he pronounced. 'How on earth could that have happened?'

'Battery acid perhaps?' suggested Bronya, with a malicious laugh. 'How would that be as a piece of evidence?'

'Absolute nonsense,' scoffed Digby.

But there was a kind of congealing of the air around them all, which was the only way Stephanie could describe it. Ant dropped the dog's foot and looked hard at his father. Thea was gazing into the wheelbarrow and at the copper strip still in Stephanie's hand. Digby and Bronya seemed to form a unit, custodians of some ghastly truth that was leaking out despite their best efforts to contain it.

'Dad?' said Ant in a low voice.

'The police are certain to fit it all together, you know,' said Thea. 'Probably thanks to Stephanie.'

'She certainly is a clever girl,' said Bronya. 'Almost as clever as me.'

'Much cleverer than you, dear,' said Digby. 'Your mistake was thinking I had anything to lose. Now Beverley's given up on me, it hardly matters what comes next. And when it comes to it, you're even more of a loser than me, wouldn't you say?'

'I'm going now,' was the reply. 'And I wish you luck.' But she only moved two steps away and then hesitated.

Stephanie thought again of her father, counting the minutes. Thea had not brought her phone with her, so he couldn't call to demand where they were. But now Bronya was leaving, much of the tension was going with her.

Digby sighed. 'She killed him, you know,' he said, as if imparting some barely relevant news. 'She enticed him into the woods, late on Thursday, and used my battery to kill him. Isn't that so, my lady? She'd intended to throttle him, I fancy, but changed her mind when I turned up. Not that I realised, of course.'

'You're talking nonsense,' Ant said angrily. 'Pure fantasy.'

'It would be nice to think so. There *was* a fantasy, of a sort, I suppose. I've dreamt for years of ways to do away with that man. Murder must be easy, I thought, if the bastard who killed my girl could get away with it. The pacemaker clinched it. Fibrillation, you see. That's the thing. If you can interrupt the heart's rhythm with an electric current, it never gets right again, and the person dies. Really quite simple in the theory, but extraordinarily complex in the execution. But thanks to loud voices and the digital revolution, I was greatly helped by this young lady.'

'Rubbish,' said Bronya. 'You know nothing.'

'I know he was after you for sex. Every time you came visiting, he'd be chasing you around, day and night. And I could see you weren't keen. Microphones, in case you're wondering. Tucked into the wall of your precious parterre all summer, and under the windowsills. Placed under cover of darkness out of view of your nasty cameras. I heard you and him go out on Thursday night and grabbed my chance.'

'Dad, be quiet!' Ant ordered. 'You sound as if you're boasting about killing someone.'

'Oh, but I didn't. That's what I'm telling you. Thanks, as it happens, to your poor innocent mother.'

'She said she came back,' Ant remembered slowly. 'When? What did she see?'

'She saw Bronya and Rufus in the woods, apparently doing the dirty deed. And because old Percy had somehow got out and followed me, when I went up there with the battery and other things, she assumed it was me rather than Rufus. She gave a bit of a shout, and tipped the wheelbarrow over. The dog might have got acid on him – I don't know. I picked it all up again, left Bronya to her fate and scooted back home with the barrow, thinking to set things right with Bev. But she just drove off and didn't come back until today.'

'Did Bronya know you were there, planning to kill Rufus?' Thea asked. The Russian woman was unmoving, saying nothing. It looked as if at least some of Digby's account was new to her.

'Oddly enough, no. The plan, you see, was to get him while he was next to his damned fence, whack him with the kit I'd assembled, preferably with Bronya's willing assistance, and hope the cops would think it was an accident. After what I'd heard, I didn't think she would raise any objection. And I was right.' He looked at the statuesque woman with something close to affection.

'Nobody will believe such a crazy story,' she said, holding his gaze. 'Or if they do, they'll charge you as an accomplice. Or worse.'

'Fair enough,' said Digby meekly. 'I won't argue if they do.'

The sound of the Old Stables landline pealing imperiously brought them all back to the present. 'It'll be Dad,' said Stephanie.

And it was.

Chapter Twenty-One

It was Wednesday afternoon before Gladwin phoned and Beverley Frowse visited. It had not snowed and Damien was on his way. Drew was doing his best to forgive the flouting of his instructions regarding Thea's return from Crossfield. Jessica was all packed up, and had exchanged five texts with Finch Graham on matters not concerning murder.

'I gather we should thank you,' said Gladwin, when she phoned.

'Is it all sorted now?'

'We're still not quite there, but at least people are talking to us. I ought to warn you, though, I think you've probably lost a friend.'

'Even the dog doesn't like us much,' Thea agreed. 'We

shut him in the kitchen and he whined all night.'

'You've got their dog?'

'Stephanie insisted. She was the only one with a clear head yesterday. That's why we went back there in the car, you see.'

'Not really, but it probably doesn't matter. You met Bronya Blavatskaya, I take it. I still don't entirely follow what went on between you, but she's being gratifyingly co-operative.'

'I met her, but I have no idea what to make of her. Stephanie says she looks like Jessica, but I can't see it myself.'

'She's luscious,' said Gladwin. 'There's no other word for it.'

'And a murderer.'

'So it seems.'

There was considerably more helpful information from Beverley. 'I've come for Percy,' she said, appearing at the Slocombes' front door. The dog rushed to greet her, as dogs so often did – claiming to have been separated for at least twenty years.

'Come in,' Thea instructed, brooking no argument.

'I suppose it wouldn't hurt to try and fill you in a bit,' the woman conceded. 'All I ever do at the moment is answer questions, anyway. Serves me right for trying to keep everything to myself, I guess.'

Thea made tea and sat the visitor down. 'Where's Digby?' she began.

'At the police station. It'll take them a while to get the story straight. I'm not sure I understand it myself, despite

Ant's best efforts. Poor old Ant – he's never going to feel the same about either of us again. He keeps insisting that Bronya's really the victim in the whole thing.'

'The way it sounded to us, Digby had been planning to kill Rufus for ages, and somehow Bronya brought it all to a head last week, and then killed him herself. In a nutshell, as it were. Have I got that right?'

'Remember I haven't seen Digby. They let me go at the same time as they took him in. I've just got Ant's account to go on. He's putting quite a lot of the blame on me, for some reason.' She gave a windy sigh. 'And he keeps saying there won't be any real evidence against anybody, and they'll have to let Digby go. He's not so sure about Bronya.'

'But you – where did you go? And why? And *when*?'

'I went early on Wednesday, before the others were up, because I was sick of the way Digby was fixating on Bronya. I caught him sneaking around the back of our house, with some gadget that can magnify voices. He was listening to her in her parents' living room, even though he tried to deny it at first.'

'A listening device?' said Thea, feeling very clever at even knowing the phrase.

'Right. You plant a little box somewhere and you can hear everything it hears, through your phone. Incredibly simple and very sneaky. I was furious with him. He thought I'd never find him out there – we hardly ever go round the back,' she added.

'Okay. So you stormed out because of that?'

'It was his *manner*. He told me it was none of my business, nothing that would affect me, and I would do

313

best to just forget the whole thing. Well, how would *you* feel? Nobody likes to be told something like that, do they? I stewed all night, and decided I should drive off to my friend to cool off.'

'You went to a friend?'

'Winnie,' she nodded. 'She'd been inviting me for ages, and it seemed the perfect solution. But she's awfully hard work. Never stops talking. So I gave it a day or two and then headed home again.'

'That was Thursday evening?'

'Right – I think. The days are all a bit of a blur now. There was no sign of Digby or the dog, and Ant fast asleep in his bed. I thought Digby must have taken Percy out for a late stroll – it was a nice moonlit night – so I went looking down by those woods. The dog heard me and came lolloping up, but no Digby. I didn't dare shout, for fear of annoying the landlord. The woods are nice, you see, because they're shielded from the bloody security lights that are on all the time round the houses.'

'Okay,' said Thea, visualising the scene. 'Then what?'

'Then I heard sounds. Heavy breathing, rustling undergrowth. Percy was all alert but not especially disturbed. We tiptoed towards the noises and I saw two people lying on the ground in what looked like sexual congress – as the police kept saying. I took them to be Digby and Bronya, although I realise now that I hardly saw anything that could identify anybody. I was furious, and went charging back to my car, determined to leave him once and for all. Then I bashed into a wheelbarrow that was under a tree, and tipped it over. Percy was under my feet at the same time, and he got hurt somehow. He yelped, and I was scared of being caught, so grabbed his collar and got us both back to the house without being seen. I'd left my car down by the road, which I often do, to save having to wait for the gate to creep open. It's quicker on foot – and I hate having everything I do caught on the rotten cameras. We figured out that a person on foot can stay out of its sight, you see. Anyway, I shoved Percy into the house and ran back to the car. Winnie wasn't best pleased to see me back at midnight, I can tell you.'

'And you stayed away all over Christmas,' said Thea, trying not to sound reproachful.

'For my sins. I took Winnie out to a hotel for lunch, and we played about fifteen games of Scrabble, and watched an awful lot of mindless television, and I tried to psych myself up to leaving Digby and getting a nice little flat in a town somewhere. I figured if he was having it away with Blackwood's stepdaughter, I couldn't trust him even to be on my side any more. It made nonsense of the whole ghastly business.'

'Your feud with the landlord, you mean?'

'Right. I'd just had enough. So I phoned Ant and said as much. Something about Digby being dead to me – which he misheard, apparently. It was a bit melodramatic, I know, but that's how I was feeling at the time.'

'I'm not sure I follow the timing. Was it all pre-planned by Bronya and Digby together?'

'I really don't think so. It all came to a head when Rufus accused me of stealing that necklace, at the same time as Digby heard things getting more and more nasty for Bronya. It's not really such a coincidence that the three of them ended up in the woods at the same time on Thursday night. Digby knew what Rufus was up to, and seized the moment.'

'When did you first know that Blackwood was dead?'

'Must have been Boxing Day, I suppose. When I phoned Ant again. I couldn't work out where that fitted in the scheme of things, and by then I knew I'd have to go back and explain myself. And I was a bit worried about Percy, as well. And I think you know the rest. It wasn't Digby rolling on the ground with Bronya – but Blackwood. And she was resisting him, not enthusiastically co-operating. It is quite hard to tell in the dark, you know,' she added defensively. 'And I still don't know where Digby was. Behind a tree, I assume.'

'Apparently Digby heard you knock the wheelbarrow over. He set it right again and ran back home without it. Maybe Bronya saw him and somehow got Rufus subdued enough to use the equipment to electrocute him.' She hesitated. 'Does that sound even remotely feasible to you?'

'Not really. She'd have to have been miraculously quick-thinking. Ant thinks she probably saw Digby arriving with the wheelbarrow before Rufus came out in his pyjamas to have his wicked way with her. It's even possible that they talked about a combined effort to bump him off. They both wanted him dead, after all. And Digby seems to be sympathetic towards her. And he can't have taken all his equipment home if Bronya used it on Rufus after Digby had left the scene.'

'It was back in the garden on Boxing Day – because Stephanie saw it and worked out the implications.'

'He must have gone back for it before they found Rufus's body, to try and cover up the truth of what happened.'

'More than likely,' said Thea, feeling sad.

'If that's so, he's an accessory at best. He'll get ten years in gaol.'

'And what'll you and Ant do?'

'Get on with our lives.' Beverley lifted her chin and stared at a corner of the room. 'Which won't be before time. All we've done for years is live like people under siege. If it's not too late, I want to do something constructive. I was thinking I might offer myself to the Citizen's Advice people.'

'Good idea,' Thea approved.

'And Ant can finally grow up.'

Stephanie was even more taken with little Kim than expected. Within an hour she was besotted. The child was chunky, with rather thin, colourless hair like her mother. But she had greeny-grey eyes that glowed with an intelligent interest and a very advanced vocabulary. Drew and Thea watched in helpless wonder as the two settled down on the hearth rug with a collection of plastic toys and lost themselves in a game of fantasy involving a cow, a camel, a small house and five dinosaurs. Timmy had presented the last as his contribution to the game.

But Timmy had chosen Damien as his preferred member of the visiting family. It transpired that they shared an interest in exotic freshwater fish.

Jessica had gone, after a brief conversation with her mother out in the lane. 'Another murder solved, then?' she said. 'I assume Beverley tied up all the loose ends for you?'

'More or less,' Thea said.

'No thanks to Detective Constable Graham, apparently.'

'He wasn't even on duty. What did you expect?'

Jessica smiled. 'I'm glad, really. I managed to stay out of it rather well, don't you think?'

'Was it deliberate?'

'Pretty much.'

'And are you staying in touch with him?'

'I might. It's a long way from Manchester. I wouldn't get too excited. As far as I can see, relationships are pretty difficult even when you're in the same house. If it's three hours' drive away, it might be impossible.'

'Or it might be a darn sight easier,' laughed Thea. 'But don't go away with the idea that there's anything wrong between me and Drew.'

'Even if you insist on going off to that woman in Northleach?'

'Even then. We'll be fine, honestly. You can trust Stephanie to make sure everything stays on track.'

'Stephanie's a marvel. You don't know how lucky you are to have her.'

'Oh, yes, I do,' said Thea.

REBECCA TOPE is the author of three bestselling crime series, set in the stunning Cotswolds, Lake District and West Country. She lives on a smallholding in rural Herefordshire, where she enjoys the silence and plants a lot of trees, but also manages to travel the world and enjoy civilisation from time to time. Most of her varied experiences and activities find their way into her books, sooner or later.

rebeccatope.com   *@RebeccaTope*